To Betty & Roy
Best wishes to a
quiet & sleutar cobe are
our team in wellness and
valued friend, Bob

LETHAL
HINDSIGHT

LETHAL HINDSIGHT

By

Robert Abel Jr., MD

"Earth provides enough to satisfy every man's need but not every man's greed."

—Mahatma Gandhi

Copyright © 2010 by Robert Abel Jr., MD.

TXu 1-620-835

Library of Congress Control Number: 2009913197
ISBN: Hardcover   978-1-4500-1111-2
                 Softcover   978-1-4500-1110-5
                 Ebook   978-1-4500-1112-9

This is a work of fiction. Names, characters, places and incidents either are the product of the author's imagination or are used fictitiously, and any resemblance to any actual persons, living or dead, events, or locales is entirely coincidental.

This book was printed in the United States of America.

To order additional copies of this book, contact:
Xlibris Corporation
1-888-795-4274
www.Xlibris.com
Orders@Xlibris.com
72458

DEDICATION

Dedicated to my aunt Valla Amsterdam whose love of literature and support of the arts has been an inspiration to so many.

ACKNOWLEDGMENTS

I would like to thank Bryan Reardon for his excellent input with the manuscript and Rose and Pat Canfield for their continual encouragement in the mystery genre. My appreciations are extended to Leann Hornung, Athena Mallen, Mary Malloy and Liz Actub for their editorial assistance

I am grateful for the constant encouragement of Lauren Cunningham whose medical acumen, physical fitness and willingness to help others is so exceptional.

Chris Cunningham's cover design adds so much to the intrigue. I need to recognize Adam Abel, Leila Buck, Valerie Abel, Ari Abel, Laura Kupferman, and my partners at Delaware Ophthalmology Consultants for their willingness to share my thoughts.

And finally, I am deeply indebted to my wife Mike Abel for her endless patience, support and infusion of energy.

FIRST MOVE:
REMBRANDTPLEIN 2001

The case dangled from his hand, a specially made Anvil brief case. Hard years reflected off its dented shell. But the thick fingers wrapped around the leather-bound handle showed something else, trust. The two, case and man, had weathered many storms together, fourteen years' worth to be precise.

Light rain hung in the air, soaking through Walter Harper's Hugo Boss raincoat. He switched the case to his left hand and tried in vain to wipe the rain off his right. Switching the Anvil back, he pulled the fedora down over his eyes. He hated the hat, thinking it made him stand out like an eccentric tourist, the last thing he wanted to do considering his profession. Since arriving in Amsterdam, it had not stopped raining. Walter was tired of being wet.

From under his soaked jacket, Walter's cell phone vibrated. Taking a deep breath, he fished it out, trying to keep it dry. It was brand new and he still had not mastered all the features. He never would, but Walter could not resist the newest electronics.

Before looking at the number, he closed his eyes. Something about this drop had him on edge. He answered the phone.

"Yes."

"Walt?" The feminine voice on the line had a Columbian accent.

"Alex?" Walter's eyes opened. His pursed lips eased. "Sorry. I didn't know it was you."

"Did you get the package?" Alexandra asked.

At first, her question confused him. His girlfriend never asked for specifics about his business. Then, he remembered the phone.

"I'm using it now."

Alex laughed. "You got the number changed already?"

"Yeah," Walter said.

"My little addict, I swear if there was a way to live your life in one of those toys you'd leave me."

Walter shook his head but his words sounded hollow. "Never."

The conversation paused for an uncomfortable moment. Walter's fingers tensed around the handle of his Anvil. He knew what was coming.

"Is it done?" Alex whispered.

"Not yet."

"Oh, Walt. Can't you back out this time? You promised me."

He shuffled his feet. Beads of moisture rolled off the polished leather of his Italian shoes.

"This is the last time," he said, his voice firm. "I have to finish it, and then I'm done. Like I promised."

There was another pause.

"It's different this time," she said.

Walter turned his head. He looked out through the mist at the far corner of Rembrandtplein toward Amsterdam's Diamond District. Something itched at his mind. Maybe it was nothing more than the haunting architecture of the city.

"I'm really sorry I couldn't bring you," he said. "I know how you love Amsterdam, but there wasn't time."

Walter heard ghostly footsteps echoing through the fog. He took a step back, withdrawing into the shadowed overhang of the coffee shop behind him.

"It's not that. This one feels . . ."

"Alex," Walter said, trying to hide the tension in his voice. "I have to go."

She spoke in Spanish first, so fast that even Walter could not understand. When she continued in English, her voice was frantic.

"Blessed Mary," she said. "Something's wrong. I knew it."

Walter lied. "Everything's fine."

"I told you to get out," she screamed as Walter pulled the phone away from his ear.

He stared down the street. The footsteps stopped.

Walter ended the call with his girlfriend and looked down at the Blackberry's display. He checked his missed calls. Nothing. Something was definitely wrong. His contact was supposed to call before the drop. He had not.

His contact, a sarcastic voice over the phone with an American accent and a German cell number, had called him at 4 a.m. that morning. The nameless man had sent him on a tiresome series of what Walter considered useless acts, some kind of Hollywood plot to cover his tracks. He had been told to pick up the package in a decaying Czech hotel and secure it in the Anvil. From there, he rented a second hand Yugo from an agent in Prague and drove the car, the interior smelling like melted plastic, into Amsterdam, where he ditched the rental.

Walter had waited for three hours outside a tobacconist shop on *Maurlstkade*. He expected his contact to call on his new cell but when a dented public phone clanged to life behind him, Walter was not surprised. Shaking his head, he answered it. The familiar voice sounded tinny through the ancient, cracked receiver.

Annoyed, Walter half listened to the man's senseless directions. Instead, he focused on the itching familiarity of the voice. He had the feeling he spoke with an old friend, but the distortion made it impossible to know which one.

"Don't worry," the contact had said. "I know all about your attachment to that bag of yours. With the bonus we're paying, you can finally buy yourself the entire set."

The next series of directions had sent him to a coffee shop on Rembrandtplein. Unlike Alexandra, Walter did not love Amsterdam. He had fumed as he walked twelve blocks along the uneven paving stones lining one of the city's concentric half-ring roads that arrayed out from the center. Briefly, the setting sun broke through the clouds, casting long, gothic shadows across the street. Along the Rembrandtplein he dodged the racks of discount clothing being hawked by an array of loud traffickers.

When he had reached the coffee shop, Walter waited again. It had been an hour of silence. He had watched the streets slowly clear out as even the locals found shelter from the confounded weather. The entire time, he had thought about the conversation that morning with the sarcastic American.

Standing under the coffee shop awning, staring out into the blanket of wet fog pressing down on the street, Walter wondered if the bonus was worth it. For the first time since he graduated from the University of Pennsylvania's Wharton School of Business and tragedy thrust him into his obscure and unexpected line of work, he questioned it. He was doing this last job for a German friend.

Not taking his eyes off the street, Walter put his case down on the relatively dry cobblestones. He typed the code on the digital keypad above the latching mechanism—82689, the long past due date of his first son. He had been warned that once he placed the package inside, not to open it again. But so much time and memories were on his hands.

The Anvil's expensive security clicked open. Walter bent over and reached inside. He pulled out a picture and closed the case again. Taking his eyes off the street for the first time, he looked at it.

His wife's blue eyes looked back at him, mirroring the infectious smile on her face. Guilt caused him to think of Alexandra for a moment. The two women were so different. Madelyn, Walter's wife, had been fair and warm. Her smile had lit up rooms and her kindness had been one in a million. In the picture, her face glowed with the early months of pregnancy.

Walter swallowed. His hand tremored. For the first time in seventeen years, the shock of loss withdrew. Walter remembered everything clearly, all the love and all the pain. He could see once again the flashing red light on his home answering machine. He could hear the crackling voice telling him that there had been an accident, that he had to get to the hospital immediately. And finally, he heard the time stamp of the message—four hours earlier. By the time Walter reached the hospital, his wife and son had already died. He was alone.

Walter's lips touched the photo. He whispered, "I love you, Maddy."

Slipping the picture into the inside pocket of his jacket, Walter reached back into the bag. His finger traced slowly, respectfully, across a silver name plate riveted to the lining of the case. He could see the name. Dr. Warren Harper, Surgeon, Walter's father. The Anvil being the only thing he had left of his father's.

Every ounce of instinct Walter owned screamed out, sensing danger, dulled only by a life too full of death. Earlier that morning, those same instincts had assured him how pedestrian this particular job was. When he picked up the package, his seasoned hands knew immediately what hid within the thick white envelope—a bundle of papers, maybe a manual, not anything more. Definitely nothing sexy, like drugs or computer components, which were particularly active as every manufacturer scurried to make their desktops and cell phones smaller and smaller. This time, it wasn't even blueprints. The package was too small and thick for that.

"How bad could a manual be?" he thought. Maybe a draft annual report, some kind of insider trading scheme, Walter knew he could handle that crew. At the same time, why all the drama, and why was he so tense?

Something moved in the gloomy shadows directly across the street. Walter squinted and pulled off the fedora, wishing he had never shown weakness by wearing the ridiculous hat in the first place.

Although his senses stood on end, Walter was a professional. As unlikely as the genesis of his employment was, he had been at it for a long time. He had seen things, absurd and deadly both. Walter would not roll over, regardless of the haunting specters of his past. He would not give up without a fight.

His eyes locked across the street, he sensed a presence. At the same moment, someone else rounded the corner behind him and he startled, reaching for the revolver he wore behind his back.

It was a woman in her late forties, obviously a prostitute. She stumbled, giggling. Her eyes met Walter's, blinking in a depressing parody of seduction.

"Twenty U.S.," she slurred.

Walter pulled his gun from the holster on his belt, his eyes never leaving the other side of the street. He knew this would be the time.

The woman cackled. "Ten if you're fast."

She stepped in front of Walter. He heard the airy sound of a silenced bullet. The woman lurched to the side, a puff of smoke rising from her jacket just below the armpit.

Walter leveled his gun. Before he could get off a shot, the woman fell into his arm. His gun fired, the errant bullet striking an awning across the street. The pinpoint flash of a red targeting laser blinded Walter's right eye.

Walter reacted. His body instinctively jerked as he dove to the side. His head whipped around. The woman moaned and hit the ground. He heard another shot and a bullet slammed into his shoulder, spinning him around. The force threw him against the plate glass window of the café.

The misty rain that had hung over the city for over a day suddenly cleared. Rays of dim moonlight cut through the gloom. Walter blinked. Someone was crossing the street toward him.

Walter tried to raise his gun and aim it at the man approaching him. The muscles of his arm did not answer his command. His gun remained at his side, held by a limp and lifeless arm.

The approaching footsteps quickened. The red light, now clearly shining on Walter's forehead was replaced with a pfennig-sized hole, announced by a strangely hollow "thwok."

Walter's head snapped. The window shattered. For an instant, his body remained perpendicular to the cobblestones lining the outside of the coffee shop. As if his bones dissolved, Walter's body flowed to the grimy sidewalk, pivoting so that he slammed down face first.

Dark blood oozed out. One hand twitched, rhythmic spasms that grew fainter with each second. His other hand remained locked around the handle of his Anvil case.

The woman pushed up to all fours beside him, still moaning. A second "thwok" sounded. The woman fell silent. He heard her body hit the sidewalk.

Shining black shoes stopped an inch from his head. A hand reached down and wrapped around Walter's and the handle of the Anvil. Outside of the circumstances, the gesture may have appeared loving, like a mother prying her son's sticky hands from the hem of her skirt.

Walter fought. He could not release the case. He would die with it frozen to his palm. He heard a low chortle. Then all strength left him and Walter lost his most prized possession.

The case lifted off the ground. A ring on the fourth finger of the hand now holding it reflected the dim moonbeams. A star-cut ruby flashed, a black flaw marring the stone's quality but not its stunning beauty. The gem hugged a platinum setting. The case lifted off the cobblestones.

Walter would have recognized that ring. The distorted voice over the phone would have cleared. He would have known his betrayer.

As the case's new owner walked into the night, a dark red stain flowed from beneath Walter's head, the viscous liquid diverting around an empty cigarette pack, trickling into the gaps between 400 year-old curbstones. It dripped through a sewer grate where it was carried by grimy water into one of Amsterdam's famous canals.

Baltimore, Maryland 2001

The expanse of Baltimore's showplace, the Inner Harbor, opened up below Lauren Chandler as she hit her stride. She was a beautiful young woman in her early twenties. A lifetime runner, her body was lean and her muscles rippled under her soft skin like a born athlete. As she ran, her auburn hair flared out behind her, reflecting copper highlights in the sun. Her lungs burned, trying to pull every particle of oxygen from the thick early September air.

It was a Thursday, so a light training day. Every third day she ran twenty miles. Today it would only be six.

As her lightweight running shoes brushed along the concrete of Federal Hill Park, her body slipped into the familiar automaton stage, when the pain pangs from her stretching muscles and pumping lungs faded into the background. Free of the distraction, her mind soared. She ran for that feeling, her only freedom from a hectic life.

At that moment she stopped noticing the looks of the businessmen out for coffee and the male tourists ushering their families toward the Inner Harbor. If she could see it from their eyes, she knew they were only eyeing her trim body encased in a Spandex running skin. For her part, the looks still puzzled her. They saw a fit, tall body capped off with flowing auburn hair. She saw a machine, engine, pumps, cooling and electrical systems, and every machine looked and ran better with good maintenance. This machine, her machine, was in good shape, but that was no accident. Some mornings she would throw a thought back at the gaping men. If you worked out almost every day and ate right, your machine would draw attention, too.

Shaking her head, Lauren used the opportunity the way she had intended. She let her mind float out to the future, to prepare herself for the "informal" meeting she had latter that afternoon.

Lauren clicked through the points she wanted to hit, cum laude in neuroscience at Wesleyan University in Middletown, Connecticut; Division III All American in the 800 her senior year; and her letters of recommendation from the Chairs of the Chemistry, Biology and Psychology departments. She had made AOA honor society in her junior year at Hopkins Medical School. Even with all that, she felt butterflies in her stomach as she headed back toward the parking lot where she had left her car.

As she stutter-stepped over the spike strip at the entrance, Lauren had one thought coursing through her head. There was one thing she did not want to talk about in her interview, though—her dad.

Lauren's concerns changed immediately when she saw her Datsun 410. It was parked toward the back of the lot, the sun shining on the driver's side. Something, however, did not look right. When she neared, her running shoes crackled over broken glass.

The driver's side window of her car had been shattered. Shards of glass littered the pavement and the worn tweed fabric of the front seat. Lauren stopped and stared, her eyes open wide.

For a blinding minute, she had absolutely no idea what to do. Lauren stood beside her car, glass puncturing the soles of her expensive shoes. Her hands dangled at her side, the skin of her palms clammy.

"Hey, you over there!" someone yelled behind her.

Lauren whipped around. An elderly woman, walking far faster than her frame should have managed, stormed toward her. Her gray hair was pulled back into a messy bun and a mottled stain marred the front of her billowing yellow shirt.

"You get away from that!" the woman yelled.

"It's my car," Lauren said.

"Yours?" The woman appeared to notice the broken window. "You broke your window."

Lauren blinked. "I didn't."

The woman stopped way too close to Lauren.

"You did," she said. "Look."

"Who are you? Someone broke into my car."

The woman stepped past Lauren and inspected the damage. She bent over and peered into the car through the gaping window.

"Definitely didn't happen here. You better go home." The old woman waved her away.

"What?" Lauren asked, her voice high pitched.

"You go home," the woman snapped.

Lauren took a step toward the car. She had no idea what to do. The woman hovered near her, threatening.

At that moment, a beat cop walked by. Lauren did not see him at first but the cop must have sensed something going on. He approached with a hand on his belt.

"Everything all right, Ms.?" the cop asked.

"Everything's fine," the old woman interjected.

The cop did not acknowledge the woman. Instead, he stared at Lauren. He was tall and well built with a crew cut and wore mirrored aviator glasses. She felt both uneasy and thankful at the same time.

"I was running. When I got back . . ."

"She broke her window," the old woman cut in.

The cop turned on her. "You have one second to get back to that shack of yours before I write you a citation for being annoying."

The old woman fumed, but hurried back to the front of the lot.

"Now then," the cop said, turning back to Lauren. "You were running?"

"Yeah." She could feel her hands shaking. "When I got back, the window was broken."

"Anything missing?" he asked.

Her cheeks blushed. "I don't know. I never checked."

The cop motioned toward the car. Lauren walked slowly to the door and opened it. Glass fell to the pavement.

"Let me get that for you," the cop said.

He stepped up and brushed the broken glass off the Datsun's driver's seat. A piece pierced the skin of his middle finger. He did not react.

"You're bleeding," Lauren said.

"It's nothing."

She looked at his finger for a second and then bent into the car. Two pennies were all that was left of her full change drawer. The glove box hung open and a few CDs were thrown around the passenger side seat and floor. A quick scan told her four of her favorites were missing.

"Change and a couple of CDs. They didn't even take them all."

The cop pretended to write on his ticket pad. "Got it. Discerning scumbag. What kind of music did he like?"

Lauren realized she was being teased. To her surprise, it calmed her down a bit. She put her hands on her hips.

"Who said it was a he?" She smiled. "My Indigo Girls is missing."

"Touché," he said, laughing. Then his tone turned serious. "I hate to say this, ma'am, but we'll never catch him, I mean, her. At the end of the day, it's going to cost you more to fix the window then what the scum got from breaking it. I'm sorry."

"Aren't you going to brush for prints or something?" she asked.

"That's TV stuff, ma'am. Stuff like this happens in this city every second. There's just not enough of us to do anything about it."

Lauren could not believe it. She started to say something else but stopped. The cop smiled and pulled something out of his shirt pocket.

"This is my card. Call me if anything else happens, or if you want to have dinner, or you get robbed by any more folk-singing female bandits."

Lauren took the card before she processed what he had said in the middle. Dinner? Did he ask her out? Her cheeks grew even hotter.

"I got to go," she said. "I have an interview."

As she turned toward the car, Lauren felt foolish for having made an excuse for herself. She glanced over her shoulder and saw the cop smiling at her.

"Stay safe," he said.

She smiled back. "You, too."

She knew she should not be driving. Between someone breaking into her car, the conversation with that crazy old woman, then the officer, the afternoon had put her on edge. She had to get past that, though. It was an important day. She had to get home and get cleaned up. She was dangerously close to being late for her meeting with Dr. J. Edgar Connor, M.D., Ph.D., Chairman of the illustrious Department of Ophthalmology at the Johns Hopkins School of Medicine.

Lauren had a small apartment in a house on Federal Hill. When she reached her street, every parking spot was taken. Pounding the steering wheel, she circled the block then turned down a side street. Two intersections later, she found a spot. Jumping out of the car, she jogged to her door.

Once inside she glanced around her Warren Avenue apartment, her mood darkening. Four spider plants hung brown and wilted atop the half-wall separating her updated kitchen from her narrow living room. Someone had told her they were the lowest maintenance plants out there. Greeted by the dying leaves, Lauren felt a familiar tug in her chest.

"I need a vacation," she whispered.

She stepped into the kitchen. A wicker basket held crumpled dry cleaning slips. In a panic, she turned and rushed back to her bedroom. Prying open the ancient closet door, she shuffled through her clothes, taking a deep breath of relief when she pulled out a pressed blue business suit.

Lauren's spandex running shirt stuck to her damp skin as she peeled it off. Walking to the bathroom, she turned on the shower and checked the clock. She had an hour to get ready and make it to the Wilmer Eye Institute for her meeting.

Tugging off the rest of her clothes, she jumped into the still cold shower and squealed. Shivering, she soaped up and washed her hair. She ran her hands over her ripe breasts, wishing someone else would do that, but she never had the time. Rinsing the last of the shampoo out, the water had just reached a comfortable temperature. She climbed out.

She dressed as quickly as she could. Picking up her hair dryer, she glanced at the clock again. She groaned when she saw the time and put it back down. Instead, she brushed her hair out and arranged it into a tight bun. She slipped into her shoes while rushing out the door.

Traffic crossing the city was abysmal. Pulling into a garage a block from the intersection of Wolfe and Monument, she tried in vain to calm her nerves. No one in their right mind kept Doctor Connor waiting.

Calling J. Edgar Connor a doctor was somewhat of a disservice. He was an M.D., Ph.D. who was chairman of the most prestigious teaching center for ophthalmology in the world. His long-term interest in genetic engineering in the management of eye disease made him a guest of honor around the world. As a senior medical student who had not even started her internship, she could not believe she was heading up to his office for a private, informal meeting made at his request.

Lauren threw her car into the first open parking space she found. She jogged through the garage toward an elevator. Reaching it, she pushed the button. Her foot tapped as she waited for the door to open.

When she had made the decision to run that morning, she had felt the need to relieve some of the stress that had built up since she received the call from Dr. Connor's office requesting the meeting. She had not expected her car to be broken into and there to be so much traffic that it took her half an hour to drive barely twenty blocks. Shaking her head, she wanted to scream. She should have known better.

It was five-thirty-two when Lauren tentatively knocked on Dr. Connor's office door. No one answered. Lauren opened the door slowly and peeked inside. A desk sat empty in the middle of a good sized reception area. An office door beyond the desk was half opened. She heard nothing but her own breathing.

Lauren stepped in.

"Hello," she said.

Something rustled inside the back office. The door swung in and Dr. J. Edgar Connor appeared at the threshold. He was a tall man, six foot-one inch, partially bald and amazingly overbearing in the vein of European aristocracy. His face was clean shaven and the gray hair at his temples was neatly trimmed. Lauren could tell even through his loose fitting blazer that the doctor took care of his body. Her respect for him immediately increased, if that was even possible.

"Lauren Chandler," Dr. Connor said. His voice filled the room. "Thank you for coming."

He walked around the receptionist desk, his hand extended. Lauren shook it, fighting to keep her pinky from collapsing under his firm grip. The palm of his hand was cool and as hard as iron.

"Thank you for inviting me," Lauren said. Her voice did not betray the nerves that raged inside. "I was surprised you called."

"Nonsense," Dr. Connor said, still holding her hand. "Follow me."

He let go and led the way back into his office. Lauren took a deep breath and followed. She still could not believe she was there. His call had been far from protocol.

The normal process for applying for residency started the senior year of med school. After selecting a program of interest, the student applied to the Ophthalmology Matching Program, an independent organization that through a computer program matched the student's prioritized list of programs and with each eye department's choice of applicants. For instance, if University of Pennsylvania was a student's first choice and the University also had the student rated highly, that would be a match. In the end, there would be only one match per applicant. He or she had to take it or leave it.

Usually the interview took place prior to the final submission to the matching program, allowing the students and the programs to learn more about each other before final matches would be set. The different programs reviewed the applications and would come up with the number of students they wanted to interview. An interview at Johns Hopkins was one of the most difficult to earn.

Lauren had submitted her application to the Wilmer Institute but had not heard as yet about an interview. To get a call asking for an "informal meeting" by arguably the world's leading doctor of ophthalmology was mind blowing. Although flattered, Lauren was a little suspicious as well. She just hoped she could not guess Dr. Connor's true reason for this meeting.

When she entered Dr. Connor's office, she looked around her, awed. The space was huge. Atop a massive credenza, pictures of Dr. Connor shaking the hands of world dignitaries were lined up with obvious care. She saw Presidents Clinton and G. W. Bush. There were others, too. One she could have sworn she recognized from a Newsweek article as the president of Argentina.

A dozen lacquered plaques with modest black rimmed frames hung on the walnut paneling of the wall. They held honorary degrees from around the world. Inside a tall glass cabinet rested an assortment of ophthalmological instruments dating back to the 17th and 18th centuries. There were moderate-sized forceps and syringes with large, bent needles. Some of the older instruments had pale ivory handles.

"Beautiful, aren't they," he said, stopping behind his desk. He seemed to think better of it and motioned toward two stuffed burgundy chairs with brass rivets. "Have a seat."

Lauren chose one, sitting on the soft leather. Dr. Connor came out from behind his desk and sat in the one beside her. He looked as if he might reach out and touch her leg. Instead, he cleared his throat and sat back.

"I am so sorry for keeping you waiting," she said.

"No problem, no problem," he answered briskly. "It gave me time to finish my PowerPoint presentation for the upcoming American Academy of Ophthalmology in Chicago next month. Tell me about yourself."

Lauren paused, gathering her thoughts, knowing every word would count. Not only was Dr. Connor a giant in the field, but he was known for having collected an all-star faculty.

"You're wondering why I asked you to come. You probably recognize this is not the traditional way we evaluate med students; however, some of my colleagues in the department have observed your level of insight and medical acumen during your elective last year, and I knew you were applying for our residency class entering in 2003."

Dr. Connor folded his hands behind his head. "I felt I'd like to get to know you even before you have the opportunity to meet with our residency application committee."

Lauren fought back an excited reaction at his mention of the residency application committee. Normally, at the time of an applicant's interview, the residency committee evaluates the applicant and the applicant asks questions of them. After all interviews the committee prioritizes the applicants. And if the program ranks the applicant high and the applicant has placed that program as her top selection, it ends up a favorable match for both.

For Lauren, the fact he had just said he wanted to meet her "before" she went before the committee hinted that a meeting was inevitable.

Taking a deep breath, she smiled. "Let me at least say 'thank you.' And tell you what a privilege it is to spend even a few short moments with one of the leaders of professional medicine from around the world."

Connor nodded. "I read your article in the proceedings of the National Academy of Science. Great stuff, especially since our dean here at Hopkins has never shown a real interest in complementary medicine. Your paper was the modern version of Pottinger's cats. Except you had taken laboratory rats and statistically demonstrated that different dietary regiments could alter vision and cognitive skills. Many researchers have evaluated mental and motor development but no one previously had charted food selection with visual status. I've always been interested in adding simple solutions to synthetic interventions. What pointed you in that direction?"

"In my junior year at Wesleyan," she said. "I began researching nutrition as it related to ocular health. After noting an increase in the incidence of macular degeneration in the country and the new projects being generated at Wilmer Eye Institute, I . . ."

"So you read Trebor Leba," he interrupted.

"Ah, yeah. Yes, I did, The Eye Care Revolution. Then I went to some of the basic references."

"I'm impressed you did this as an undergraduate," he said.

Lauren had scored a point.

"Yes," she said. "Thinking back, that book inspired me into going into ophthalmology. I realized the old saying was true. We are what we eat. We can redirect our personal physiology, perhaps even our mood, through nutrition and how we lead our lives. I realized that the eye is an active biological system and can be significantly influenced by dietary choices."

"Thus your thesis," he said.

"It seemed logical to me, dietary alterations in visual physiology in rats. I found that we could alter visual acuity in the subjects by selecting specific diets and using objects that had no scent trace, thus creating a controlled experiment.

"I also had to include the effect of tobacco, alcohol excess and lack of exercise as factors in visual status in later life and longevity. I truly believe that in the debate regarding nature verses nurture, it is obvious when it comes to the eye, that one's lifestyle and diet are crucial and too often ignored."

Dr. Connor closed his eyes. "I hear it earned you highest honors. And the Academy published it."

Lauren nodded. "And my freshmen epidemiology course at Johns Hopkins Medical School deepened my interest in developing the clinical correlations between dietary patterns and medical diseases. I was fortunate to have the opportunity to participate in the vision testing for the ARED Study."

Lauren understood that Dr. Connor had worked with the National Eye Institute to set up the ten-year Age Related Eye Disease Study evaluating vitamin supplementation and the course of macular degeneration. She had volunteered on Saturdays during her sophomore and junior years to help collect the data on the patients. Dr. Connor also knew the study was terminated at seven years because the results were statistically significant that the vitamins beta carotene, C and E, and zinc reduced the progression of the disease in more advanced cases of this degenerative condition.

Dr. Connor sat forward, nodding. Lauren knew she had impressed him, filling her with a sense of confidence. For the first time, she thought, her merit would be the deciding factor.

Dr. Connor cleared his throat again.

"I look forward to hearing about your interview with our residency selection committee but I really hope that your first choice will be our institution." He looked into her eyes. "I hear that my colleague Dr. von Fricke has also shown some interest. I hope you select Hopkins over Massachusetts Eye and Ear Infirmary."

He got up and gently grabbed her elbow. It surprised her but she did not show it. It also surprised her that he knew about Dr. von Fricke, the Department Chair at Massachusetts Eye and Ear Infirmary at Harvard Medical School. She had met him years before while doing a summer internship set up by her father. Lauren admired him but his distant, German demeanor intimidated her more than she let on.

Helping her up, Dr. Connor kindly escorted her to the door.

"So," he said. "Please extend my best wishes to Benjamin?"

Lauren's stomach sank. So much for her first interview without mention of her father.

FRANKFURT, GERMANY 2001

A large black Mercedes sedan glided up to the curb near the corner of *Kaiser Strasse Rossmarket* and *Neue Mainzer Strasse*. Gerhardt Kugler stepped from the rear of the car, pausing to tug the bottom of his vest a bit closer to his belt. He sniffed at the damp air blowing off the nearby Main River and then walked in crisply measured steps toward the entrance of a soot-darkened, nine-story office building.

A man of average height and medium build, he would be barely noticed in a crowd but for his harshly straight back and eyes that appeared a little too small for his face. Kugler nodded curtly to one of his workers as he approached the doorway. The morning sun shined off his smooth head as he stood just outside the door, making no effort to pull the handle. Finally, a uniformed guard hurried to push the door open from the inside.

Kugler walked past the guard with another nod. His footsteps echoed off the marble floor as he headed toward a bank of elevators. A small knot of office workers, who watched the scene at the entrance, had already pushed the "up" button. They sidled out of the way as he approached.

The elevator doors opened. Kugler stepped inside, alone. He turned to face the crowd and stared wordlessly as the doors silently closed. His hooded eyes partially covered his dark brown unreadable irises, much like Peter Lorre. Nonetheless, he never missed a detail. Shaking his head, Kugler pressed the nine. It lit up a pale yellow, the color of old bones.

"Weaklings," he said, as the elevator rose.

The chairman of the board of directors of Teleplunkt, a moderately successful electronic and optical engineering firm, Gerhardt Kugler still traveled under his father's shadow. He had inherited the privately held company from him five years before.

From birth, young Gerhardt had been primed to follow his father's footsteps. Teleplunkt provided for the best private schools and a degree in business management from the University of Berlin. On breaks, he would join his father at the office, watch the old man preside over the board and run the company with a steady, uncreative hand.

Gerhardt had also been told what sports to participate in, track and skiing, and what social clubs to join. He still attended the clubs, but now they reeked of what he took to be condescending indifference he received from the other members. They would glance at him for only an instant before returning to their conversation. He knew that they would welcome him if he approached. But what would he have to say to them? They could not understand his desires, his goals. Their talk could not interest him.

Alone in the elevator, Kugler smiled, knowing that this day would change all that. His father's shadow would be put to rest, along with the failures of the past.

The door opened on the ninth floor and he stepped off onto the plush cranberry carpet. He walked straight past his secretary's desk without a word, not even pausing to collect that day's edition of Frankfurter Allgemeine Zeitung that rested in anticipation atop her desk, unfolded and ironed as per his demands.

Kugler opened his office door and peered back. His secretary looked away as if caught doing something wrong.

"Hello, Fräulein Griswold. Lovely day, isn't it? Thank you for caring for my paper. Have the board members arrived?"

She did not make eye contact. "Yes, Herr Kugler, they have."

As soon as he closed his door, he noticed the scarred Anvil case on his desk. His heart leapt with excitement. Finally, it had arrived.

Kugler walked slowly to his massive oak desk. No papers marred the shining surface. Only the case awaited his attention. He stood over it like a father might his newborn son.

The top of the case had been pried open. Kugler ran a finger along the damaged security lock. He paused, prolonging the moment out of excitement and a tinge of apprehension. Once he looked, there would be no turning back. His destiny would be committed. Thinking once again of his father, he opened the case.

Kugler pulled a manila envelope from the case, ripping it open. Turning it, he dumped the contents on his desk. A bound report and a small plastic packet of white powder fell to the polished oak. Kugler grabbed the report first.

Flipping it over and sliding it under his desk lamp, he took a closer look. Large-print characters embossed the top of the page. Under an official looking government seal, familiar characters spelled out the only few words Kugler could make out. He did not read or speak Korean, but he recognized, *Democratic People's Republic of Korea*.

Smiling, he leaned forward and pressed the intercom button on his phone.

"Helga, call Kim. I need something translated, *schnell*."

He let go of the button and reached for the packet of pure white powder. Kugler hesitated for a moment, then picked it up. He held it up to the light.

This was the chance he had been waiting for his whole life. He knew that if he left it up to the dried up men on the board of directors, they would tell him to wait, consider, plan, or worse, pass up the opportunity.

Kugler, on the other hand, saw the contents of the case as the one piece he needed to make the leap to world-recognized business leader, legend maybe. This powder was richer than any pension fund he could rob, or any no-interest "loan" from one of the unofficial banks that existed on the second floors of the buildings by the river.

One person had already died to get this case on his desk. More may follow. The one thing Kugler knew for certain, though, was that he would not leave it up to the board to decide.

A tap on the door interrupted his thoughts. The cleaning women entered. Most of her face was hidden behind a burqa. Only her dark eyes could be seen, and they met Kugler's without embarrassment.

"Out," he barked at her.

The woman bent and picked up his full trash can.

"Out," he repeated. The anger boiled inside him. "Get out and know your place, woman. After I have you fired, I will get you deported."

The woman smiled and walked out of the office with the trash can. Kugler stared, his eyes blazing. He knew he needed to control his words, his actions, until he was free to act openly with the public support. But at that moment, with the case at hand, he could not abide by the woman's presence. To him, she was a blight on his *Vaterland*, and she must be swept away. Soon, he thought, she would be.

"The end, father," he said, and quietly laughed.

The boardroom was laid out to his father's specifications. One of the few tricks Kugler's father had passed on to him was to seize the advantage in any situation. Following that rule, he had arranged the room with the mullioned windows facing to the west. He sat down with his back to the window. Normally, like his father before, he would call meetings for late in the day. Like his father used to say, "A fighter pilot always attacks out of the sun."

To Kugler's father, business could best be described with military analogies. Ironically, the old man had never taken up arms in the country's defense. His weapons during the war had been his cunning, his ability to know almost instantly who would survive, and thus latch himself to the winner.

It began so mundane. His father started a small company that made, of all things, pipes—for tunnels, industrial uses and residential sewers, concrete down to plastic. When the war broke out, he saw an opportunity. He approached a man, Heinz Becker, who worked with Hitler's SS on infrastructure plans. Heinz used whatever methods he deemed fit to obtain the lands the war machine would need. Kugler's father, seeing the future, donated materials and time to make Heinz's work easier.

His work won him the regard of the Reich. He was awarded contract after contract. When the momentum of the war changed, he read the winds. As sly as before, he used his good fortune to hire officers, young and old, and in the end, gave them alibis that saved them from the trials in Nuremburg. Thus, he built a workforce that would die for him before betraying Teleplunkt.

Kugler took his seat at the table, another of his father's favorite sayings coursing through his mind, "Take whatever advantage you can find; there is no such thing as a fair fight. Honor is only awarded to the winner."

"Guten Morgen!" Kugler said to the men sitting around the table.

"Guten Morgen, Herr Chairman," they answered.

Kugler cleared his throat. "I called the Board of Directors of Teleplunkt together this morning for we stand on the threshold of a bold future. Today, I will ask you all if you are prepared to follow me forward.

"We, Teleplunkt, have been a successful player in the electronic and optical engineering market for over three generations. Successful, but not universally respected. Not yet."

One of the board members protested but Kugler silenced him with a stiff hand gesture.

"When I inherited this company from my father, all of you were already on the board. We were the men my father hand-picked to lead Teleplunkt into the future. He dreamed of comfort, the status quo. I, my brothers, see things differently.

Kugler smiled. "Our current path will keep us all in our Daimler-Benzes, or comfortable in our winter chalets, or provide the upkeep for our modest *schlosses.* That is what my father wished for. Grab our place in the world economy and fight all comers."

Kugler swiveled in his chair, glancing at the oil portrait of his father hanging perfectly level on the wall.

"I have done that," he continued. "None of you can deny that. You have all spent the money I earned for you."

Kugler watched the men arrayed about him for their reaction. Most claimed their chairs not as a result of working with Kugler on any day-to-day operations or projects for Teleplunkt, but due to his father's wily dealings. It did not hurt that many of the names contained the aristocratic "von" that continued to signify superiority generations after the accomplishments that earned them, added prestige to the firm. Such names looked good on an annual report.

More than half of them were so obvious in their disinterest that it bordered on rudeness. Willem von Gungen, a man who strived to do nothing but live off his father's success, appeared to be nursing a mild hangover. Otto Spartin, one of the original backers of his father, with capital his family had siphoned from the collection sheds at camps in Poland and East Prussia sixty years before, suffered from sleep apnea appeared near falling asleep.

Watching the rest, Kugler found the handful who returned his gaze with steady-eyed interest, obviously aware that this was not shaping up to be a rubber stamp board meeting. These were the men Kugler had appointed since his father's retirement.

There was Hulger Schmidt the financial wizard. He had taken a small telecommunications company and secured lucrative government contracts that helped them grow close to being a monopoly. More importantly, Schmidt was the nephew of the Prime Minister, and was now a successful broker on the German market. He and his wife lived alone in the heart of Bonn.

Next to him sat Dieter von Brock of the Bundesbank, a young executive with a list of accomplishments well beyond his years. While the world enjoyed an economic bonanza, von Brock saw the future. He reevaluated the market and said, "Cash is king. This has always been the case with the Wallenbergs of Sweden. Keep cash and prudently reinvest. Buy distressed assets at low prices. Then sell good assets at their peak." Although his true genius would not be apparent for years, Kugler saw the truth in his words.

There was also Juergen and von Müller. Both stars of Germany's reunified government, they were known best for their staunch opposition to the European Union. Gunter Jeurgen, an asset manager and Arnold von Müller, an executive at Daimler Benz, would surely see the future Kugler knew was his destiny.

These were the men he directed his address to.

"The old days are gone," he whispered.

He bent and picked up the scarred case off the floor. Kugler held it over his head for a second and then slammed it onto the conference table. The framed portrait of his father shook. Old Otto awoke with a start.

Kugler's voice grew more firm as he continued. "In here is the future of this firm, this country, the very society we live in. The path I, and those who join me, take forward will be hazardous, even more than the one our fathers took after the war."

Eyes widened at his comment. Some of the older members in the room could have been arrested and found guilty at Nuremburg had luck turned a different way. Kugler had everyone's attention.

"Those who do not wish to risk all, who do not envision a day when the world will know each and every one of the names on this board of Teleplunkt, for better or worse, those who are not willing to put all that they and their families have at risk, this is the end."

Kugler paused.

"Are you prepared to go with me?" he asked in a voice that might have shaken his father from the grave. "I will not tell you where this path leads, but I will promise you it will be perilous. I will not tell you the risks, but I can tell you they will be substantial. I will tell you that the decision you make here today at this table, will be the most important decision of your life."

Kugler stood, case in hand. His tone returned to normal as he turned his back on the board.

"I will leave now by the door to my private office," he said, his eyes closed. "Those who decide against a continued involvement in Teleplunkt will be free to leave by the main door. Their investments, along with a sizable lump sum payoff will be delivered to them upon signing of the documents of resignation from the board. You will find the necessary documents on the table just outside the boardroom. Sign them, take your money, and we will appreciate seeing you at the annual Christmas party."

Kugler turned, looking only at the men who had paid attention to his speech earlier.

"Those who will go forward into this adventure with me are asked to join me in my office. And be assured, gentlemen, once you walk through that door, you are committed unto the end."

He walked as slowly as he could toward his door. Over his shoulder, he added, "You have ten minutes to decide. Good day."

Kugler disappeared into his office, leaving the shocked board of Teleplunkt behind.

Kugler was not surprised by the men who filed into his office ten minutes later. He sat at his desk, nodding at each one in turn. He could still feel the sweat that had soaked into his Egyptian cotton shirt beneath his waistcoat as he waited for his door to open. He finally let himself smile as the men took seats arranged around his desk.

He knew he could never have fired the dead weight of the board. The legal ramifications would have destroyed any chance he had of moving forward. And he could not allow any loose lips aboard a ship sailing into uncharted waters.

Only four of the nine members sat before him, Schmidt, von Brock, Juergen and von Müller, all sons of Nazi war heroes. Old Otto, of course, had hurried out the front door, happy to take his riches and scuttle back into a safe den to end his days. The playboys were gone as well, unwilling to risk their decadent lifestyle.

The number meant nothing for now. There would be new appointments, men who Kugler had already handpicked for their ability to help the cause, including an ally in America, the man whose expertise made all this possible.

Looking at the men who had stayed, though, Kugler knew he had guessed right. Although the four came from different circumstances, one factor was common among the group. Each one had the cold, unblinking eyes of men who would do whatever it took to achieve their goals.

"Ruthless," Kugler thought. "Perfect."

"Gentleman," he said, still smiling. "You have chosen wisely. I see in your eyes you feel as I do. Since the war, we have toiled in a world without a true opportunity to shine in our own greatness. That has changed now. We will make the world forget the failures of our fathers, of our grandfathers. They will only remember us.

"The West will falter. Their allies will turn against them; it is inevitable. They have been left alone in the world. Their economies will tumble. With a push, the right push at the right time, they will fall. And when they do, we will be poised to regain our rightful place.

"Our country is contaminated. We have allowed the weak and useless to cross our borders, live among us, take our jobs and our handouts. We are shackled by a war lost decades before. Steps must be taken to return the *Vaterland* to what it should be. The invaders must be expelled. Our people must be cleansed. Then, and only then, can our enemies be defeated."

Kugler smiled. "We need money and influence to succeed. I have a plan that will win us more of both than you can ever imagine."

The men slid to the ends of their seats. Their hungry eyes stared at Kugler. He ate it up.

"From what you said," von Brock said. "I assume such a course would need muscle as well."

Kugler smiled. He thought of the case and the man that brought it to him. Becker was his name. The son of the man who helped his father weather the war.

"I have that well in hand," Kugler said.

The men nodded. He felt a trust building, one that would be necessary to stomach their next moves.

"Today," Kugler continued. "We are going into the medical device market. And the market share we capture will be beyond your wildest dreams."

Baltimore, Maryland 2006

The gym was crowded. Lauren ate the miles, her shoes pounding on the treadmill. Out of the corner of her eye, she could see Justin running on the treadmill beside her. She increased her pace, matching, and then topping his. He sped up, gaining on her, but she stayed a beat ahead.

Looking out the window across Wolfe Street, she watched the cars jostling to get through the overcrowded intersection down the block. Through the heavy glass of the gym's storefront, she could hear horns blaring out and people shouting over the pouring rain.

Baltimore—she had lived there now for so many years, all through medical school and now into her residency at Hopkins. Dr. Connor had come through for her, or maybe for her dad. She had deserved it though. Since then, her life had consisted of night calls every third day. The other two nights she finished clinical studies and inpatient rounds.

Regardless of the years, the city still did not feel like home to her. She missed Connecticut particularly the campus at Wesleyan. Her time there had been a utopia filled with hard but stimulating work and surrounded by well tuned, open minds, so different from the gray streets of the city.

Her glance fell to the treadmill display. She was a fraction from finishing mile eight. Listening to the rain pelt against the glass, she wished she had been able to run outside. It was one of her big days. She had planned on doing thirteen miles, but not in the gym.

Her paced slowed as she adjusted the incline down. She half-noticed Justin matching her speed. Shaking her head, she looked over. He was staring at her.

"Done for the day?" he asked.

Justin was tall and dark with tightly cropped hair and a muscular build. He worked in hospital administration at Hopkins. For almost a year, he "accidentally" bumped into Lauren at the gym. He'd make small talk, and when she turned around, she could feel his eyes on her, but he'd never built up the nerve to ask her out. For her part she was ambivalent. He was an attractive thirty-something man, and she had no ties to worry about. At the same time her life moved way too fast for additional complications.

"Yeah," she answered, slowing to a walk.

Justin did not say anything right away. When she glanced over at him again, his cheeks were red. He looked away. When she stopped the treadmill, however, he spoke up.

"You want to go get a juice?"

Lauren turned, her eyebrows furrowed. "Juice?"

He stammered. "I mean, there's a new juice bar. Down the street. I'll buy."

Lauren looked out the window. The rain continued to fall and the traffic appeared more snarled than it had a minute before. She had an hour of time free, due to her run being cut short by the weather. She had no reason to say no.

"Uh, I . . ."

Justin's face fell in an expression of rejection. For some reason, it got to Lauren. She thought about her life for a second. How many friends did she have? How often did she go out? The answers were a stark reminder of moments just like this one, moments where she had a choice but her drive checked her hand and her walls stayed up.

"You know what," she said. "Sure, let's go. I'll meet you out front in five minutes."

"Great," he said, smiling. "I'll see you in five."

Lauren walked back to the women's locker room. She already regretted having said yes. Not just that, though. She had said she'd meet him in five minutes. There was no way she could shower and put make-up on in that amount of time. She knew that's what she should do. Although it wasn't a date, per se, it was the closest thing she'd been on in a while.

Peeling off her exercise clothes, she toweled off her body and squeezed back into the khaki pants and blouse she wore to work that day. In front of the mirror, she pulled her damp auburn hair, which matched her hazel eyes, back and put it up with a spare hair band she kept in her bag. She did not look bad, but she felt like it would be obvious to Justin that she was not putting in much of an effort. Glancing at her watch, however, there was little she could do about that.

She met him in the front of the gym and they hurried through the rain. Throwing open the door to the juice bar, he held it for her. Thankful to get out of the rain, she turned and smiled. Water dripped down Justin's face and his hair was drenched. That was when she saw the look in his eye. He was taking this very seriously.

Cowed somewhat, she let him lead her to a raised table in the corner. The place looked like a modern café and everything was so new that she had the feeling they might be their first customers.

A young woman with a nose ring waited on them. They ordered healthy juice blends and some oatmeal energy bars. It took a second after the waitress left for Justin to find the nerve to start up the conversation.

"How do you like it here in Baltimore?" he asked. "You're not a native, right?"

"No," she said. "I'm from Connecticut. Baltimore's okay. Did you grow up here?"

"No," he laughed. "I'm from New Jersey."

"Oh."

The conversation stalled for a second.

"You're a great doctor," he blurted out.

Lauren laughed. She had not meant to but the comment sounded so absurd to her.

"No," he said, blushing. "I didn't mean it like that. I just meant that you look like you really know what you're doing, and what you want. It's cool."

"Thanks," she said.

Something about what he said touched her though. It was the first time in her life, she thought, that someone had told her she made a good doctor. She had the grades and the letters of recommendation to prove the point, but what Justin said was different. To her at least, he was saying that she "made" a good doctor, like her life choice had been the right one.

Lauren zoned out for a second. She thought back to when she was finishing up medical school, right after her impromptu meeting with Dr. Connor. It was the day she had taken her Hippocratic Oath.

Her class, days from graduating medical school five years before, was led into an auditorium above one of the operating rooms. Down below, surgeons worked on a man's chest. He was having a triple bypass, along with a valve replacement.

While everyone was getting situated in the room, Lauren had wandered over to the window. She peered down at the operation, looking at the patient, not the doctors. Although covered partially by a blue shroud, something about the man felt familiar to her. A mask covered most of his face and his hair was bunched under a blue skull cap. But when she looked closer, she saw a black dreadlock poking out from under the hat.

That was when she recognized who the man was. Although it seemed impossible that she could tell from just one lock of hair, she knew she was right. It was a homeless man that wandered around the streets outside the hospital. She had given him five bucks one night, mostly because he hadn't asked for it. Instead, he had just been sitting up against the wall outside the parking garage muttering to himself. The realization that she recognized the patient shocked her. Up until that point, her work in medical school had made her view the human body as a machine. There were times when she was working on a faceless patient or some random cadaver, that she felt more like a mechanic than a doctor.

Suddenly, the patient was human, a person, someone with a life. Not just that, but this man had nothing. She had never seen him talk to anyone. He had no money, no house. Yet, the doctors were working on him just like they would work on a neighbor or a family member.

In that instant, she saw her choices in a new light. She had loved the coursework, no doubt. She liked the idea of being a doctor. And, admitting it to herself in that moment, she liked the fact that her father could not help but be proud of a daughter who was a doctor. Looking down at the patient, his life in the hands of those surgeons, she realized that no matter what other thoughts she might have, that was why she would become a doctor, the best doctor she could.

When the professor asked her to take a seat, she had to pry herself away from the glass. Lauren felt warm inside, full for the first time in her life.

Days later when the dean of the medical school walked into their classroom to administer the Hippocratic Oath, her heart raced. He stood before them and said:

"Today, students, you will take your Hippocratic Oath. From this moment forward, your lives will change. You will no longer live only for yourself. You will have dedicated your life to others. When you see illness, you will be honor bound to fight it. When you see death, you will be honor bound to push it back.

"Medicine is power. When patients need us to help them, when they can no longer help themselves, we must be there. We cannot sit by and let people be harmed. We are the protectors from this moment until the day we die."

The dean's words hit Lauren more forcefully than anything had in her life. After seeing the homeless man, after how it changed her, his words reinforced her epiphany. She would be a doctor. She would help those in need. Their lives came before hers.

Justin cleared his throat. The sound jolted Lauren out of her reverie.

"What?" she asked.

Justin laughed. It was a nervous sound and she instantly felt bad for daydreaming.

"You're so beautiful." His voice shook when he spoke. "I was afraid to even talk to you the first time. And I've never felt like that before with anyone. You just seem, I don't know, untouchable I guess."

"Me?" Lauren was shocked. "I'm totally not."

Once she said it, though, it felt like a lie. She was untouchable, but it had nothing to do with whether or not she was beautiful. No, it had everything to do with walls she had built inside herself.

She had friends in college, girls, who had walls, too. Most of them had trust issues. Maybe their father left the family or was a bastard or something. Lauren's was different. She knew that. Her walls had nothing to do with trust. Instead, they had everything to do with a burning need to make her father proud. She bet that if she founded a support group for children of United States Senators, there would be no shortage of people feeling exactly the same way she did.

Although her childhood laid the foundation for her wall, she knew the height came from somewhere else. It came from that day in the auditorium, overlooking the homeless man's operation, hearing the dean speak of responsibility and sacrifice. Her life was no longer her own.

"I'm sorry, Justin," she said. "But I really need to be going."

"I figured," he said with a dejected shrug.

Lauren laughed. Justin looked hurt for a moment and then seemed to understand she was not being mean. He laughed, too.

"You're a pretty cool chick," Justin said. "Someday, you'll make someone pretty lucky."

She smiled. "Thanks, Justin."

They walked out of the juice bar and went their own ways. Lauren would see Justin from time to time. They would talk. But she would never forget his words. She already felt pretty lucky.

WASHINGTON, D.C. 2006

Senator Benjamin Chandler hurried down the wide hallway of the Dirksen Senate Building, his chief of staff rushing to keep up. He was a fit looking man of sixty with silver hair and the air of a man used to female attention. His aquiline face and Roman nose presaged his meteoric rise in politics. He was six feet three inches, a four-year tight end at Yale in the early sixties, and a law school graduate at the same institution.

He quickly rose to partnership of a small but prestigious Danbury, Connecticut, firm. Soon afterwards, he ran for city council with the full intention of moving up from there. He was a state senator for four years after that. When Connecticut's senior Senator Timothy Fowler II passed away suddenly from an aneurism, the party came to him. It had not been luck, however. Every minute he had been in the state senate, he traveled far and wide and laid the foundation for his political career. Attending every developer's dinner and every Republican fundraiser, Chandler had ensured his name would be atop the list.

In the end a few well timed words earned him the Fowler family's endorsement. He sailed to the Senate by the largest margin for a non-incumbent in state history. From there, he never looked back. Chair of the Armed Services Committee was only the newest notch in his belt.

When the Senator reached the stairwell, he headed down.

"Are you ready for this?" his Chief of Staff Isaac Abrams asked.

Senator Chandler did not turn around. "Of course, Isaac. Why are you so worried? This is no big deal."

"There's a lot of chatter," Isaac said. "I don't like it."

They reached the basement level. After flashing their credentials at a security check point, they stepped into an underground tram system. On one side of the tracks, tourists and visitors waited in line to ride the silent trains to the Capitol Building. Senator

Chandler bypassed the wait and used the tram designated for Congress and their staff.

On the way, they passed two Senate staffers that he did not recognize. He noticed the looks on their faces. At times the attention was like a drug. Drinking it in, he chose a seat two cars back and Isaac joined him. The tram slid out of the station and into the underground tunnels that connect the Senate and House of Representative offices to the Capitol building.

"What kind of chatter, Isaac," he asked.

"I'm not sure, Ben," his aide said. "Strange. All of a sudden people are talking about our bases in Germany, something about closing them and moving the troops to Afghanistan."

"That's absurd." The Senator patted Isaac on the shoulder. "So there's chatter. It can't mean anything. Don't get your panties in a bunch. Understand?"

Isaac frowned. "I know you think this is just my personal opinion clouding judgment, but I have a feeling, Ben. Just pay attention and be ready. Something weird is going on."

"It's Brown, isn't it?" Chandler asked.

"Partially," Isaac admitted. "He's started the chatter, I think."

"We all know he's got his own agenda," the Senator said. "No one is going to side with him. You know the party line. And do you think he'll sway some Ds? He's still angling for my seat. Thinks if he annoys me enough I'll step down and he'll get the nod."

Isaac laughed.

"See," Chandler added. "Nothing to worry about. Let's get this meeting done with. I'm supposed to golf with Kerrington, a hundred a skin."

Isaac smiled. "Drinks on you at Mitzy's fundraiser tonight."

"It's open bar, Isaac." He shook his head. "You are stressed, aren't you?"

The tram eased to a stop two stories below the rotunda. Senator Chandler exited and headed toward the Senate wing of the Capitol. A tourist recognized him and called out. Feeling magnanimous, the Senator stepped over and shook the man's hand over the plush velvet rope that separated the two sides of the station.

Walking up the stairs, Senator Chandler glanced up into the rotunda. He had served his country in the Senate for over a decade but walking under the great dome still touched his soul. His eyes lost focus as the full effect of the spiraling gold, brown and white design became a child's kaleidoscope. It warmed him and made him wonder for the millionth time if he had done enough to deserve the wonderful life he had been granted.

"I still love seeing it," the Senator said. "I'm as bad as the tourists."

"Sometimes, I still feel like one."

Chandler laughed. "Sorry, old friend. We are becoming the furthest thing from a tourist possible."

In general, committee meetings were held in one of the many rooms surrounding the Senate Chamber. Chandler, however, veered away from the corridor leading in that direction and instead headed straight across the lobby. When he reached the corner, he nodded at one of the pages who had corded off the entrance to the Old Senate Chamber. The page scurried to remove the velvet rope and the Senator walked inside.

Although Senator Chandler had only been the Chair of the Armed Services Committee for four years, coming into power when the Republicans regained control of the Senate, he was responsible for one of the largest coups in the Chamber's history. Using his considerable charms, he had convinced the head historian, a young woman in her early thirties who was known for wearing formfitting skirts and cat's eye glasses, into letting him use the Old Chamber. Prior to that, the room, in all its colonial grandeur, had become a museum.

Standing inside, Chandler looked around. Polished cherry desks formed a half circle before a large, raised dais. A two-tiered bench stood at the top, a high-backed chair at its center. An antique gavel sat propped on a stamped leather base.

The senator breathed in the musty air. Closing his eyes, he could see the Senates of the past busily working to shape a fledging republic. As far as he knew, no lawmaker since 1859 had sat behind that bench. When he did, presiding over the Armed Services Committee, he felt like a modern founding father righting the ship after a century of raging waters.

"I love this room," he said.

"Me, too."

Isaac walked up to the bench and arrayed the Senator's notes across the shining surface. Chandler took a moment to walk the perimeter of the chamber before joining his aide. Once seated, the other members, accompanied by their staff, filed in. Ten minutes later, the meeting was called to order.

It progressed as most Congressional committee meetings did. Some posturing, some feigned emotion, and a lot of side conversations. That all changed when Senator A. Richard Brown from Montana stood up in the middle of an innocuous conversation involving funding for a new mess hall for the US base in Germany.

Chandler saw Brown stand and ignored him for a moment. The bylaws of the committee clearly stated that all wishing to speak must be recognized by the Chair first. Senator Brown ignored that protocol and began anyway.

"My fellow senators," Dick Brown said. "I believe it's time for us to pull our troops out of Germany."

Senator Chandler had been about to silence the right-wing Montanan but the reaction of the rest of the committee stilled his hand. The room filled with open disdain for the senator's bizarre outburst.

"You scoff," Brown said. "But face the facts. Times are changing quickly. We have no right to occupy a peaceful country, a country that considers us an ally. The troops are unhappy. The German people are becoming more indignant. And the current Christian Democratic leadership may lose its majority because of issues like this. Our deficit is mounting and we need more troops in Afghanistan. And quite frankly, if we are not going to reinstitute a draft, which would be condemned by the American public at this time, we have no other source of trained soldiers other than those sitting around doing nothing in Germany. I call for this committee, and you Mister Chair, to introduce a resolution to consider a total withdrawal of American troops from German soil by the end of 2009."

The Senator from Delaware, Kerrington, stood. Smirking, Chandler recognized his young friend.

"You could introduce it yourself," Kerrington began, "if you feel so strongly about it."

The entire chamber watched the exchange and waited for the inevitable entertainment that would ensue.

"Give it to him hard," Isaac said into Chandler's ear. "Or this thing won't be going away."

Chandler nodded. He banged his gavel.

"I let this blatant disregard for procedures go too far." Chandler stood. "Senator Brown, you will not disrespect me, this committee, and even more dire, the Senate of the United States of America with these shenanigans."

For the first time since he was appointed Chair, Chandler walked out from behind the bench. He paced in front of the committee, his days as a prosecuting attorney flaring back to the forefront.

"Are you saying, Senator Brown, that the Germans want a total withdrawal of U.S. troops?"

Brown nodded.

"How can you know this?" Chandler asked. "What are your sources? I have heard no such thing from mine. And I will be glad to have them come speak before this committee and say just that."

Chandler saw his colleagues react. Always juiced for a good fight, they looked on Senator Brown with unabashed amusement. Senator Brown did not share in the fun, however. Instead, he leaned back and whispered to his aide, who shrugged in return.

Basking in the moment, Chandler walked right up to face Senator Brown.

"You stand up like this in my chamber again, sir, you can kiss your dreams of my chair, and maybe your seat, goodbye."

An uncomfortable silence dragged out after Senator Chandler's remarks. Brown stood his ground staring back in defiance. The tension broke when a Blackberry chirped from Senator Brown's pocket.

"And turn that thing off," Chandler said, turning his back on the Senator from Montana. "This meeting is adjourned."

After the meeting, Chandler caught up with Senator Brown outside. Their conversation was short but heated.

"How dare you make a mockery of my meeting?" Chandler stood so close to him that the shorter man had to look up. "It's

personal now. You understand that? Whatever it is you're up
to, I'm going to dog you every step of the way. Whatever this
is about, I'm going to be the thorn in your God damn side.
Believe me."

Chandler walked away, fuming.

Striding into his private office, Chandler shut the door once
Isaac was clear. His aide sat on the shining leather sofa and
Chandler walked to his credenza. He poured two scotches. He
handed one to Isaac, then took a seat behind his desk.

"Get German Minister Hans Krauss on the phone," the Senator
said.

"Already on it," Isaac said. "I texted him during the meeting."

"He's in Bonn?" he asked.

Isaac nodded dialing his Blackberry. After a hushed greeting,
he handed it to Chandler.

"Hans," the senator said. "How are you? Listen old man, is
there any chatter among your people about closing our bases over
there?"

There was a long pause. Chandler's facial expression turned
sour. He looked at Isaac and nodded.

"You keep up the fight," Chandler said. "I doubt any of it has
legs especially over here. But you never know."

Chandler hung up and looked at Isaac.

"Hans says there is a rising sentiment in Bonn and throughout
Germany concerning the continued US military presence. He said
he gave the usual argument that his colleagues should understand
the financial relief on the *Bundestaat* of not having to fund a
majority of the cost of maintaining armed forces.

"Prime Minister Koffler has always expressed his desire to keep
some American military forces in Germany. Who really knows
what the German people want?"

Isaac's eyes looked dark. "I told you, Ben."

"Still," the senator changed. "It would take a miracle for the
committee, let alone the Senate and House, to go with Brown. He's
an island unto himself."

"Let's hope so," Isaac said.

"No," Chandler said, his voice firm. "I know so."

Unbeknownst to both Chandler and Isaac, a microphone had been placed under a desk in the smaller room adjoining the committee chamber. The listeners understood the plan for relocation of American armed forces was far more detailed and further along than either the Senator or his aide knew.

FRANKFURT, GERMANY 2006

Gerhardt Kugler stood on a catwalk that ran the perimeter of a large factory floor. He stared down at the lines, scanning the length of it with a wry smile on his face. Other men stood around him. They chattered and he acted as if he listened. It was a talent he had learned from his father and had perfected over the years.

The sound of machinery echoed off the high steel beamed roof. It was peppered with thin windows, reducing the need to light the building artificially, a cost-cutting feature Kugler himself had designed. The air inside was crisp, another savings. Fine gray dust floated on rays of sunlight cast from above. A handful of workers stood along a series of assembly lines, performing a single, menial task, over and over again.

All but one line looked worn, purchased twenty-five years ago. They pushed various electronic components along, soldering microchips onto circuit boards and attaching motherboards to tan plastic casings. The hydraulic arms moaned and lurched, threatening to tear away from years of overuse. A mechanic scurried up and down those lines, holding everything together with a prayer.

One line, however, stood out. It snaked along a back corner, partitioned away from the rest of the floor by a half-wall. The robotics along the conveyer belt were state of the art and so new that their metal reflected the sunlight in tiny rainbows. The largest, most state-of-the-art machine had a small ID plate with a U.S. flag, and the words "Made in America."

This line appeared totally different from the others. It ran silently, like a ghost. A large arm stirred ribbons of melted plastic as a nozzle released a white additive that spun quickly into the viscous mass and disappeared.

The melted plastic pushed through a series of presses until impossibly thin. Then an array of pistons stamped out half-inch discs. The discs fell into another vat, this one filled with tiny glass beads. The discs were tumbled with the beads, polishing the surfaces to a silky smoothness.

It was this line that held Kugler's full attention.

"What do you say, father?" he whispered.

"Did you say something, Herr Kugler?" the plant manager Hubert Krentz asked.

"Nothing," Kugler said, smiling. "Nothing at all. How is Dr. Kim coming along?"

"Very well," Hubert said. "Very quiet. He rarely leaves the lab. But the lens additive has tested very well. He has been efficient, no doubt."

"Good, good," Kugler said. "And how is your son?"

Hubert's cheeks flushed. The sight of it did not shock Kugler. The plant manager had been with the company for near twenty-five years. He had worked his way up from messenger to plant manager and never let a chance go by to thank the Kugler family for it.

"He is well, Herr Kugler," Hubert said. "Thank you for asking."

Kugler put his arm around the man's shoulder. He leaned in and spoke good naturedly.

"You have proven me right, Hubert," he said.

"How so?"

"Our board wanted to acquire a lens manufacturer. Von Brock and I talked them out of it. I am happy to keep this work so close to the vest. I am sure you understand.

"Make sure you speak to the men. Remind them of the incentives for higher productivity." He spoke softly. "I've already seen the enthusiasm your people are showing for our new program. Teleplunkt will reward its heroes."

The two men walked down the catwalk, talking about the old days like great friends. He knew that Hubert, like he, understood. On his own the plant manager had decided to carefully screen each line worker. All were of good Aryan blood.

Before they reached the end, Dr. Kim arrived. He was short, no more than five and a half feet tall, and wore thick framed glasses with oversized lenses. Although it was difficult to tell from his youthful appearance, Kim was nearly sixty. Kugler and Becker had paid a fortune to smuggle him out of North Korea.

"Ah, Dr. Kim," Kugler said. "Good to see you out of the lab."

"Hello, Herr Kugler," Kim said. The scientist prided himself on his proper German. It was one of the reasons Kugler trusted him.

"How is our additive?" Kugler asked.

"It is mixing with the lenses nicely," Kim answered. "See."

Kim pointed down to the line. He directed their attention to the vat with the white powder and explained how it was added to the lenses before they hardened, ensuring no change to their clarity.

"You have done an excellent job," Kugler said.

"Our friend from America has been a huge help. His expertise in this field is second to none."

Kugler nodded. Kim waited for a second, and then spoke up.

"There was some confusion in the lab. There is talk of another additive?"

Kugler shook his head. He nodded to Hubert who understood immediately and left the two alone on the catwalk.

"There is another chemical we are obtaining," Kugler said. "But this one does not go into the lenses."

"Is it the same technology," Kim asked, interested.

"Oh, no, doctor. I believe we are the leaders in that little venture. Even your home country had not found such an ingenious way to utilize their advancements. They are still in the lab using mind control to get monkeys to scratch their asses."

Dr. Kim laughed. "Ah, but this is my country, Herr Kugler. So, what is this other chemical? Is it something we will be working on here?"

"Someday. We are obtaining it from an American pharmaceutical company first. Unlike your work, it is far less sublime. This is just the tool so that we can ensure your work will reach the masses."

"I see," Kim said. "You wish to increase the number of patients. Brilliant. I have some experience with pharmas. I am sure I can at least recreate any work over here for you to avoid any messy customs issues."

Kugler laughed, putting his arm around Kim. "We are lucky to have you, my friend."

Kim smiled. "No, I am the lucky one."

Kugler sat in the back seat of his Mercedes as it neared Teleplunkt's offices. The driver looked over his shoulder.

"You should be back in plenty of time for your 2 p.m. meeting, Herr Kugler."

Kugler nodded but did not respond. Instead, he stared out the window at the Germans walking along *Neue Mainzer Strasse*. He marveled at their stupor.

He marveled as well at how oblivious the others were. They cluttered the streets hawking useless baubles and asking for handouts. He watched a dark-skinned Turk meander through a park harassing mothers out with their children.

They all had no idea what was to come. But Kugler had seen firsthand. The line was running; the product would be ready for the market in a matter of months. There was only one more step left. Then all of Germany would know Gerhardt Kugler, all the world.

The Mercedes stopped and Kugler got out. He walked briskly through the building and rode the elevator to the ninth floor. His secretary stood as he stepped off.

"They are all here," she said, "including Herr Becker."

"Good," Kugler answered. "Thank you, *fräulien*. How long have they been waiting?"

"Five minutes," she said.

"You look nice today," he said smiling, "as usual."

Foregoing his usual entrance through his office, Kugler went in the main door. The four old and four new board members stood when he entered. He shook each of their hands before taking his seat at the head of the table. Becker nodded to him from the corner.

Although squeamish at first, the Board had grown used to having their "muscle" around. Heinrich Becker was a well dressed man in his forties with salt-and-pepper hair and an expensive blue suit. His ruby studded ring flashed in the light as he rubbed his hands together. Kugler peered into his eyes.

Kugler remembered his father speaking of Becker's father. He had mentioned the man's lifeless eyes. The apple had not fallen far from the tree. Becker stared back, his light blue eyes hiding any hint of intent or deeper purpose.

His eyes, however, belied the man's strangest characteristic. For such a daunting man, Becker's voice was surprisingly high especially when he laughed. On another man it might have been comical. On Becker, however, it added to his generally intimidating presence. Even after Kugler took his seat, he remained standing.

Before he spoke, Kugler took a moment to look at the portrait of his father again. Questions streamed through his mind. Would his father be proud? Yes, he thought so. Would his father have followed the same path, though? No, Kugler was sure he would not have. The thought filled him with pride.

"Gentlemen," Kugler said. "Have we succeeded?"

Hulger Schmidt stood. "I have made contact and the scientist has agreed to terms."

"That is good progress," Kugler said, feigning surprise. He and Becker had already spoken before the meeting.

"Yes." Schmidt seemed to do anything he could to avoid making eye contact with Becker. "The scientist is ready to deliver upon receipt of the transfer."

"How did you find this scientist?" Kugler asked. Again, he knew the answer but the question was for the benefit of the other board members.

"Our newest board member was of great assistance. His contacts in the U.S., especially in the medical field, are quite astounding, not just in his field. The scientist has assured us he can use a failing cholesterol drug to fit our needs nicely. He just needed to increase the portion of a certain additive, a side chain to a commonly available statin drug. We just need to know how to manufacture it in the correct dose." Schmidt laughed. "He does not know why we want a medicine to have a more pronounced side effect."

All eight men laughed with Schmidt. Kugler, joining in, glanced at Becker. His face never broke into a smile. Turning away, Kugler felt tears forming in his eyes and rubbed at the bridge of his nose.

"Let him think us the fools," he said. "That will change soon enough. I visited the plant today. The machinery we received from our newest board member seems to be working to perfection. The lenses for implantation could hit market in a matter of months. So we should encourage our American colleague to develop the faculty to capture the appropriate American and German markets.

The many advantages of our lens, including price and flexibility, will tantalize the doctors when presented by credible sources. We need to get our phenomenal TeleLens data into publications in both markets as well."

"Where is this mysterious new member?" another of the board members asked. A marketing director at the largest German pharma company, he had been integral in formulating the use of a statin drug to rapidly induce cataracts.

"I have asked him to stay in America just to be safe. We do not want any unneeded attention, no?" Kugler asked. "There is no need for you to know any more than he exists at this point."

The board agreed.

"Plus," Kugler continued. "He is more useful there than here. He is well connected. It was no problem for him to get us the machines we needed to outfit the plant and he was a large help to Schmidt, who happens to be his distant cousin. And I think he will become more helpful in the months to come, as we get other ophthalmologists in our target areas to use the TeleLens. As our plans continue to unfold and cataracts become more frequent, he will be instrumental in securing our position in the American eye surgery market. We already have the key target areas in Germany defined. First, Bonn, when that is established, we will move to Berlin."

"Are we still on schedule?" Juergen asked.

"Of course we are," Kugler said. "With Schmidt's good news, Becker can handle it from here. Right, Becker?"

Becker nodded but said nothing.

Kugler continued. "And the lenses are near completion. We have done much in a short time, no?"

"Yes, Herr Kugler," Schmidt said.

Although he forced back a reaction, Schmidt's use of Herr did not go unnoticed. Things were changing at Teleplunkt, everywhere really. Kugler felt the respect surrounding him like a physical being. He drank it in and it made him stronger.

"Good," he said. "Now we should discuss the first wave. Becker has laid out a plan involving McMillan Reservoir. A map is in your briefing packets. Thanks to our newest member, we secured a visitors pass to the nearby hospital on the right corner. Easy access to the water and the reservoir serves the entire city."

Schmidt spoke up. "Seems to me we are hitting far too great an area. Might it not draw attention, and do we want to affect so many people? Won't that become obvious?"

"Should we not select a more defined target area and then we can decrease the dosage of your Dramastatin? With a more specific dose we will see the desired results within weeks. Our American colleague can get us electronic access to Medicare data indicating when there is an increase in cataract exams and cataract surgery in Washington, D.C."

"What do you think, Kugler?" von Brock asked.

Kugler made a simple hand movement, a gesture that said, "Let it stay as is for the moment."

"We'll discuss this again," Kugler said. "This will be a clue to adjusting the dosage for a more defined target area. For now, it is difficult to know the correct dosage to develop cataracts rapidly without other side effects. But what a first strike it will be."

Kugler stood up, his expression stern. "I am sure I do not need to remind you that everything we discuss in this room is done so in the utmost secrecy. Any hint of our true path will compromise us all. That will not be tolerated."

"Of course, Herr Kugler."

"Good," he said. "I must go. Thank you all for coming today on such short notice. I am sure you can show yourselves out. Please leave your expense receipts with my secretary." Kugler raised his hand, "To the future of Germany."

Kugler exited into his office without a backward glance. Becker followed silently behind him. Once the door was closed, Kugler fell into his chair, legs spread out in front of him. Slowly, he turned to look out the window. Frankfurt sprawled below like a long sleeping beast. He would awaken that beast. Of that he was sure. And when he did, the wrongs of the past would be erased.

"Should you fly to the U.S. tonight?" Kugler asked. "Check out this scientist?"

Becker nodded. "But it is not the scientist that worries me," he responded in his strangely soft voice.

Kugler spun around to face him.

"No?"

"There are other impediments," Becker said.

Kugler lifted an eyebrow. "Human?"

Becker nodded.

"Who?"

"A politician."

Kugler smiled. "Yes, I heard the recordings we captured. But that won't be a problem once the first wave is complete."

"I believe he may be a problem, regardless. His antagonism to Senator Brown is extreme. He has a personal agenda to thwart Braun no matter what. It's too early for a road block like that.

"Plus, his daughter is a young ophthalmologist opening a practice in the area. Can that just be a coincidence? I have a hard time believing that. The man knows more than we think."

"I'm not sure." Kugler shook his head. "Taking out a U.S. Senator is not what I had in mind, especially not at this point. I think we should wait and see. This impediment could become an asset later, no?"

"Could," Becker said. "But he is more dangerous than you think." Becker smiled, a reptilian curl of thin lips. "I would like to take him out now."

"No," Kugler said, shaking his head. "We can't afford that kind of attention."

"I'll make it look like an accident."

Kugler laughed. "You, Becker?"

Becker's expression darkened. He stared into Kugler's eyes. Kugler fought not to look away. As the moment stretched, he felt sweat running down the inside of his silk shirt.

"I said, it *will appear* an accident," Becker said.

Kugler blinked. "One chance, with your assurance no one will know."

"Done," Becker said, leaning back. "I will be in the U.S. tonight."

"Fine."

Becker laughed. It was a chilling sound, almost womanish if it did not sound so dangerous.

Shaking his head, Kugler turned to look out the window again. Becker's father had also been sadistic. That was half of what allowed the two men to survive and flourish after the war. Drastic change took resolute people. Down below he could see the riff-raff cluttering the park across the street. Gypsies and

Turks, and probably Jews as well; the sight made his skin crawl. He thought of his father.

"Do you trust the American? Even if he is of German background, does he need to know everything?" Becker asked.

"I do believe he is loyal to the *Vaterland*," Kugler said. "He was born here and is Schmidt's father's sister's son. He left for the United States at age ten where he received the finest education. Although completely Americanized, he was disturbed by the weakness of the melting pot society that lacked true character and principle. He, being a great researcher, approached me with the idea of how to develop the cataracts in exchange for shares in the company, understanding how much money the company could make from such a move. And lastly, he learned of the Korean formula while attending an Asian Pacific ophthalmology conference. Not to mention that without his expertise, we would not be where we are today. But no, he does not have to know everything. Especially what you do, Heinrich."

Becker smiled. "Whatever you say, Gerhardt. You pay the bills. We are our father's sons."

"Wrongs of the past," Kugler whispered.

"What?" Becker asked.

Ignoring him, Kugler thought of his own son. A long-haired news reporter, they did not see eye to eye. But they would soon, Kugler was sure of it. They all would learn what was best for the *Vaterland*, for Germany.

WASHINGTON, D.C. 2006

Lauren walked into her father's townhome. She paused in the formal foyer under an antique chandelier. Furniture dating back to the American Revolution filled the house. She could hear her father in the kitchen, the ice in his glass of scotch rattling softly.

"Hi, dad," she said.

"How are you, sweetie," he said. "Glad you could make it. How's Hopkins treating you?"

"Great," she said. "Dr. Connor says hello."

"Who?" her father called from the back of the house.

Lauren hung up her coat. "My mentor."

"Oh."

Lauren smiled. It was not odd for people to think they were friendly with her father. Dr. Connor had met him twice, and looked for a sponsorship to approve NIH research funds some of which would go to Johns Hopkins. Tens of thousands of people had met her father twice. Everyone remembered a senator, but a senator could not remember everyone.

She walked slowly into the kitchen. He stood leaning against the marble counter sipping at his drink.

"Would you like one?" he asked.

She shook her head. "No thanks."

"How much do you have left?" he asked.

"Of my internship, six months."

"What's next?"

Lauren shrugged. "Dr. Connor wants me to do a fellowship in Hopkins. But I'm . . ."

"That sounds great."

"Yeah."

Lauren looked around the kitchen. It didn't look like a meal had not been cooked there for at least three months. The only dishes in the sink were two wine glasses. One had lipstick on the rim.

"Where's mom?" she asked.

"Oh, she's up in Connecticut," he said. "Some socialite thing with her friends."

"Hmmm."

She walked up to one of the cabinets and opened it. Sitting on the shelf inside were vials of pills. Most were ibuprofen, decongestants, and other over the counter meds. Her eye immediately went to a large vitamin bottle with a colorful label. The sticker read: Protect your eyes with ABLE-EYES, now with DHA and Vitamin D.

"Checking up on me, huh?" her father asked. "Told you I listen."

Lauren looked at him. "Just because you have the capsules, doesn't mean you take them."

He looked hurt. "I do, every day with meals, like you said. And I learned that capsules are better absorbed than pills, which depend on stomach acid. Since I have to take Tums all the time because of the job, I might not be able to dissolve the cheaper tablets."

"Have you had any change in your vision since?" she asked.

"Not really," he said. "I notice I see much better at night than I used to. You told me five of the ingredients specifically improve dark adaptation and night vision."

He laughed but Lauren did not. Instead, she reached in and shook the bottle. It sounded half empty. She nodded and shut the cabinet door.

"Next you're going to be hiring a PI," he said.

"I'm glad you're taking them, dad," she said.

"Well, I do have sense. And when you said take them or have surgery on my eyeballs, it was a pretty easy choice."

"Are you ready to go?" she asked.

He nodded and downed the rest of his drink. She shook her head.

"You know," she added. "You could cut back on that, too."

He put his hands up. "Come on. What's life if you don't enjoy it?"

"Longer," she said, deadpan.

He laughed. "You always did have your mother's sense of humor."

Lauren and her father walked along Wisconsin Avenue toward M Street. Shops and restaurants lined the way and the sidewalk was packed with both tourists and locals. She noticed many of them, mostly the locals, recognized her father. One or two young adults in suits said hello with sycophantic politeness.

When they reached the corner, Lauren looked up at the Riggs National Bank. The golden dome at the top of the building reflected the sun in bands of bright white light. It made her think about her father's life. She had always felt she had not lived up to his expectations. Even though she did not come naturally to the competitive drive he felt as an attorney and politician, she knew she had been competitive and effective in her own way. She hoped that as they communicated more like they were that night, the little girl inside her could be replaced in his eyes by the successful adult she had become.

"You know," her father said. "Wisconsin is one of the only streets left in D.C. that was around before L'Enfant planned out his grid."

"Hmmm," Lauren said, still looking up at the dome.

They continued to walk, neither saying anything. When they reached the restaurant, a small French café, it was not crowded. To her surprise, the hostess flirted with her dad as she led them back to their table. For his part, her father acted the innocent victim.

"What was that?" Lauren asked after the girl left.

"What?"

"That thing with the hostess," she said.

"Oh, Lauren," he said. "Come on. I know it doesn't mean much to you but I am a U.S. Senator. Around here, it's a big deal. That kind of stuff happens all the time."

Lauren shook her head. She picked up the menu, not wanting to talk about it anymore. The waiter came and took their orders. He was a young man, well put together. Lauren thought he might be flirting with her father, too. She wanted to scream.

"I don't know how you do it," she said.

"What?"

"Live here."

"You live pretty close," he said.

"I know. And I like D.C. But all this." She waved her hands in the air. "As a senator you're like a celebrity living in LA."

"Nature of the beast," he said. "I worked hard to get here. I know you think this was all handed to me. But don't forget. If it weren't for your uncle passing away, I'd probably be working some paper mill in New York."

"What do you mean?" she said leaning forward.

"You know my brother died when I was in high school."

She nodded.

"He was seven years older than I," he continued. "He was working down here as an editor for some science magazine."

"I knew that," she said. "But what does that have to do with a paper mill."

"Well, my brother had life insurance."

"So?"

"He left half of it for my college," he said, closing his eyes. "Didn't you ever wonder why you never knew your aunt and cousin?"

"I just figured they went back to her side of the family after your brother died," she said.

"They did. But part of the reason was that she was angry. My brother probably shouldn't have done it. But we, my mother, brother and I, were poor. My brother went to school on a baseball scholarship."

"He gave you the money?" she asked. "What about his daughter?"

He shrugged. "I don't know. I guess he figured his wife would be okay. She was a nurse."

Lauren stared at her father. He looked away, waving to someone in the far corner of the restaurant.

"What happened to your niece?" she whispered.

"Not sure," he said, still not looking at her. "I think she was married. She was home with her kids. And her husband died, about the same age as her dad was."

"Oh, God," Lauren said.

He turned, looked her directly in the eye. "Every day, I feel guilty about it. I worked my butt off trying to make my brother's decision the right one. But who knows."

Their food came at that instant. She watched her father as their plates were placed in front of them. He looked tired, and something more. For the first time in her life, she felt her relationship with him change.

"I never knew all that," she said.

He smiled. "I wish I didn't, either."

When they left the restaurant, it was already dark. They picked their way through the growing crowd until they reached N Street. From there they went two blocks, taking a right onto her father's street.

Most of the interior lights were on inside the row of federal homes lining the street. Inside, magazine type décor was clearly in view through parted curtains. As she passed one house, Lauren saw a real gas lamp sconce burning in one of the living rooms. At the same time, she happened to notice the streetlamp in front of her father's house was out.

"This is an amazing place," she said. "Really makes you feel like you're back . . ."

The sound of an engine rumbling around the corner cut Lauren off. She heard the bump and screech of tires jumping a curb.

She saw something coming at them through the dark. Lauren grabbed her father by the upper arm.

"Oh God!" she screamed.

Lauren pushed her father. Together, they fell off the sidewalk, down a flight of stairs leading to a basement apartment entrance. At the last second, her arm protected her head from slamming into the concrete. The Senator screamed next to her.

An instant later, the sound of shattering glass and rending metal erupted above them. Lauren's vision cleared in time to see a rearview mirror slam into the brick wall beside her head. A woman screamed from the street above.

"Dad," she said.

He did not answer. Her voice turned frantic.

"Dad?"

He groaned. "I think my arm is broken."

"Are you okay?"

"It hurts like hell."

She stood, the dizziness almost knocking her back to the ground.

"I'm going for help," she said.

Lauren staggered up the stairs. Before she got halfway, a middle-aged man in a blue business suit appeared at the top of the stairway.

"We need help," she said.

The man stared at her. There was something odd about him. She did not see him blink. The man stood there for a second. His hand slipped behind his back. Lauren heard footsteps approaching from every direction. People were talking loudly about the crash. The man looked over his shoulder as two women rushed into view. He turned and walked away. Lauren saw a flash of red on his finger before he disappeared into the night.

WASHINGTON, D.C. 2006

Heinrich Becker was not used to failure. From across the street, he stared at the white van as white smoke billowed up from under the hood. The driver stirred, working on the door handle from inside.

Nonchalantly, Becker crossed the street. His mind ticked off possible actions. He could off the driver, put a bullet through the man's head. Although preferable, it would draw too much attention. Instead, he reached into the bag he carried and pulled out a small black device. It looked like a tin of chewing tobacco. Inside, however, was a enough Semtex to blow the van and driver ten feet off the ground.

He chose the explosive because the bomb was specially made by an expert in his outfit that assured him that only faint traces of the Semtex would be found on the scene, enough to detect but not enough to attribute as the cause of the explosion. Although counterintuitive, it would be less obvious than the bullet.

When he approached the car, the driver's side door opened. The man he had paid ten thousand dollars to simply run over two pedestrians, tried to get out. He stuck his head past the frame, blood dripping from a laceration on his forehead.

Becker kicked the door. It slammed shut on the man's skull. As the door swung back open, he pushed the driver, knocked senseless from the blow, back into the van. Becker closed the door and bent down. He reached under the van as far as he could and placed the Semtex near the gas tank.

He looked around. There were people running toward the van, dialing on their cell phones and calling out for help. Few, however, seemed to have seen the two pedestrians who dove out of the way and down a flight of stairs. Even from there, he could hear the man screaming out in pain.

Becker walked up to the top of the stairs. The girl was up. She appeared unhurt. She looked up at him, but he knew she could not see clearly through the darkness. He reached back and drew his gun.

Before he could pull the trigger, a siren rang out. More people appeared. A curtain right in front of him parted and an old woman peered out, directly at him.

Cursing, Becker holstered the gun. He took a step back and then turned to walk down the street. Furious at Kugler for not letting him just shoot the two in the head, he detonated the Semtex. The van exploded and Becker disappeared around the corner.

WILMINGTON, DELAWARE 2006

Kermit Steinmetz sat in a nondescript white sedan he had rented at the Philadelphia International Airport. He glanced at his watch for the fifth time. It was 4:53 p.m. on a Monday. He picked up the phone and dialed Becker.

"What is it?" his boss abruptly asked.

"He has not shown yet," Steinmetz said.

"Give it time. You need to be patient."

"I don't get it, though," Steinmetz said. "We already have the chemical. You got it from the North Koreans, right?"

"Don't be stupid," Becker said. "Even with what we stole from the North Koreans, and the work Kim has done on it, we still need to make sure that the people we want to have the lens must need to get it."

"What does that have to do with some two-bit American scientist and a failed cholesterol drug?"

"Steinmetz, you are not paid to think. We'll leave it like this. We need to be able to make sure that certain people get cataracts or they will never need our lenses, right? So get the chemical and call me back. Stop asking idiot questions."

Becker hung up. Steinmetz tapped at his steering wheel, annoyed. He had parked the car in the parking lot of an Acme market off U.S. 202 about two hours before. The wait had been long but he knew he was close. When the silver BMW rolled into the parking lot a minute later, he restarted his engine.

The man driving the BMW looked lost. He glanced nervously around the parking lot. Steinmetz flashed his lights three times. The BMW flashed back once.

Steinmetz pulled his sedan out as the BMW passed his spot. From there he followed the car through a back exit of the shopping center. They wove through neighborhood after neighborhood before crossing a major highway. Down another and back around, the BMW rolled into the parking lot of a small warehouse. The large buildings of a pharmaceuticals campus rose above the trees behind it, secure behind a high barbed wire fence.

When they got out of the car, Steinmetz walked up to the man. His name was Harvey. He was short and balding, wearing a short sleeved oxford shirt and slacks that hung two inches above the top of his shoes.

"Isn't that your company?" Steinmetz asked, pointing at the campus behind the fence.

Harvey nodded.

"Then why did we drive around like that?" Steinmetz asked.

"Because," Harvey said. He talked through his nose. "Someone might have tailed me."

Steinmetz rolled his eyes as he followed the little man to the entrance of the warehouse. Next to a huge loading dock, a set of stairs led up to a single door. The man leaned forward like an elderly lady at an ATM and punched in a security number. The lock clicked open and the man slipped inside, beckoning Steinmetz to follow.

The building opened up into a large, empty space. There were hundreds of boxes stacked up to the ceiling in one corner. A nondescript white van was parked behind them. The man led Steinmetz past all this and to another door at the center of the back wall. He punched in another security code and turned before opening the door.

"In quick," Harvey said, "can't have the odor escaping. People might notice."

Confused, Steinmetz stepped closer. When the man opened the door, a blast of fetid air struck him in the face. The stench of caged animals enveloped them. Steinmetz reared back. The man looked annoyed and pulled him into the back room.

"Hurry," he said. "We need to shut this quickly."

In the dark Steinmetz could hear small animals scratching at metal. Rodents cried out. The sound seemed to come from everywhere.

After securing the door, the man hit a light switch illuminating the lab. Steinmetz walked into a good-sized laboratory. It was in pristine shape, belying the strong smell in the air. Instruments and equipment lined floor to ceiling shelves, everything clean and in order. Cages of animals were stacked neatly in the far corner. There were rats and rabbits, even a Rhesus monkey languishing in the shadowed recesses of its cage.

"*Mein Gott,*" Steinmetz whispered.

"Great, huh?" Harvey asked. "This is where I do my best work, all the stuff that the company doesn't let me do. They're idiots. They want us scientists to come up with the next great drug but they put all these restrictions on us. We can't do this, we can't do that. You know, they took the animals out of our lab. Can you imagine?"

Steinmetz shrugged. "So, no one knows about this place?"

"Are you stupid?" the man said. "I told you, I am very careful. Even my family has no idea."

Thinking, Steinmetz glanced at the closest cage. One of the rats teetered, moving as if blind. The man noticed and scurried over to a work station. He jotted something into a notebook. Without looking back, he spoke.

"You know, it wasn't so easy getting the stuff you needed."

Steinmetz looked at the man. "Our associate assured us that the drug would be available to you."

"I got the statin," Harvey said. "Producing the chain additive, on the other hand . . . Come here, look."

The man pulled Steinmetz to his desk. Flipping through pages, he turned to one. It was the chemical formula for Dramastatin, the concocted statin derivative they had paid the scientist to create from the formula he had stolen from his employer, Pharmoletia. They called it Dramastatin because of the high level of secrecy attached to the entire project. The diagram on the left was the original statin. Attached to it, however, was an additional molecular side chain.

Steinmetz quickly assessed the material on the page. He saw a list of the exact amount of the side chain components and enzymes to bond it to the parent chemical structure. The details were complete and the animals in the warehouse testified to its effectiveness.

He stared at the scientist for a second. The man was a chemist with curly brown hair and thick glasses. He had a long career with a big company, and Steinmetz was sure the man felt he was undervalued and underpaid. He was the typical spy. But Harvey was not a typical spy. He was receiving $50,000 from Teleplunkt for doing ordinary work in secrecy. And he was a total amateur.

"Beautiful huh?" the scientist said.

"This one on the right is the formula?" Steinmetz asked.

"It is, and it wasn't easy to develop."

"That is why you are being paid," Steinmetz said. "Do you have your drawings on the computer?"

"No." Harvey rolled his eyes. "Someone could hack it."

"The final product is clear, correct, and untraceable when immersed in water?"

"Of course, my work is excellent. I earn my salary, which only paid for half of my Beamer."

Harvey never looked back at him. Steinmetz reached behind his back. His fingers moved with the grace of a practiced musician as he loosed the handgun in its holster.

Harvey reached down and picked up an egg crate. Two gallon jugs rested inside. Steinmetz could see the silver, viscous liquid through the fogged plastic of the jugs.

"That's it," the scientist said. "And it's all you get for now."

One of Steinmetz's eyebrows arched. "Hmmm. Will it work?"

Harvey looked too excited. "Of course. Come here, come here."

He pointed at a set of five cages away from the rest. A rabbit huddled in each one.

"Watch this," the man said.

Steinmetz leaned over and peered into one of the cages. The man took out a penlight and shined its beam into the rabbit's eyes. They glowed cloudy green.

"Total vision loss in only three weeks." The man's voice quivered. "Mind you, that's eighteen times the necessary dose in milligrams per kilograms for humans."

"What does that mean?" Steinmetz asked. "For humans?"

Harvey laughed. "That is the question, aye. The one you paid me so much for. At the dosage you spoke of, like you requested, we're talking symptoms progressing slowly over the matter of a month, depending on concentration and sunlight exposure."

"And you are sure?" Steinmetz asked.

The man blinked. "Of course I am."

"You're bonus will be deposited tonight then," Steinmetz said.

The scientist appeared giddy. He moved closer to the caged rabbits and began to shine the light directly into their eyes.

Steinmetz heard a squeal. Ignoring it, he took the gun out of its holster. He attached a silencer behind his back. Why disturb the animals any more than was necessary.

"So, all your work is safely here?" he asked.

"Geez," Harvey said. "I didn't think Becker would send an idiot. Of course it's all safe here! I said no one even knows this place exists."

"Good," Steinmetz said.

He knew that all of the now identified ingredients in the lab would be readily available to Dr. Kim, the scientist at Teleplunkt in Frankfurt. With the formula in hand, there would be no more need of a loose end.

He lifted the gun and fired in one movement. The bullet took the man in the forehead. His legs lifted off the ground and he slammed into the stack of caged rabbits. They crashed to the ground on top of the dead man's body.

Steinmetz reached down and pulled a set of keys out of the man's pants. One of the rabbits tumbled through an open door. Steinmetz, disgusted, kicked it. He turned and walked out of the lab.

In the other room, he walked over to door. He pulled out his phone.

"Becker, Steinmetz," he said. "I have everything." He paused. "As you directed, I have the recipe. Totally untraceable. I will stay until you give me my next assignment. I'll be using the name of Miller."

"Fire the lab," Becker said.

"But it's safe. I thought . . ."

"Just do it," Becker ordered.

Steinmetz hung up the phone and loaded the white sedan He took all of the chemical plus every record he could find. He took pictures of the animals and the white boards that Harvey used. He took the notebook and the chemical jars containing the altered statin. When he was done, he planted Semtex all over the lab.

Pulling away in the white sedan, Steinmetz detonated the building. Flames engulfed his rearview mirrors. Harvey and his rabbits would be difficult to identify.

Baltimore, Maryland 2006

The patient, a forty-three year old male, rested comfortably on a hospital bed in Surgery B. A large microscope hovered above, aligned with his eye. Lauren leaned in and placed a single drop of 4 percent xylocaine, an anesthetic, on the outside of his eye. The man blinked.

"Everything looks great, Mr. Derringer," Lauren said. The bruises from her accident still bothered her. She smiled through them. "This shouldn't take long at all."

Using a sticky drape, the nurse secured the eyelids so they could not close during surgery. Mr. Derringer smiled.

"I wondered how I wasn't going to blink," he said.

Lauren smiled back, although her mouth hid behind a surgical mask. "I hear that all the time. During surgery I'll be numbing the eye several more times. You shouldn't feel a thing. The hardest thing for you is going to be looking into that bright light from the microscope for twenty-five seconds."

Lauren made a partial incision on the edge of Mr. Derringer's cornea. A small wound opened on the eye, just about an eighth of an inch.

"Now look into the light as best you can," Lauren said. "Five quick steps and we'll blur the light."

After injecting several drops of anesthetic, Lauren removed the front of the cataract capsule. Then, she injected saline into the lens to reduce glare and make Mr. Derringer more comfortable.

"I see lights," Mr. Derringer said. "Beautiful, and not too bright."

"Try to stay as still as possible," Lauren whispered.

The nurse handed her a short, tapered instrument. Lauren aimed it at the lens. When she activated it, the instrument emitted high-speed sound that shattered the center of the lens, the nucleus, into pieces that were easily aspirated. She then removed the soft, outer cortical portion of the cataract.

Working quickly, Lauren injected the eye with viscoelastic material to ensure that the anterior chamber did not collapse and the pupil remained dilated. From there, she affixed a finely polished artificial lens into the now empty lens capsule. These intraocular lenses were developed to replace the focus power of the natural lens of the eye.

The new implants were able to reduce a six millimeter optic for plastic cataract lenses to three millimeters because of the current folding technique. Rarely did the wounds require suturing. The prices of some of these implants were still beyond what many of her non-professional patients could afford. Ophthalmologists had been selecting implantable lenses which could be billed to the patient as a way of countering the loss of Medicare reimbursement.

Lauren prepared to finish the operation. The final procedure inside the eye was to aspirate the residual viscous material and replace it with normal saline. The wound was then tested to ensure that it was water tight. As a last step, a contact, soaked in antibiotics, was placed as a clear bandage over the eye.

"All done, Mr. Derringer," Lauren said.

"Wow," he said. "No big deal at all."

"Everything went smoothly," Lauren answered over her shoulder. "I'll talk to your wife."

Outside of surgery, she shook her head, having finished her fifth and final case of the day. She appreciated his faith in her and his statement that the procedure was "no big deal." At the same time she wished she had not had to operate at all. In her opinion, there was so much the man could have done to prevent it. Although she disliked stereotypes, the patient was a 240-pound fisherman who most likely did not eat right nor did he wear sunglasses.

Lauren smirked. "But at that point, what good could a lecture have done."

A nurse entered the dressing room behind her.

"What?" she asked.

"Nothing," Lauren said.

"Are you all right?" The nurse asked.

"Sure," Lauren said.

She paused only long enough to strip off her scrubs. She nodded to the nurse and pushed open the door. It swung shut as she hurried down the hallway.

At the elevators a doctor from the department walked out as the doors opened. Her name was Melanie Stonebridge. Lauren had known her since medical school and they were frequent running buddies. Melanie was one of Lauren's few confidants.

"Hi, Lauren," she said. "Dr. Connor was just talking about you."

"Oh," she said.

Normally, the idea of Dr. Connor mentioning her name would have piqued her interest. This time she just did not have the energy. She felt tired and more stressed than she could remember. She tried to smile at Melanie but she knew her friend could see through it.

"You okay?" Melanie asked.

Lauren considered talking to Melanie. Maybe they could go get lunch. Lauren could unload exactly what was on her mind. But on second thought, she knew that was not an option. She trusted Melanie but her friend was too close to what was troubling Lauren.

"Just tired," she said.

Melanie nodded. "I understand. You have clinic today?"

"Yes," Lauren said.

"Maybe we can run this weekend?" Melanie asked.

Lauren answered before she thought about it. "No, can't. I'm heading out of town for the weekend."

At first, Lauren felt bad, thinking she had just lied to her friend. But when she considered it again, getting away seemed like a good idea.

"Sounds nice. Have fun," Melanie said.

Lauren pushed the up button and forced a smile again. "You, too."

Lauren walked quickly down Wolfe Street. She stopped at the juice bar next door to her gym. She pushed the door open.

Inside, the place was quiet but for the soft music playing on the sound system. About a dozen small, round tables sprinkled the sitting area, all empty. Another dozen stools lined the service counter. Atop the counter, a long rectangular planter held perfectly trimmed wheat grass.

The door rang a bell as it closed and a young, long-haired girl poked her head out from the back.

"Dr. Chandler," the girl said. "The usual?"

Lauren nodded. "Hi, Aria."

"Bad day?" Aria asked.

Lauren nodded again. "More like a bad month."

She walked across the café, her stride comfortable. She sat softly on one of the stools, resting her elbows on the counter. The sound of a blender drowned out the calming music. A minute later Aria was back with her drink, a blended mixture of carrot juice, soy protein, yogurt, plum and ice.

"So, what's up?" Aria asked, leaning on the counter.

"Just life stuff," Lauren said.

Aria looked around the empty café. "Not like I don't have time to listen."

"It's been a weird week," Lauren said.

"How so?"

"My dad and I almost got hit by a car."

Aria's eyes widened. "Are you kidding?"

"No," Lauren said. "We were walking in Georgetown not more than a block from my father's place. It drove up onto the curb."

"On purpose?"

"No, don't think so. The driver died, though. The van blew up. Weird thing. The accident didn't look all that bad for him. He sideswiped the front stoop of a house and then hit a pole, but not too fast. Life's strange like that. It was so close. I mean, my dad and I could have been the ones that didn't make it."

Aria shook her head. "You never know. I hear that kind of stuff all the time. I like to think it all has a reason. But who knows?"

"But that's not what's bugging me," Lauren sighed. "It'll probably sound trivial."

Aria laughed. "Not as trivial as sitting around here all day."

"It's just that I'm confused about my future and I think the close call really brought it to the forefront," Lauren said. "My mentor wants me to do a fellowship here at Hopkins."

"Isn't that a good thing?" Aria asked.

She nodded. "Of course, I mean, it's not like I don't know how lucky I am."

"It's not luck," Aria said. "You earned all this."

Lauren thought about her father, about how she had never felt she lived up to his expectations. At the same time after hearing the story about his brother, she knew he felt the same stress.

"Maybe. The thing is that I'm not sure I want to stay here. The city seems to be getting worse."

"*Balt-mer*," Aria said. "Nah, it's the same as the day I was born."

"I don't know." She took a sip of her drink. "I feel like I need to get out of here. Plus, I want to do clinical work at my own pace, independently. Another doctor from Boston is courting me hard. He's a different guy, but a great mind. I've been offered a fellowship at the National Eye Institute in Bethesda, too."

"That sounds cool," Aria said.

"Yeah, it does." Lauren smiled. "To me and you, not to my dad, though. He would never understand my leaving an opportunity to stay with my mentor."

Aria smiled back. "How old are you?"

"Huh?"

"Aren't you, like, twenty-five?"

"Thirty," Lauren said. "But who's counting?"

"Your dad's just a guy now," Aria said. "You have to make up your own mind. You think my dad is happy I work here?"

Lauren shrugged.

"He isn't. He's a banker. This isn't exactly what he wanted for his little girl. But I don't care. I know how unhappy I'd be if I followed his path. You can't be happy doing things for someone else's benefit all the time. You'd lose yourself."

"You're right," Lauren said. "Plus, I could probably get a faculty appointment down in D.C., if I wanted to."

Aria rolled her eyes. "Well, at least you kind of got it."

Lauren laughed.

"Now," Aria said, "how's your love life?"

Lauren dropped her head to the counter. "Don't ask."

Lauren was five minutes late for clinic. Luckily, it was a surprisingly light day. The tech on duty gave her a little attitude so, to make up for being late, Lauren offered to handle the tech's responsibilities for the next patient. The tech, a twenty-five-year-old woman born and raised in Baltimore looked suspicious but nodded.

Lauren walked to the waiting room and ushered the next patient back. Normally, the tech would do that and most of the exam, and Lauren would only see the patient toward the end, after his or her eyes were completely dilated. This allowed the doctor to see more patients each day.

Instead, Lauren showed the teenage girl to the exam room and helped her get comfortable in the chair. Lauren smiled. Seeing patients was just what she needed right now. It would distract her from everything else.

The girl fidgeted in the chair, clutching a worn backpack that rested on her lap. Immediately, Lauren started a game she played while in medical school. She and her friends used to guess at a patient's personality based on their eye exam. It was amazing what they could learn just by paying attention.

"This will be nice and easy for you," she said. "Just sit back. Keep your glasses on and read the chart."

Lauren clicked on the projector and a standard eye chart appeared on the far wall. She watched the girl for her reaction. The patient looked nervous but read the letters down to the second to last line.

The girl leaned in. She fidgeted in her chair again.

"I can't," she said.

Lauren smiled. She knew what would happen next.

"Just look at the top lines. E, V, O."

Hesitant at first, the girl read the letters off. She reached the fourth line.

"Great job," Lauren said.

"Great," Lauren said. "Keep your glasses on. I'm going to slide this occluder in front of you so we can test your vision one eye at a time."

The patient improved when the pinhole was place over each eye. As Lauren continued the exam, checking the eyes with a flashlight, asking the patient to track her finger, Lauren thought about the old saying, "the eyes are the windows to the soul." It was truer than people thought. Just watching someone take an eye exam, significant observations of personality could be made.

Right from the start, some people were timid, some were suggestible. A doctor could tell if a patient had been the goodie-goodie in school, someone unwilling to make a mistake. Other patients just blundered through the process, not caring.

The young girl was of the suggestible variety. Lauren knew that if she began the test for her, the girl would finish it fine. She knew that there were all sorts of aptitudes and attitudes from an eye exam, although the test was not a perfect measure of vision, it was all they had. In her studies, she knew that vision had many components such as: near (reading), distance, accommodation (focusing), color, peripheral, tracking, converging, and hand-eye coordination.

More impressively, as shown by the girl's suggestibility, the eyes did not just influence vision, but also higher brain functions. Vision played a large part in intuition and clearly influenced the mind. In fact, she had recently read an article by Francine Shapiro which described her work on EMDR, a technique using hypnotic eye movements as part of a treatment for Post Traumatic Stress Disorder.

Still thinking about that article, Lauren put drops in the young lady's eyes, one for testing eye pressure and two others to dilate the pupils. She then moved the slit lamp in front of the patient and had the girl put her chin on the rest. Lauren could then look in and examine the external ocular structures and the front of the eye. She moved a device in place that allowed her to measure the intraocular pressure, which would normally be between twelve and twenty-one millimeters of mercury.

She had a few minutes until she could finish the exam, so Lauren found a quiet office in the back and pulled out her BlackBerry. Scanning through a dozen emails, she paused when she saw one with a Massachusetts Eye and Ear Infirmary address. She quickly clicked it open and read:

> From: Dieter von Fricke, M.D.
> MESSAGE:
> Please call me at your convenience. I heard about your
> recent accident. Hope you are well.

Lauren looked around, as if checking to see if anyone was watching. Whenever she heard from Dr. von Fricke who tried to woo her away from Hopkins to do a fellowship in Boston, she felt like a cheating spouse. Despite that, she dialed his number. She was curious how he knew about the accident when the Washington Post article did not mention names.

"Hi, Margaret," she said when his assistant answered the phone. "It's Lauren. Is Dr. von Fricke around?"

"Hi, Dr. Chandler," Margaret said. "He's expecting your call. Hold on."

Lauren had to wait no more than a minute before Dr. von Fricke came on the line.

"Lauren," he said with a gruff German accent. "How are you? I heard there was an accident."

"Almost," she said. "But I'm fine, how are you?" Lauren answered smiling.

"Good. But what is this I hear?" he shouted over the phone.

Lauren cringed, but this was not the first time she had spoken to Dr. von Fricke. Regardless of his bedside manner, his expertise was second only to Dr. Connor. And it was a close second.

"I'm not sure I know," she answered.

"Bethesda?" he snapped. "This is unacceptable! What keeps you from coming here? A Mass Eye and Ear fellowship will augment your clinical and surgical experience."

"Dr. von Fricke," she said. "You know how much I'd love to come work with your illustrious institution. I've already accepted an NIH fellowship that will allow me to start my own practice. I already turned down Dr. Connor's offer at Hopkins."

"Are things better with your father then?" he asked.

She sat forward in her chair. "What? Well, I guess maybe they are."

"Humph," he said. "At least, if you were here, you would be out from under that pompous windbag."

She laughed, getting her hand over the receiver just in time to mute it. "Who?"

"Connor, of course."

"Oh," she said as innocently as she could. "He does want me to stay here in Baltimore full time. This whole thing has been difficult for me."

"I would like to have your worries," he said, patronizingly.

"I don't mean . . ."

"Do not worry, *fräulein*," he said. "I am just a jealous old man. Someday, you must come up for a visit again. I truly believe I can provide you with the grants and faculty appointment that you really want."

"Thank you," she said.

When she hung up, she could have kicked herself. She had meant to ask him how he knew about the accident. With that accent of his, he had a way of boggling her thoughts when they spoke.

She stared at the far wall. At once she felt overwhelmed and guilty. She had no idea what her future held. At the same time, she knew she had no right to complain.

If that was true, she thought, then why couldn't she shake the feeling that she faced a dire choice. It made no sense to her, but the anxiety was there nonetheless. She recalled her encounter with Melanie Stonebridge at the elevators. She definitely needed to get away.

WASHINGTON, D.C. 2006

Senator Chandler picked at the nylon wrapped cast covering his forearm and wrist. The bone inside was almost healed after six months. He told most of his staff that it had happened playing handball at the gym. Isaac backed up the story but he knew the truth.

Sitting alone in his office, he closed his eyes. The night flashed through his memory again, the sense that something large and fast bore down on him and his daughter. One snippet of the picture caught his mind every time.

It had been dark. After getting patched up, he had gone back to the scene at night. As he remembered, the streetlight was dark. He had noticed it before the accident. It had been broken.

But that night, it should not have been dark. There was no flash of errant headlights. The guy must have been driving with them off.

A soft knock sounded on the door.

"Benjamin, it's me."

"Come in," he said.

Isaac opened the door slowly and slipped into the office as he had for so many years. Chandler nodded toward the credenza and the half-empty carafe of scotch. Isaac shook his head and took a seat.

"How are you feeling?" he asked.

Chandler rubbed his arm. "Not too bad."

"How's Lauren?"

"She's fine, I think." Chandler looked out the window. "I haven't talked to her since."

Isaac shook his head. "You should call her."

"I will," he said. "I just don't want her to be worried."

"She should be. Pretty freaky accident. Do you think that someone tried to kill you?"

"I don't know that," Chandler said. "Not for sure."

"What else could it be, Ben," Isaac said. "You told me that the sidewalks were pretty busy that night. No one else got hit. That's a big coincidence, don't you think?"

"Well, there was something else," Chandler said.

"Something else?"

"Yeah," he said. "I've been thinking about that night a lot. You know, I'm pretty sure that car didn't have its headlights on."

Isaac's eyes widened. "Are you serious?"

Chandler nodded.

"Why didn't you say so before?"

He rubbed his cast. "I've been in a little bit of pain, you know."

"Ben, we have to call them in."

"Are you kidding?" Chandler asked. "If we do, they'll be tailing me by the end of the week. I can't handle that."

"You have to," Isaac said. "An attempt on a senator is a big deal. They need to look into it."

"It might not have been . . ."

Isaac cut the senator off with an askew look. "I'm calling them, Ben."

He shook his head. "You're infuriating."

Isaac smiled. "Only when I'm right."

Lewes, Delaware 2007

Lauren stood in the stone driveway of her father's home in Lewes, Delaware. It was a cedar-shingled three floor summer home her parents had owned for as long as her dad was in Washington. It was the perfect place for her to get away from the city and maybe contemplate leaving it for good. She let the briny sea air fill her lungs, instantly reinvigorating her mood like nothing in Baltimore could have.

Lauren's shoes kicked up the loose stones of the driveway as she stretched the two-hour trip out of her leg muscles. She enjoyed the ride in her Acura. This was the first break during her NIH fellowship and the commencement of her practice. She cruised across the Chesapeake Bay Bridge, the last of the day's picnickers and day trippers on the brown sand beach of the Eastern Shore just visible through the ozone-induced smog on the Bay. Lauren made a quick stop at the Fisherman's Inn on Kent Island, a place she and her mother sometimes visited years ago, for a sandwich and a mineral water. Then the Acura ate up the miles of U.S. 50 for the long run through the fields of horse corn and soybeans that helped make the Eastern Shore such a stark contrast between marine and farm environments.

Smiling, Lauren approached the vacation home. Unlocking the door, she strode through the house flinging open windows to allow the salt breeze to replace the stuffy air trapped inside, most likely since the last time she had visited. She made sure the refrigerator was plugged in, turned on the water to the ice maker, and then opened the door to the side porch. From there, if she tilted her body at the right angle, she could just see the stacked crates in the yard of the old Lewes Boatyard, and beyond them, the tips of outriggers and masts. She leaned against the splintering cedar shakes, and let the last six months of tension and anxiety leak out.

A flash of movement at the far side of the yard caught her eye. A shining black cane held by a weathered hand appeared from behind the neighbor's privacy fence. The fingers unlocked the gate between the two yards. A tanned, well muscled man walked into the yard, juxtaposing with the cane she had first seen. He wore long cargo shorts and a faded blue T-shirt with the outline of a badge and the words "To Protect and Serve" underneath it. The man, relying only slightly on his cane, moved to the overgrown tomato garden next to the fence and began to help himself to some of the ripened fruits.

"Can I help you?" Lauren asked.

Like an awkward dance, the man spun around toward Lauren's voice, dropped the cane, dropped the tomato and crashed into the splintering fence.

"God, but you scared the shit out of me!" he said.

He gingerly extricated himself from the tomato plants. A perfect circle of red appeared on his forehead from the impact with the fence and squashed tomatoes stained his shirt.

Lauren fought to keep from smiling. She stood with arms crossed while watching the man attempt to pull himself together.

"So, are you protecting or serving?" she asked.

"Right now I'm wondering how I'm going to convince you I wasn't stealing these tomatoes." He grinned and reached a hand out. "Mark Bartholomew, I'm from next door."

"Lauren Chandler. I own the tomatoes."

"Chandler?" He looked up at her, squinted, and then nodded his head. "You're the daughter. Your father told me about you."

Keeping his left leg stiff he bent down and grabbed the cane. After straightening up with some effort, he ran his other hand over his graying black hair, leaving a bit of crushed tomato in the tight curls.

"I met him when I came down here," he said. "And he asked me to keep an eye on the house when he was gone."

Lauren arched an eyebrow. "My father was down here?"

"Sure," he said. "About a month ago."

"News to me," Lauren said. "Did the arrangement include raiding the garden?"

"Well, if you don't thin the crop out, the bears get to it, and that's a problem," Mark said.

"Seen many bears lately?

"No, I've been pretty good about taking care of the surplus."

"I suppose I should thank you," Lauren said, allowing the smile to stay on her face. She had a decision to make here. She made it although it was out of character for her.

"The least I can do is let you get yourself cleaned up. C'mon in." She turned around and walked into the house, letting her new neighbor find his own way.

As she walked into the kitchen, she heard the old screen door slam behind Mark as he followed her in. He went to the kitchen sink and turned the water on, using his cupped hands to rinse off his face. She gave him a dish towel to dry off with.

"I just got here, and I haven't been to the store yet, so I don't have anything to offer you," she said.

"That's okay," Mark said as he finished wiping his hands and threaded the towel through a cupboard door handle. "Listen, today's my grocery day, too. I was going to go this afternoon. If you have a list, I'll be glad to pick up whatever you want." He looked at her, his dark eyes meeting hers directly again. She did not look away. The exchange gave her a thrill, a little bit of control peeled away.

"I think I'll go, too," she said. "I'm not sure of everything I want; I usually just pick and choose from the aisles."

A few minutes later they were riding in Mark's rusty Jeep toward the old IGA market in town, across from the hospital.

"You're a doctor, right?" he asked as they parked along the shaded street. "You could work there," he nodded at the red brick hospital.

"I'm already working a fellowship and starting a practice in Bethesda. I did my training in Baltimore," she said.

"*Bal-tee-more*?" he teased. "I was born and raised in Dundalk there. We never heard it called *Bal-tee-more*. C'mon, learn to say it like a native. *Bawlmer*, hon, *Bawlmer*."

They were laughing together as they walked into the market. Mark directed the trip, showing Lauren what aisles held what, all the while greeting shoppers throughout the store.

Most of them were locals. The vacationers and owners of the million-dollar beach homes either had somebody do their shopping for them or went to one of the newer, larger supermarkets out on

Delaware 1. The IGA was an old-time town market, only six aisles and one checker, a gum-snapping blond teenager who spent more time peering at the crew-cutted boy outside than she did ringing up groceries.

"Here you go," Mark said while peering into the small refrigerated meat section. "Tripe. Didn't you say you were looking for some nice tripe?"

"Ugh! It's bad enough your scrapple is sharing the basket with my broccoli," Lauren said.

Passing a basket of oranges, she playfully tossed one over her shoulder. Once she did it, she whirled around to make sure he caught it. Her cheeks blushed.

Mark executed a perfect hook shot, returning the orange to its display. He picked up two sirloin steaks, some of the last good corn of the season and some Delaware potatoes.

"Got what you need?" he asked Lauren.

"I think so," she answered. "But it's close enough that I can run back tomorrow if I forgot anything. I got a couple of frozen dinners, and some tea and bagels, that'll be good for me."

Mark picked up one of the frozen dinners.

"This is for tonight? I can't believe you, a doctor eating this stuff"

"I know, I know. I should know better," she said. "I do know better. But I'm only here for a couple of days, and I don't feel like doing a lot of cooking. I feel like my brain has been cooking all summer."

"I'll tell you what," Mark said "I'll cook dinner tonight, to pay you for all the tomatoes I've been taking all summer. Couple of steaks, some potatoes, some corn, maybe a salad, it'll be easy, you'll be fed, and my conscience will be soothed. Deal?"

Lauren looked at him warily. She'd been a single woman in a big city long enough to have her defenses up.

"Dinner and what else?"

"Oh. Hey. Nothing?" he backed up. "I didn't mean anything by it. Look. Your old man and I get along okay. He asked me to look after things." He smiled. "I figure you came under 'things.' I'm not coming on to you."

He looked at Lauren again and tried another tack. "I've been down here, going out of my gourd, for the past two months. I wasn't even able to walk too much until about two weeks ago. I do some fishing. I do some drinking; I do some reading. I am flat-out bored. You seem like a nice person. I'm a nice person, too, and just thought we could have a meal together. Nothing else."

She looked at him, gave a small scowl, and then a quick smile. "Okay, dinner. Let's get back."

He put her groceries, along with his, in the back of the Jeep and limped to the driver's seat. Even with leaving the windows open, the August heat left the interior shimmering.

"No air in this thing?" Lauren asked after he got in and started the engine. "Sure I do. It comes on when you roll your window down."

He pulled out onto the street again, past Victorian houses painted in pastels and onto the drawbridge crossing the Lewes & Rehoboth Canal. It was mid-afternoon, and the charter fleet was coming in. Mark craned his head to note what boats were in, and then continued on to their houses.

"Look, all my cooking stuff is at my house, obviously," he said to Lauren. "Why don't you come over there?"

"You know, why not? That would be great. I'll bring the salad," Lauren said.

Something about Mark made her feel safe and relaxed. The rational side of her mind knew she was acting out of character though. Regardless, a thrill tingled her spine and she followed Mark over to his house.

Washington, D.C. 2007

Steinmetz drove the white sedan down 1st Street in downtown Washington. The city opened up to his left. The gray expanse was replaced by a field of green grass. Beyond that, water sparkled in the morning sunlight.

A few blocks passed and 1st street became Washington Hospital Center Road. A large campus of buildings sprung up where the water ended. Steinmetz took a left onto an access road for Washington Hospital. He stopped at an automated gate.

Steinmetz reached across the passenger side seat and picked up an ID card. On the front it read, Maintenance, Washington Hospital. He flashed it across the magnetic reader. The yellow and orange banded arm rose, opening the way for Steinmetz. He drove onto the grounds of the hospital, following his GPS to the designated parking area behind the Children's National Medical Center.

No one gave him a glance as he stepped out of the car wearing the blue coveralls of a hospital maintenance worker. Walking around to the back, he opened the trunk. A green metal tank with shoulder straps lay next to an empty egg crate. He slung the tank onto his back and walked away from the hospital.

Michigan Avenue ran behind the Children's National Medical Center. Steinmetz stood on the curb, watching the traffic race by. Calmly, he attached a self-adhering patch to the front of his coveralls. It read National Park Services. He then attached a spray hose to the nozzle of the tank.

When the traffic thinned, he raced across the four lane street. He picked his way down a grassy slope onto an open field. Birds sailed over head and people walked along a footpath that spanned the water's edge. Many were parents wheeling small children.

Steinmetz walked across the field, pretending to spray the grass. The people on the path saw him coming and hurried past, not wanting to breathe in what they took to be pesticides. Emboldened by how well his plans were progressing, he waved to them.

Up ahead, he saw the corpse of trees right on the water's edge. He eased into them, and they provided enough cover that people from the footpath could no longer see him. Once out of view, he knelt by the water's edge.

Working quickly, Steinmetz slipped the tank off his back. He laid it by the bank and extended the hose out into the water. Turning the nozzle to the right as far as he could, Steinmetz stood and watched the viscous liquid snake out into McMillan Reservoir, the primary source of water for metropolitan Washington.

Diligently securing the tank to his back, he made sure not to leave any trace of his action behind. He strolled out of the trees and back toward his car, acting as if he sprayed the grass as he went. Without a backward glance, he walked away from the scene of the single most damaging terrorist act that had ever taken place on American soil.

Bonn, Germany 2007

Becker drove a nondescript Mercedes out of the city, heading south toward the spa town of *Bad Godesberg*. His cell phone rang.

"Hello."

"It's Steinmetz."

"Is it done?"

"Yes."

"Good," Becker said.

"I can move onto the senator now if you would like." Steinmetz paused. There was a hint of disrespect to his tone when he continued. "I can finish the job."

Becker seethed, but he refused to let his voice betray his emotions.

"He's no longer a target," he said.

"No?" Steinmetz asked.

"No, I said. The FBI has put a tail on him and his daughter. Any more attempts would be too risky. I'll have them both watched. If things get worse, we may have to act. But not now, it's too early."

"Whatever you say," Steinmetz muttered.

"Exactly."

Becker hung up the phone and took a deep breath. With one hand still on the wheel, he opened a folded map of the area. Outside the city limits, the land turned a lush green. He traced a blue line as it meandered through, ending in a larger body of water.

"A target-rich environment," he thought. He had heard the phrase used during the televised coverage of the Gulf War.

Becker felt slightly envious. He had wanted to be the one to start this wave of the plan. Even more, he had dreamed of the challenge inherent in attacking the United States. Yes, he had come up with the plan that Steinmetz followed. Everything had been his idea, but he wished he had been the one who pulled the trigger.

What was done was done. The first wave had begun in Washington, D.C. Now it would continue in Germany. For Kugler trusted no one else to succeed, not in the *Vaterland*.

His finger followed the path to the target. Becker found it ludicrous to think that facilities so necessary to life were so unguarded. Banks filled with currency and precious metals that were, in the final analysis, meaningless to the miracle of life, were locked up and closely monitored every hour of the day, every day of the year. But water, without which human life, all life, was impossible, water was left unguarded and unwatched. And unsafe, he thought.

The sodium vapor lights arranged in the empty parking lot of a train station cast a yellow sheen to his face as he cruised along the empty street. In a dichotomy he was used to in industrial Germany, the rearview mirror showed flare towers from refineries even as the trees began crowding the side of the road.

He passed several more intersections with traffic lights ordering cars that weren't there. Suburban developments, blue lights from televisions stealing through the upper windows of some of them, passed by on either side of him. Sleepy Germany, he thought. These people were the heart of this country. And it was this heart that Kugler and Teleplunkt hoped to awaken. To Becker, it was a heart that beat already, full of contempt and hate that bred men like Kugler, men who let him play the game he loved more than anything else — the game of destruction.

Everything was progressing too easily, he thought. At that exact moment, he got a scare. Stopped at a red light, a small automobile drew up next to him. He glanced across, and hid his reaction when he saw an official-looking seal decal on the black door, and a number of short, stubby antennae jutting from the rear deck of the car. He looked at the driver, and a shaft of excitement, tinged in fear, shot through his chest when he realized the officer was studying him. He worked to keep his face still, lowered his head less than an inch in a show of respect, and then turned his eyes front.

The light turned green, the police car slid away and turned left. Becker moved his foot from the brake to the accelerator and rolled ahead, slowly building speed. He let out the air he had held in his lungs until the police cruiser vanished from view. His entire face rose with a wide smile as he fed on the adrenaline.

Across one more major roadway and the road went from four lanes to two. Out the window, he saw some sort of fallow farm field on his right, woods on his left, and long, low stone walls crisscrossing the fields. Following the map, he turned onto a winding back road and continued over a series of hills, each one a little steeper than the rest. The headlights cut brightly across the darkest hour of the night, flashing glances of straight tree trunks, clumps of wild flowers, and once the glowing red eyes of another creature of the night.

The final hill died out, and Becker let the car slow to a stop. He looked to the left, already knowing from the photos that were now just burned ashes in a dustbin back in Frankfurt, what he would see.

The car stopped on a causeway. To the right a small pond overflowed under the bridge into the widening reservoir to the left. A pole-and-cable safety rail lined both sides of the two-lane road, with just a narrow, weed-filled shoulder between the road and the rail.

Becker rolled the window down, smelling the thick aroma of the water. He started the car again and at the end of the causeway turned onto an even narrower road. About 200 yards further on, in the gloom of mature growth evergreens, he saw the drooping cable blocking the entrance to a dirt lane that wound down to the edge of the water.

As promised, the cable was secured only with a hook at one end. He got out, unhooked the cable, drove the car over it, and carefully hooked the cable back up. He extinguished his headlights at the water's edge.

It was clear that he was not the only one to know the secret of the unlocked cable. The charred remains of several campfires dotted the packed dirt at the water's edge, and a collection of discarded beer bottles was visible in the pale light reflecting off the moon and the moving water.

He climbed out of the van and opened the trunk, pulling out two heavy tanks. They were filled with the same chemical, the Dramastatin, Steinmetz had secured in the United States. He had encrypted the formula and sent it to Dr. Kim in Frankfurt, who easily produced the viscous silver fluid in Germany. Two chemicals, Becker thought, two different things—one, the liquid, to create the need; the other, stolen from North Korea, to change the world.

Under the canopy of swaying pines, he walked up to the water. Carefully, he lifted one prepared tank. It was heavy and awkward. He poured the contents into the reservoir. In the moonlight, it slowly flowed as a silver tube from the neck of the bottle into the dark water. He did the same with the second jug. In the distance a fish slapped the surface of the lake, adding its own splashing noise to the sounds of the bottles' contents running into the lake and diluting into another city's water supply.

Phase two was completed. Soon everything he had done to steal the secrets of North Korea and the good man Walter he had to kill, would pay dividends.

Becker smiled and drove away into the night.

Lewes, Delaware 2007

Lauren found herself wandering around Mark's house. She could hear him in the kitchen fixing dinner. The aromas wafted into the room causing her mouth to water. Lauren realized that it had been a long time since she had actually enjoyed an eating experience.

She expected Mark's house to be messy and was surprised to see it crowded, but neat. An old china cabinet in the small dining room had been converted into a bookshelf. The living room held a couch and a recliner. From the corner, the screen of a PC softly glowed.

As Mark busied himself in the kitchen, Lauren ran her eyes over the books. Most, but not all, were hardbacks. The classics were well represented, including what appeared to be a well-used Penguin Edition of Shakespeare's major works. Mixed in were some philosophy books that appeared to have been college textbooks, some with "Used" stickers still on them. One row consisted entirely of police procedural novels and mysteries, including all of Ed Dees' stories, and a good collection of Hammett.

"So, a cop who reads?" Lauren asked, half in jest.

"So," Mark replied, "a doctor who eats junk?"

"Touché."

The second she said that, a memory slipped to the front of her mind.

"Hey," she said. "I think we've met before."

"Huh?" he called out from the kitchen.

"A few years back," she said. "My car was broken into. You saved me from this crazy woman."

He stuck his head around the door jam. "What are you talking about?"

"You said you were a cop in Baltimore, right?" she asked. "Well, I think we met back then in a parking lot near Charm City."

"Doubt it," he said, ducking back into the kitchen. "I worked vice the last five years. Unless you were a dealer, I don't think our paths crossed."

"Huh." She frowned. "Maybe I'm wrong."

"And you know," he said. "We're not all brainless brutes."

"What are you talking about?" she asked.

"You're comment about my books. In fact, most of the guys and women on the force have associate's degrees at least now."

"And you?"

"Well, I'm a brute."

"Yeah, a brute who travels with a case full of the classics. No, I mean, do you have a degree?"

"Is it a prerequisite for you?" His voice had a sudden chill to it.

"No, I do like my friends to know how to read though." She walked into the kitchen so he could see her when she spoke.

"I try not to make any other judgments until I get to know them. College doesn't always mean class."

They looked at each other for a moment more and then they both relaxed.

"I know how to do brute though," he said with a laugh.

"Good. Comes in handy sometimes, I'm sure," Lauren said.

In the next hour, they sat on the back porch, wine in hand, and each gave the condensed version of childhood, upbringing, major life decisions, and thoughts on their respective paths forward. At one point Mark leaned back in his chair and stared at the ceiling.

"You know what?" he said. "I lived in the same red brick row home my whole childhood. I went to the same little Catholic school from K through 12. I used to walk past the front gate at the Sparrows Point shipyard where my father was a welder."

Lauren's amber eyes narrowed. "I don't mean to be rude, but . . ."

Mark cut her off. "Anytime someone says that, then they are about to be."

Lauren paused, rethinking her question.

"Don't stress," he said, smiling. "I think I know what you were going to ask. This isn't my house. I'm house-sitting for my sister. She married a guy from D.C., some lobbyist, a ton of money."

"I wasn't," Lauren laughed. "Actually, I was. You're a mind reader."

"Comes with the job," he said.

They sat in silence for a minute, sipping at their wine. Lauren glanced at Mark. He sat with his legs out, his one arm dangling loosely over the arm rest. A content grin warmed his face.

"I grew up in Danbury, Connecticut. Half the time, I was in an empty house," she said. "My father was always on the stump."

"I guess that comes with being a senator's kid," he said.

"Yeah." She took another sip. "And my mom played the part, too. You know, the socialite wife of a young up-and-coming attorney with dreams of politics in his future. I had a nanny and my little sister. Most days after school, I just laced up my shoes and went running with my team or by myself."

"Alone?" he asked. "Wasn't that dangerous?"

Lauren laughed. "In Danbury? No. It was pretty upscale. I remember I used to do my homework while I ran. It always seemed so easy to me."

"You know, anyone else talking about how easy their homework was would really turn me off."

She laughed. "I finished two years of high school in Connecticut before he moved to Washington. I decided to go to Wesleyan University because of their broad liberal arts program and access to full professors. They were very flexible with selecting majors. Since my sister went to boarding school, I wanted to stay closer to my mother. But my mother ended up moving down to Washington. I majored in neuroscience and did laboratory and clinical research and did my thesis with a great man, Professor Peterhagen, who ended up becoming my advisor. He always made me feel like I would be a success no matter what I went into. I decided medicine because it would give me greater access to both patients and research grants.

"I chose Hopkins; they chose me. Then I interned at Washington Hospital Center, which allowed me to rotate through the subspecialties of internal medicine. I went back to Hopkins as a resident, turned down the offer to become Chief Resident, which would have entailed two more years, and decided between fellowships at Hopkins, Harvard or the National Institute of Health."

"Sounds so simple," he said, smirking.

"Oh, please," she said, shaking her head. "You like playing the less-than-smart cop role, don't you? I've seen your books and I can tell from your vocabulary, it's an act."

"Says you," Mark said, sheepishly. "So, you're a big runner?"

"I guess so," she said. "It seemed that my endurance increased along with my dad's stature. I ran my first marathon after he got elected to the Senate."

"I don't even know, is he a Democrat or Republican?"

"Republican," Lauren answered. "But he's pretty middle of the road. He was a big activist actually, especially on AIDS. But he's a total patriot on issues like national security.

"So, how'd you end up a doctor?"

She shrugged. "You guessed it, huh? He wanted me to be an attorney. It wasn't for me, especially the politics."

"So why'd you pick medicine?" he asked.

"It was never really a question," she said. "Everything just seemed so clear to me. Biology, psychology, physiology, I just got it. You know?"

"I do," he said. "It was the same for me. I was the youngest detective in Baltimore history."

She sat up. "You were?"

"I know, I know," he said, patting himself on the back. "Amazing aren't I?"

She threw a pillow at him. It almost spilled his wine. He picked the pillow off the floor and put it behind his head.

"Thanks."

The night sailed by as the two sat together on the screened porch. Frogs chirped from the canal and the soft sound of the outboard motors rumbled from the fishing boats inching back from a night on the water. Lauren ran a finger along the rim of her empty wine glass. They had been quiet for a few minutes. When she glanced at Mark, he was looking at her.

"I kind of get how you feel about your father," he said.

"You do?" she asked, teasing him.

"Yeah," he said. "My dad died when I was in high school."

"Oh, God," Lauren said.

"He was a rock, my dad. Never sick a day in his life. Then he just collapsed over his lunch one day at the yard. My mom called the school. I remember the look on the assistant principal's face when he came to get me from class."

"I'm sorry," she whispered.

"He had a massive coronary. My dad, not the assistant principal," he said. "Doctors told my mom that he hadn't felt a thing."

"I feel like a whiney kid," Lauren said. "My dad was there, at least. Not like with you. No matter how we get along, I can't imagine that."

"It was tough. Back then, it was all just emotion. My mom was a mess. I ended up staying with her and working construction. A friend of my dad's got me the job."

"I guess that kind of stuff made you who you are," she said. "You're so . . . I could tell you were strong when I first met you."

He looked her in the eye and laughed. "I guess I told you all that because I wanted you to know why."

"Why what?" she asked.

"Why I became a cop," he said. "I had a scholarship to Loyola in Baltimore. I was going to study English."

He laughed again then finished his wine. He put the glass down on the cedar planked floor.

"What's so funny," she asked.

"Can you imagine me an English prof?" he asked.

Lauren paused. She looked him in the eye this time.

"Yes," she said. "I could."

He stood up, grabbing his cane, and walked to the screen. She thought his leg must still pain him. Normally she would never dream of asking someone she had just met personal questions. Somehow, though, the conversation had opened an intimacy she had never felt before.

"How'd it happen?" she asked.

"What?"

"You're leg?"

"Okay. The Life of Mark Bartholomew, Chapter Two." He looked at the ceiling for a moment and then continued. "I was a beat cop for eight years. Then a corruption scandal decimated the vice unit. That's how I became the youngest detective in the PD's history."

"Vice is pretty rough, right?" she asked.

"I know," he said. "Worse, I was vice in Baltimore. At the time, I figured my commanding officer volunteered me just to get me out of his hair. English profs don't mesh well with the true cop type. I didn't speak their language, and he took that as insolence."

"Sixteen months in and I was working undercover. I was deep in this group of meth dealers from Dundalk. They were cooking in a row house just three doors down from where I grew up. The stink from the chemicals just got lost in the neighborhood's general stench. They were making pretty good money selling to the biker crews.

"We were about to raid them. The day before, I stupidly reported to my new lieutenant that I had a line on some cops who were on the take. I told him I'd have names in a couple of weeks.

"When the final raid went down, so did I. A 38 caliber slug tore through my femoral artery and hammered into the bone, smashing it into three pieces. The paramedics said I was lucky I didn't bleed out on the filthy row house floor among the glass envelopes and empty Kool cigarette packs."

"One of the dealers shot you?" she asked.

He turned to look at her. "That's what they say. Some scum named Slater Cole. Afterwards, they offered me a disability pension."

"Do you want it?" she asked.

"Hell, no. I've almost got my 20 in, but I'm not ready to quit. Thing is," he stopped.

"What?"

"Well, it's weird. I've never told anybody this." He refilled his glass of wine. "Not all of it, anyway."

"What?" Lauren looked at him, one eyebrow cocked.

"That night, the one thing I really remember about that night was how loud it was. I remember the door splintering open and a bunch of uniformed cops in riot helmets cramming into the house. I remember looking over at Cole, seeing him draw a gun, and then it sounded like the room was blowing up.

"I mean, I've been to the range. I've burned through boxes and boxes of Remington. I know gunfire. I know what it sounds like. But I've never been in the kitchen of a Baltimore row house when everybody started shooting. And let me tell you, an inside gunfight is loud. It's loud and it smells. Gun smoke smells and it burns your eyes. Did you know that? You never see TV cops crying from the gun smoke in their eyes, do you?

"Anyway, I was looking at Cole as I dove for the floor, saw him pull out his gun, this whopping great Glock forty, and then I hear this boom and somebody smacks my leg with what feels like a baseball bat, and I'm down, And I'm thinking, how'd Cole do that, from way over there, without ever firing? I wasn't hurting, as much as confused."

"Turns out, I'm the only one who gets hit. This crime scene guy tells me fourteen shots were fired in there, like eight of us in this little stinking kitchen, everybody pulling out and blazing away. One slug went through a window and buried itself in a corpse in a casket at a viewing in a funeral home across the street. I mean, how ironic is that?"

"And I'm the only sap who collects one. The only live one, I mean. How fair is that? Anyway, the next thing I remember is the EMTs slamming me on this gurney into the ambulance, and that's another thing. You see that on TV all the time, the ambulance attendants sliding the gurney into the ambulance smooth as silk, and the patient damn near smiles everything is so smooth. Never a word out of a TV patient. Well, I'm here to tell you, those gurneys have anything but a Cadillac suspension, and it hurt like hell going into the back of that thing. Everybody on the street knew it when I was pushed into that ambulance, I can tell you.

"And then this uniform, this guy I don't know, but then I wouldn't recognize him since I never worked uniform in Dundalk, this uniform asks the senior EMT, 'Is he going to make it?' and I realize he's talking about me."

"EMT says, 'If you let us get out of here, he might,' and then, and this is the part I remember best, then the uniform tells the driver, 'Take your time.'"

Mark stopped and turned away from her. "Take your time." He shook his head. "I've never told anyone that before."

Lauren looked back at him. "They shot you?"

Mark smiled at her. She half expected it to be an angry thing, or maybe sardonic. It was not.

"It means, I think, that I might consider a career change."

"Aren't you going to . . ."

Lauren paused. She thought about how Mark had compared his experience to what happened on TV. She was about to ask if he was going to do anything about it. She realized, though, just how "TV" that would sound. One person taking on a police department, it was just not possible.

"What?" Mark asked.

"Nothing," she said. "I want to take a walk on the beach."

Mark patted his cane. "What, you trying to get rid of me?"

"Oh, come on," she said. "It'd be good for you. And I would know. I'm a doctor."

Together, they walked along the shore. Lauren found herself leaning into Mark. At the same time, she did not want to touch him. She felt afraid and excited at the same time.

For his part, Mark seemed oblivious. He walked along, his leg handling the sand very well. They spoke some more, nothing more intimate then their earlier conversation.

When they returned to their homes, Lauren expanded the distance between them. She fidgeted awkwardly, not making eye contact.

"I'll stay here until you let yourself in," Mark said. "Give me a wave when everything's okay."

"Oh," Lauren said. "Yeah, sure."

She walked up the driveway, looking back once. Mark gave her a friendly wave. Lauren turned back and closed her eyes. She felt like a little kid at Christmas, half excitement, half disappointment.

When she reached the door, she opened it and then waved down to him. Mark smiled.

"Maybe I'll see you tomorrow," he said.

"Maybe," she said.

Lauren stepped into the house and shut the door. Then she leaned against it and tilted her head up. It took a few minutes for her to catch her breath.

BETHESDA, MARYLAND 2008

Lauren leaned back in a rolling chair beside the receptionist. She glanced at the institutional wall clock. It was 9:45. Although she could hear the soft chatter of a full waiting room, her nine o'clock was late.

With a second to spare, she took a breath. She could not believe how things had changed since she left Baltimore and opened her practice in Bethesda. She was very fortunate to be able to start a practice while doing her ophthalmic epidemiology fellowship at the National Eye Institute at NIH. Her plan had been to join the faculty at Hopkins, but her practice had been far busier than she had expected, giving her little time for anything else so far.

Her cell phone rang. Lauren shook her head.

"Hello," she answered.

"Please hold for Senator Chandler."

She rolled her eyes. Lauren hated when her father did that, like it was a burden picking up the phone and calling his daughter. Or maybe he was just reminding her how important he was.

The phone up to her ear, Lauren rolled the chair over to the sliding wall-to-ceiling filing cabinet. She flipped through the color coded tabs until she found the patient she wanted. Pulling the file out, she rolled back to an open desk.

Although only in business for a little more than a year, Lauren had more patients than she thought she could handle. She had purchased the practice from the most renowned ophthalmologist in the metro area. He had been so prominent that many D.C. dignitaries traveled all the way to Bethesda for their appointments. When she purchased the practice, she had expected some drop off. There had been little to none so far.

Lauren heard a click and her father was on the phone.

"Lauren, how are you?"

"Hi, dad."

She opened the case file, scanning it quickly.

"Are you at the office?" he asked.

"Of course I am, dad," she said, her tone short.

"I ran into Dr. Connor at the Lincoln last night. His offer still stands."

"Dad, we've gone over this before," she said. She rolled a long strand of her auburn hair around a finger, a habit she thought she broke when she was eleven. "I like my practice. I like direct patient care over a full time academic setting. I can still be on the faculty of the Washington Hospital Center or even the Wilmer Institute."

"And next you're going to tell me you like Bethesda over D.C.," he said.

"I like Bethesda," she said.

"What's so wrong with Connor's offer? You could be co-chair of the department one day," he said.

Lauren felt the emotions bubbling up inside her stomach. She pushed them down and tried to keep calm. Using an old tactic, she remained silent until her father spoke again.

"I heard you took good care of the freshman Senator from Delaware for me," he said.

She had figured that was why he called. Senator Chandler probably needed the freshman's vote on some security bill.

"I tried," she said. "But your other 'friend' is late."

"Who?" he asked.

"I can't say." She smiled. "You know, doctor-patient confidentiality."

"It's Bobby Yost that's late, isn't it. That sleaze." The Senator laughed. "He owes me dinner."

"Isn't he a tobacco lobbyist," Lauren asked. "Why does he owe you dinner?"

Her dad laughed even louder. "He owes everyone dinner, sweetie."

Lauren's skin crawled. She wanted to change the subject.

"Dad, have you noticed how many of your colleagues are having cataract problems?"

"Washington's full of old men."

She ignored him. "I looked it up. The U.S. Health Department statistical abstract noted an increase in the regional frequency of cataracts and cataract surgery."

"Senator Carter told me you were great, too." Her father continued, ignoring Lauren's question. "Yeah, he told me he wasn't so sure goin' in. Said he thought all that nutrition stuff sounded like so much mumbo jumbo. But he's singin' a different tune, now."

Lauren shook her head, listening to her father laugh at his own joke. He was not the first to ignore her growing concern with the sudden rise cataract rate she had noticed.

"So he's forgoing surgery?"

"Looks like it," her father said.

"What about you, dad?" she asked.

"Me? I'm following every rule you gave me. I only eat whole foods and I'm down to one cup of decaf a day. I never go out without my sunglasses. All my colleagues are jealous as hell," he said.

"So your eyes have been fine? No blurred vision, pressure?"

"Nothing," he said. "Everything's great. Maybe you should take Connor up on his offer. You can do your studies on all this stuff, prove to everyone you're right."

Lauren's face reddened. At the same moment, the office door opened. A man in an Armani suit with black, slicked back hair walked in. He appeared to be talking to himself in a sickeningly smooth way until Lauren noticed the Bluetooth. He walked briskly though the waiting room, ignoring those already there.

"I gotta go, dad," she said. "Your dinner buddy just walked in."

"Tell that son-a-bitch he owes me," Senator Chandler said.

"Sure, dad," Lauren droned.

"Bye." She stopped when she heard the click of her father hanging up.

Bobby Yost, big tobacco lobbyist, walked up to the receptionist window. He looked right at Lauren.

"Tell the doc I'm here, doll," he said. "And I'm in a hurry."

Lauren sighed.

When Lauren got into her car, she was still laughing at how pompous the tobacco lobbyist had been. It was like meeting a character from a bad television drama. Traffic was awful but she didn't care. She had an hour to make it to Union Station.

First she stopped at a small shop on the way out of town. The store specialized in hard to find gifts. It was located in a row home. Inside, tight aisles ran between racks heavy with curios. An older woman with dyed red hair approached and asked her if she needed any help.

"Sure," Lauren said.

"Who are you shopping for?" the woman asked.

Lauren loved that question. Usually store employees asked, "What are you looking for?"

"My . . . a friend."

"A friend?" the woman asked with an arched eyebrow. "This a man friend?"

She nodded.

"Who is he?"

"Pardon?" Lauren asked.

"Who is he, inside?"

Lauren thought about that. Her mind immediately went to her time with him at the beach. She thought about what had happened to him, when his fellow officers shot him.

"He's a police officer. An honest one."

The woman laughed. "I have just the thing."

She took Lauren by the arm and led her deeper into the store. They stopped in front of a glass case. Inside were an array of antique weapons and tools. Some of the pistols, though, looked like they might still work.

"I don't know about . . ."

"Hold your horses, sweetie," the woman said.

She unlocked the case and reached in. She pulled out a pocket knife. Lauren was not impressed.

"Maybe something . . ."

The woman interrupted her. "It belonged to Elliot Ness."

Lauren's eyes widened. "You mean, like, the Untouchable Elliot Ness?"

"The same," the woman said. "He used it once, to pry open a desk drawer. As the story goes, inside he found evidence that uncovered corruption throughout the Chicago Police Department."

"Are you kidding?" Lauren asked.

The woman shook her head.

Going from Bethesda into Washington, D.C., she could have taken the red line of the Metro. She had thought about it but wanted to have her car with her. She did not know what time she would be leaving the city and did not want to risk missing the last train.

Choosing a more scenic route, she merged onto Clara Barton Parkway. The road wound along the bank of the Potomac. Driving along, she could see the water out of her passenger side window. Smiling, she fished her BlackBerry out of her bag.

"Call Mark," she said.

On speaker, the line rang.

"Hello," Mark said.

"Hi, Mark."

"Hey, Lauren." He sounded as excited as she felt. "Are you on the Metro?"

"No," she said. "I decided to drive. Are you already at the station?"

"Yeah, I got here early."

Her smile broadened. She had not seen Mark for over four months. Over the last year, their paths had crossed more than she would have expected. Although it seemed more like fate, at times Lauren wondered if he was following her. He did not strike her as the stalker type.

When she had returned, she searched through her house, looking for the card the police officer had given her that day her car was broken into. She could have sworn it was Mark. But she could not find it and he had said it was impossible, so she let it stand.

With all their accidental meetings, the relationship, if that was what it was, had stalled somewhat from the distance. She was heading to the first official date they had been on in months.

"I should be there in about twenty minutes," she said.

"Great! You feel like Asian? I love the place on the second floor."

"Me, too," she said. "They have great noodles."

He laughed but did not say anything. Lauren tried to restart the conversation but she faltered as well. The moment grew uncomfortable and Mark cleared his throat.

"Me, too," he said. "Drive carefully, and I'll be right out front by the newsstand."

"Great," she said. "See you soon."

Lauren hung up and turned the radio on. She found a station that played songs she knew. Singing along to an eighties rock song, she could not wait to get to the city.

Approaching the city, Lauren took M Street across town. At Thomas Circle, she turned onto Massachusetts Avenue. Seeing the sign, she thought about Dr. von Fricke. She owed him a phone call.

Grabbing her phone from the passenger seat, she dialed his number. The line rang twice and the doctor answered.

"Hello."

"Uh, hi Dr. von Fricke, this is Lauren Chandler. Where's your assistant Margaret?"

"Ah, she's left me. Gone to work for some nonprofit in the city. How are you?"

"Good, how are you?" she said.

"Are you coming up for a visit?" he asked.

"I want to," she said. "I'm finished my fellowship with NIH, and my practice is keeping me really busy. It's busier than I imagined when I bought it. I can't complain, though. I love the work."

"You're turning me down again?" he asked.

Lauren paused. She could never tell if he was kidding or actually mad.

"I don't want to," she said. "But I am."

"Some day, Lauren Chandler, some day."

"I know. I promise." She looked out the window, the sun catching her eye as it slanted between two buildings. She squinted. "I have a question for you, though. Have you noticed more cases of cataract surgeries up your way?"

Dr. von Fricke was silent for a second. She heard a rustle from his side of the phone.

"I'm sorry, Lauren, I must be going."

Dr. von Fricke hung up. Lauren lowered the BlackBerry from her ear, feeling confused by the abrupt termination of the call. Absently, she took a left onto H Street.

Stopping at the first light, a flash of white appeared in her rearview mirror. Before she could look up, something exploded behind her. The car lurched forward. Her body lurched forward. The seat belt struck her like an iron pipe across her chest as it locked up. Her head hit the windshield and then whipped back, striking the back of her seat. Lauren's vision flashed brightly and then went black for an instant. She gasped for air, her ribs feeling as if they had been pulverized.

The sound of excited shouting filled the car. Dazed, Lauren's eyes cleared. She wondered how she could hear the outside so well with her windows closed. Absently, she reached a hand out to check. The driver's side window was gone. Little cubes of glass peppered her lap. It reminded her of the day her car had been broken into. That felt like a lifetime before.

Still not thinking clearly, Lauren unbuckled her belt and tried to open her door. It would not budge. Wincing, she crawled across to the passenger side and climbed out. Blinking, she took in the scene.

Smoke plumed from the crushed front end of a white four-door sedan. Its hood had folded in on itself and now pointed straight up toward the sky. One side of the white car's fender hung from the smashed grill and the other rested halfway under Lauren's car. It looked as if the sedan had tried to eat her Acura.

Still in a daze, Lauren walked toward the white sedan. Her neck hurt. Car horns erupted, belatedly issuing a warning, or maybe callous impatience. The din of anxious pedestrians replaced the morbid silence following the accident. Lauren let out a huge breath held in her lungs and winced.

"Call 9-1-1," a man next to her yelled. A cell phone hung in his hand like a forgotten finger.

As she neared the sedan, Lauren's shoe splashed into a growing trail of green antifreeze. She dodged around the steaming front end of the car to the driver's side. Bending over, she hesitated before looking inside.

An elderly man sat behind the wheel, blood trailing from a triangular gash on his forehead. It covered his face like a red net, dropping in fat globs onto his shirtfront. His hands lay folded in his lap and he stared ahead at the spider web of cracks that had been his windshield. Teetering on his thigh, one earpiece broken off, were a pair of dark, oversized sunglasses, the disposable kind a patient received after a visit to the eye doctor.

Lauren reached into the car, her hand resting gently on the man's shoulder. She looked into his eyes. From outside the car, the faint wails of an ambulance siren drew closer. A sheet of paper on the passenger seat caught her attention. It was a pre-printed prescription slip.

The feel of hot breath on her cheek startled her.

"See it," the elderly man whispered.

"What?" she asked.

The man's voice gurgled as he spoke. "I didn't see it. My eyes—the glare—I didn't see . . ."

"Quiet now," she said in a soothing voice. "Shssh. It'll be all right."

Lauren stood that way for a few minutes, holding the man steady in case of a spinal injury. An ambulance rolled to a stop on the other side of the damaged white sedan and a young woman wearing a blue paramedic's uniform jumped out of the front seat. She quickly sized up the scene as another EMT appeared behind the ambulance wheeling a gurney out of the back.

The young woman threw open the passenger side door of the car. She shot Lauren a questioning glance.

"Dr. Chandler," Lauren said. "His pulse is accelerated, scalp laceration, a little bit shocky. I haven't moved him, possible head injury. Both pupils dilated, but I don't think it's from the impact. Look at these." She pointed at the broken shades, then at the prescription slip. "And that."

"Christ," the EMT said as she unfastened a foam cervical collar and began to fit it around the man's neck. "He was probably half blind when he left the doctor's office. Why did he think he could drive?"

Lauren shrugged, feeling a deep and unexpected sadness for the elderly man. At the same time, a wave of nausea caused her to take a step back. The EMT turned to her partner, a middle-aged man with a thick mustache, who approached with a backboard.

"Pops here had an eye appointment. His eyes look like a stoner's. When you can't see something the size of a car, you probably shouldn't be driving."

The EMT turned to look at her. "Thanks," she said dismissively, then paused. "Are you okay?"

Lauren nodded.

"Well, we'll take it from here. Go talk to the uniform." She motioned Lauren toward a Baltimore PD officer just pulling up. "He'll need help with the report and I don't have time to deal with him. Tell 'im we'll be taking the old man to Mercy."

"Okay," Lauren backed away from the car, noticing the growing crowd for the first time. She stumbled but caught herself. "I'd do a MRI on him anyway, just to be sure."

"Sure thing, honey," the EMT said, her tone sarcastic as she worked on the man's scalp wound. "We have any problems, we'll be sure to call you right away."

Lauren blushed. "I just thought,"

"Sorry," the EMT said. "We've done this a couple of times. Thanks for the help."

Feeling dismissed, Lauren walked over to the officer who now crouched behind the car looking for any trace of skid marks. He stood up, appearing bored, and Lauren gave him a short statement and left her name and work number.

"Why don't you go over to the EMT," the officer said. "I think you need to be checked out."

Lauren shook her head. "No thanks. I need to get out of here." After a few steps, she said to herself. "Something's telling me to get out of here."

Wandering aimlessly away from the accident, a pain seized up her neck. She kept walking until her BlackBerry rang. In a daze, she picked it up.

"Lauren." Mark sounded worried. "Where are you?"

"I'm not sure," she said.

"What happened? Are you okay?"

"Someone hit me," she said.

"Hit you?"

"Accident," she said, looking around.

"Where are you?" he asked. "Stay with people. Find a police officer."

"Huh?"

She could hear his breathing over the phone.

"Just stay still. I'm coming."

The phone went dead and Lauren sat down on a bench. She closed her eyes and the world began to spin.

WASHINGTON, D.C. 2008

Senator Chandler watched his colleagues filing into the Armed Services Committee meeting. Senator Brown was the last to arrive. He walked in wearing a crisp blue suit, a red tie and a shining new American flag pin on his lapel. Chandler shook his head when he noticed the pin was upside-down.

He called the meeting to order. For the first hour he waited for Brown to pull something. For the last year the Senator from Montana's behavior had progressed from annoying to obstinate. Not only had he continued to introduce a Senate Resolution to close U.S. bases in Germany, but he had attempted to bully other members to vote his way. It had never worked, nor would it, but Senator Chandler's patience was growing thin.

As the meeting neared its end, Senator Chandler began to relax. There was one last item on the agenda considering funding for a small air services museum in Georgia. The expense was menial and the museum sat smack in the middle of the Senate Pro Tem's district.

Chandler banged his gavel.

"Our final order of business, gentlemen. The Fightin' Airmen Museum in Atlanta is asking for our backing. They're looking for a small allocation for renovations and the acquisition of a spitfire from a private dealer in Akron. Total cost, $100,000. Can I have a second?"

Senator Kerrington raised his hand.

"Thank you," Chandler said. "All in . . . "

Senator Brown interrupted. "Discussion."

"What?" Chandler asked.

"I call we discuss the motion, first," Brown said.

Chandler shook his hand. "It's a rubber stamp."

"No, it is not," Brown said.

Abandoning protocol, the Senator from Montana stood. He walked out and stood below the dais, facing the other members of the committee.

Chandler spoke up but Brown ignored him, talking louder.

"Vote no," Brown said, fiddling with the pin on his lapel.

Chandler slammed his gavel down. The leather base flew off the desk, striking Brown in the shoulder. The Senator turned to look at the Chair.

"Sorry," Brown said, and he took his seat.

Chandler was flabbergasted. He could not find the words to express his anger. Instead, he just stared at Brown for a minute. When he glanced at his colleagues, expecting to find support in their angry expressions, many of them looked blank, confused.

Clearing his throat, Chandler found his voice.

"What in God's name was that all about?" he asked.

Brown nodded.

"That's it!?" Chandler said.

Brown nodded.

Shaking his head, Chandler frowned.

"All in favor," he said through clenched teeth.

The motion passed seven to three.

Chandler watched the other senators walking toward the door. Of the three dissenting votes, Brown was not one of them. But Kerrington was. And all three acted as if nothing had happened. Chandler could feel his blood pressure rising. When his friend from Delaware caught his eye, he motioned for Kerrington to join him. With a smile, the young senator complied.

"What the hell was that all about?" Chandler asked once everyone but Isaac was out of the room.

"What?" Kerrington asked.

"What!?"

Kerrington's brow dipped. "Yeah, what?"

"You just voted against Justin's pet project."

"What are you talking about?" Kerrington asked.

"The air museum in Justin's district. You opposed. He's going to blow a gasket."

Kerrington took a step back. "You okay, Ben?"

Chandler fumed. "Of course I'm okay. Obviously you aren't."

Kerrington looked at Isaac. "Maybe he needs a rest."

Chandler's mouth fell open but he didn't say anything.

"See ya at Mitzy's tonight," Kerrington said, slapping Chandler on the shoulder.

The Senator from Delaware left the chamber. Chandler looked at Isaac.

"Did that just happen?"

Isaac nodded.

"So it's not just me?"

Isaac shook his head.

"I need a drink," Chandler said.

Isaac took a step toward the door. "Me, too."

Bonn, Germany 2008

Becker pulled into the office complex near the train station in downtown Bonn. The building looked like a jumble of modern architecture mixed with a brightly painted gingerbread house. The sign on the closest door was for the most prominent ophthalmologist in the area, a close friend of Kugler and board member of Teleplunkt.

Parking the aged Mercedes, Becker walked quickly across the parking lot and entered the office. Directly in front of the door was a large, vibrant poster. A beautiful blonde woman with strong bones and amazingly blue eyes stared out at him. Under her picture a caption in German read, A Vision of Beauty, TeleLens.

The receptionist, a young woman in half glasses and a bun, looked up at him.

"May I help you?" she asked.

"I am here to see Dr. von Gruden."

"And your name?" she asked.

"He is expecting me," Becker said.

"I . . ."

The young woman was interrupted by a door opening behind her. Dr. von Gruden smiled and waved at Becker, guiding him back to his office. Becker saw the doctor shoot an annoyed look at the receptionist and he smiled.

Sitting in the doctor's office, Becker eyed the man's furniture. It looked to have survived a Renaissance castle. The walls were paneled in thick walnut and reminded him of the deep forests of Germany.

Behind his desk, the doctor folded his hands and smiled. He was in his early sixties with slicked back, thinning hair and a cleft chin. He looked well fed and softened by too much comfort. Becker frowned.

"Your practice is doing well, I assume," he said.

Dr. von Gruden continued to smile. "A good time to be an ophthalmologist."

"Looks it."

"I just finished my fifteenth case this week," the doctor said."

"Anyone interesting?"

Von Gruden squinted. "That I can't tell you."

"Oh," Becker said, leaning forward.

"Just tell your boss that many in Bonn have enjoyed success with the TeleLens."

"Decision makers?"

"Of course," the doctor said. "I only cater to the best."

The doctor laughed. Becker smiled through closed teeth.

"One thing," von Gruden said. "It is not my practice to mention patients, but I thought Herr Kugler should know. I diagnosed a fine woman yesterday, someone you may know. Her name is Ida Schmidt."

Becker frowned. "No, I . . . as in Herr Schmidt's wife?"

Von Gruden nodded.

"Will she have surgery?"

"I believe so," the doctor said.

"And Schmidt knows?"

"Yes."

Becker shook his head. "I will tell Kugler. Thank you."

Becker walked quickly out of the office. He had a phone call to make before his next meeting.

An hour later Becker walked through one of the poorer sections of Bonn. The shop fronts were barred and there was not a church or tourist in sight.

The sidewalk was filled with gypsies and Turks selling contraband from shabby tables. They yelled out, calling to anyone who passed. One touched the sleeve of Becker's overcoat. He spun around and grabbed the grimy little man's arm by the wrist. Applying pressure, he turned it and the man fell to his knees, pleading. Becker left him there and walked on.

At the next block, he found the warehouse. The entrance looked rusted closed but the loading bay door was open. Climbing onto the dock, he walked confidently into the shadowed interior. From the far corner, he could hear heavy music, the bass reverberating off the building's steel walls.

"Marcus," Becker shouted.

There was laughter from deep in the back of the building. Then two young men, both built like athletes, sauntered into sight. Their shaved heads reflected what little light filtered into the warehouse and their thick black boots clicked on the cement.

"Greetings, Herr Becker," the taller one said.

"Same to you, Marcus," he said.

"What brings you to this part of town," Marcus asked.

Becker glanced down. He could clearly see the bulge of a handgun at the young man's waist. His friend wore a thick chain as a belt.

"It is time," Becker said. "Our friend has asked you to begin the cleansing."

Marcus smiled. "Gladly."

He whistled and several more young men, and a couple of hard looking women, appeared. Marcus turned to them.

"We have fun tonight," he said.

They cheered, a feral sound that gave Becker a thrill.

"Excellent," he said.

Becker walked out of the warehouse. The sun had set and the few working street lamps flickered to life. He walked down a block. Screams of pain and fear erupted behind him. Smiling, he returned to Frankfurt.

WASHINGTON, D.C. 2008

Lauren opened her eyes. A throbbing headache radiating down her neck made it difficult to focus her mind. She stared at a stark white drop ceiling, totally lost.

Confused and frightened, she tried to sit up. The pain in her head exploded and she fell back down. Turning her head, she noticed the IV stand beside her bed. She followed the clear line into her arm.

A nurse walked into the room. Her eyes wide, Lauren stared at her.

"Where am I?"

"Washington Hospital Center. You were in an accident."

Lauren closed her eyes. "What's wrong with me?"

"Concussion," the nurse said. "Probably whiplash. We need to keep you here for observations. You passed out."

She groaned as the nurse checked her shunt and the bag of fluids on the stand. Still in a daze, Lauren did not at first recognize the man that walked into her room. It only took a second, though, for it to come back to her.

"Mark," she said.

He was carrying a large arrangement of flowers, mostly bright colored lilies. He set it down on her rolling table and took a seat beside the bed.

"How are you?" he asked.

"Oh, geez," she said. "I was supposed to meet you."

He grinned. "You never made it."

"What happened?"

"You were in an accident. Some guy hit you from behind," he said.

"The old man," she said, remembering. "Is he okay?"

"Yeah, you both had concussions though. I guess you spoke to an officer and he had no idea."

"How'd I get here?" she asked.

"An ambulance." Mark winked.

She arched an eyebrow. "Is there something else?"

"Well," he said. "You kind of wandered away from the scene. I found you on a bench a few blocks away."

"How did you know where I was?"

"I called and you were out of it. You didn't even know where you were. So I called the PD and they put me on with the officer you spoke with."

"You talked to the officer," she said. "How'd you get to him?"

"I still have a lot of friends on the force," he said.

"Oh." She rubbed her neck. "It hurts. Whiplash?"

"That's what the doc said," he answered. "I guess you'll need some therapy."

She was not going to worry about that. But looking at Mark, she swallowed.

"I'm so sorry I messed everything up," she said.

"You didn't mess anything up," he said.

"I did. I really wanted to see you."

He smiled. "You're seeing me now, aren't you?"

"Yeah," she said with a laugh. "I guess I am."

They spoke for awhile, catching up. Before, she had forgotten how much she enjoyed being with him. She liked the way his mouth moved when he talked, and the subtle arch of his eyebrows.

"I've really missed you."

The words tumbled out before she had time to think. Once said, she blushed and looked away. He touched her arm.

"I've missed you, too," he said. "Talking on the phone, it just isn't the same thing."

"And I go mess it up by getting hit," she said. "You probably have to get back."

"Nah," he said.

"No?"

He shrugged. "I have a room at the J.W. Marriot for the rest of the week."

"You do?"

"Yeah," he said. "I couldn't leave you."

Her eyes narrowed. "But the Marriot's expensive."

"Don't worry about that," he said.

"I could help you."

"Look," he said. "I don't want you to think I can't afford to take care of myself. Don't worry about it, okay?"

"Sure," she said. "But . . ."

"But, we're having dinner tomorrow, if you're up to it."

She smiled. "I think I will be."

Not long after Mark left, Lauren was released. When she was gathering her things, the nurse handed her a small bag. Inside, she found the pocket knife. The story came back to her in a rush of memory, and she could not wait to see Mark again.

Lauren met Mark at the Red Sage the next night. She knew the place. The downstairs level was a five star restaurant serving southwest inspired entrees in the one hundred dollar range. When he asked for a seat on the top floor, a more casual, bar atmosphere, she was relieved.

They were seated at a perfect table in a dark corner. Glancing at the menus, they leaned in and spoke softly together under a shaded chandelier.

"I have something for you," she said.

She handed him the bag over the table. Lauren watched as Mark opened it. He pulled the pocket knife out and smiled.

"This is cool," he said.

"There's more to it. Guess who it belonged to."

Mark shrugged.

"Elliot Ness," Lauren said, smiling.

She told Mark the rest of the story. When she got to the end, he swallowed hard. Leaning over the table, he gave her a kiss. When he spoke, his voice was raspy.

"Thanks," he said.

"No problem."

"No," he added. "I mean it. This is the most thoughtful thing I've ever been given."

Miming one of his favorite moves, she patted her own back. He laughed. But when she restarted their conversation, he could not take his eyes off of her.

"How's the beach?" she asked.

"Not the same without you," he said. "But I haven't made it down there in a while either."

"And your leg?" she asked.

"Good. I can run now without any pain. Still aches when it rains though. Your neck?"

"Much better," she answered. "I'm glad you stuck around."

"Me, too."

The waitress came and Mark ordered a Dos Equis. Lauren did the same. And they agreed to share a plate of lobster nachos. When the food came, they ate and laughed, and Lauren found herself touching Mark's arm and brushing her knee against his. By the time the food was done, he had moved his chair closer to hers.

"So, how's your dad?" he asked. "You two getting along?"

Lauren sighed. "I guess so. He still wishes I had stayed at Johns Hopkins with Dr. Connor."

"Do you regret taking the Bethesda offer?" he asked.

"No," she said. "I love it there. And my practice is doing really well, almost too well. I enjoy getting to know the patients. I think it makes a difference considering my philosophy."

"Yeah," he said. "It's got to make more of an impact changing their eating habits if you see them on a regular basis."

Lauren looked surprised. "I'm impressed."

"With what?"

"That you remembered my 'philosophy,'" she said.

He patted himself on the back. "I'm a world class listener."

"Shut up," she said, smacking him on the forearm.

They laughed.

"He's a good man, though," Lauren said.

Mark looked confused. "Who?"

"My father," she mocked annoyance. "I don't want you to think he's just a slimy politician. I feel like I'm always complaining about the long hours he had to work to become a partner, or how little he was around when he ran for city council, then state senate.

"I was always really proud to be his daughter. I have to admit, it was great when I was younger. It's just that as I got older, I wanted to blaze my own trail, you know?"

"Sure," Mark said. "And I never thought of your father that way. I just know he stresses you out sometimes."

"I remember when it all changed. He was in the state senate. I liked that. We got to go to the state fair and all these cool concerts and events. My friends thought I was some kind of celebrity. But then, one night, these men showed up at the house. I recognized a couple of them but they all kind of looked alike. My father took them into his study. It was the night he decided to run for U.S. Senate."

"I bet that campaign was crazy," Mark said.

"Kind of, see, the day before those men showed up, one of our senators had died of a massive stroke. It wasn't until later that I put it together, but when I did, my opinion of this whole thing changed. I imagined that same night, the Senator's kids were at a viewing, looking at their father in an open casket, his face packed with white powder. It made me feel a little sick."

"Life goes on," Mark said. "If I learned one thing when I was shot, it would be that."

"True," Lauren said. "He won the election and two years later we moved here. It's kind of funny. If he hadn't, I'd still consider Connecticut my home. Maybe I would have taken Dr. von Fricke's offer to go work for the Eye Infirmary."

"What about you," Mark said. "I mean, how did a lawyer's daughter end up becoming an eye doctor? I thought that was the kind of thing that ran in a family."

"Aren't you getting tired of hearing about me?"

"No way," he said. "Keeps me from talking about myself all the time."

She smiled. "Well, I guess I was going to go into anything but law. Seriously, though, when I was in school, I loved biology and chemistry. When I was an undergraduate, I was obsessed with neuroscience and biochemistry. I had a class on the physiology of the brain. The professor, Dr. Peterhagen, was a neuroscientist. I loved the class and he really inspired me.

"That's when I started to really get interested in the effects of diet on health, far beyond what was considered commonly accepted beliefs. I used to spend entire nights in the biochem lab while all my friends were out sharing pitchers of beer and kielbasa. What a geek, huh? There I was, in the basement collating data on the effect of nutritional supplements on rats. Even in med school, while all my classmates were doing pharmaceutical research projects so they would be more competitive, I kept on working in my own little arcane world."

"I like that," Mark said. "It shows gumption."

"I wish that was how I saw it," she said. "Most of the time, I just felt like an outcast."

"And now?" he asked, smiling.

She shook her head. "Who knows?"

Mark stared at her for a moment, and then drank from his beer. He leaned back and continued in a nonchalant voice.

"So, I heard the man that hit you was having eye trouble."

Lauren had not recalled that until Mark mentioned it. Once he did, the visual of the broken black glasses flashed behind her closed eyes. Luckily she had checked on him before her discharge and the man was fine. Although she had seen far worse in medical school, she could never forget the image of the man's blood running along the cracks of the shattered windshield.

"Yes," she answered.

"Hmmm," he smirked. "Ironic, huh?"

"How so?"

"You, an eye doctor, getting hit by an eye patient."

She shook her head. "He wasn't my patient."

"True, true," he said. "Has work been busy?"

Lauren was about to answer when something dawned on her. Her patients, the man, she suddenly remembered the concerns she had shared with her father. There were so many cases of cataracts in the city.

She looked at Mark, assessing the possibility of talking to him about it. Her father had blown her off. He was, or used to be at least, a police officer. Maybe he would be interested.

"It has been," she said, answering his question. "More than usual. In fact, I've been looking into some strange numbers. It seems that in the metro area the incidence of cataracts has gone up by nearly one hundred percent in the last few years."

She half expected him to be outwardly disinterested, so when Mark leaned forward, Lauren was surprised.

"Yeah," she said. "I checked with the U.S. Department of Health. Although they feel it isn't statistical yet, considering it's not a controlled study."

"What do you mean?" he asked.

"There are a lot of contributing factors to cataracts. A lot of people believe that the higher levels of UV rays and the general decline of nutritional health in the country have a lot to do with any increases in incidence. I can't argue with that, but it seems strange to me that an increase could be so concentrated to one area. It's not like there is a huge hole in the ozone right above D.C."

Mark shrugged. "No, I doubt that. What do you make of it?"

"I don't know," she said. "I haven't gotten too deeply into it."

He suddenly looked very serious. "Maybe you should."

"You think?" she asked. "But how?"

"Have you talked to anyone?" he asked. "Maybe you can check a national database. Talk to people who you think are knowledgeable."

"Yeah," she said. "Maybe I will."

"You should," he said.

She smiled at him. "Thanks."

"For what?"

"For taking it seriously."

Mark laughed, but his eyes did not meet hers. "How could anyone not take you seriously?"

Frankfurt, Germany 2009

Kugler sat in his office, thinking. Things were moving fast now. The years of planning and preparation following the fateful day he received the formula from South Korea were coming to fruition. Other than the botched attempt on the Senator and his daughter, things could not have gone better.

As if beckoned by his thoughts, someone knocked on the door. One of his board members, Herr Schmidt, stuck his head through the doorway.

"Herr Kugler, may I enter?"

"Definitely Hulger, come in."

Schmidt stepped into the office and took a seat opposite Kugler. His face looked grim.

"What is wrong?" Kugler asked.

"I have troubling news," Schmidt said. "I was visiting our colleague, von Müller, at Daimler Benz the other day. I found this in his office."

Schmidt pushed a manila envelope across the desk. The sight of this caused Kugler's heart to miss a beat.

"What is it?" he asked.

"Take a look."

Kugler opened the envelope. The first thing he recognized inside was the cover page for the South Korean report. After that, he found dozens of documents outlining every step Teleplunkt had made over the past decade.

"What is the meaning of this?" Kugler whispered.

"I had my suspicions," Schmidt said.

"How so?"

"At the last meeting, von Müller said some things that troubled me. He alluded to a prostitute that took pictures."

"Blackmail?" Kugler asked.

"I believe so. I had not expected it to have anything to do with the company though. I went to help him, but he was called from the office. The envelope was on the top of the desk, the Korean report sticking out. It was almost as if he was calling out for help."

"You took the envelope?" Kugler asked.

"Of course I did," he said. "I don't know if he has copies, but I could not leave it there."

"Has von Müller contacted you? Certainly he must know you took it."

"No," Schmidt said. "I think he is a desperate man. Like I said, I think he wanted me to see it."

Kugler shook his head. "Thank you, Hulger. You are a loyal man."

Schmidt nodded. "What will you do?"

"I'm not sure yet," Kugler said.

Schmidt said goodbye and left the office. Once alone, Kugler dialed Becker's cell phone.

"I have work for you," he said.

"Interesting?" Becker asked.

Kugler closed his eyes. "It is right up your alley."

Baltimore, Maryland 2009

Lauren walked into the lobby of the Sheraton Baltimore City Center. A sign hung in front of the reception area. On it was written, Massachusetts Eye Infirmary/TeleLens Symposium/Ballroom A. She followed the arrow and found the session already started. As quietly as she could, she slipped into the door and sat toward the back.

Two hundred seats, well below the room's capacity, were arranged in rows facing a low stage. On top of it sat a wired dais and four chairs arranged in a semi-circle. She recognized three of the four VIPs. One was a doctor from Washington Hospital, one was G. Edgar Connor and the other was Dr. Dieter von Fricke.

The fourth man stood and approached the dais. He leaned forward, his mouth near an expensive microphone.

"Welcome," he said. "My name is Brett Taylor, U.S. Territory Manager for Teleplunkt. I would like to thank you all for coming today. And I would like to especially thank Dr. Dieter von Fricke for organizing this gathering. The ophthalmologic community in the United States has been asking for the latest technology in order to help their cataract patients attain the most natural vision possible.

"The one thing I know, is that the TeleLens makes people happy. Your patients will be happy with the outcome of their surgery and their improved vision. They will be telling their friends who will want to have their cataract annoyance taken care of earlier.

"You, the ophthalmologists will be happy. Not only will you have more patients, but you will find you have to spend less time and effort in post operative management. When you say hello to TeleLens, you will be saying goodbye to complications and dissatisfactions.

"This is our third symposium already and by the time we're done, I expect we'll hold nearly twenty all over the country."

Once he introduced himself, Lauren did recognize the man. She had seen him around, haunting the hallways of the Washington Hospital Center. He was a salesman, his specialty lenses for cataract surgery. With a smile she realized he had not paid her burgeoning business a call yet. That was not odd though. She was already using the TeleLens. Dr. von Fricke had suggested it to her months before and it was a very good lens. Plus, due to her philosophy, nutritional and lifestyle changes before surgery, she performed maybe a quarter of the surgeries compared to doctors in similar sized practices.

She had not paid attention to most of what the salesman said; her mind was wandering. When he mentioned Dr. Connor, she perked up.

"I feel truly lucky today that, thanks to Dr. von Fricke, we have Dr. J. Edgar Connor here to speak on behalf of our new TeleLens. Dr. Connor."

The audience clapped politely as Dr. Connor approached the dais. He shook hands with Brett Taylor, who smiled and took a seat.

"Good morning colleagues." Dr. Connor began. "I, too, want to thank my old friend Dieter for sponsoring these symposia. For once, he's right. There is nothing on the market like the TeleLens. From my experience, I know that the TeleLens allows the eye to naturally focus once again, far more so than any lens I have used in the past. I call it the Ponce de Leon affect.

"For over a year, we have been using their new polymer lens on all patients requiring surgery at the Wilmer Eye Institute. Not only are they less costly than their competition, I have found the results to be astounding. Brett over there asked me to put together some numbers, some success stories we've had at Wilmer. I told him that would not be necessary."

Dr. Connor pushed up his half-glasses and continued. "I told him that my colleagues know that if I like something, it has to be good. But here are the stats. We've done 120 implants with the TeleLens. Ninety-eight percent of the patients have 20/40 vision or better without correction and of those, 80 percent have 20/25 vision without correction. Almost all of them can read a newspaper without having to put on reading glasses or bifocals. We've followed these 120 patients for more than a year and none have had a serious side-effect. The TeleLens has become our lens of choice for our patients who come from a wide referral area and need to return to their local eye doctors with good results and easy management."

The audience clapped.

"In the coming weeks," Connor continued. "I am going to accompany Dieter and Brett to Washington, Richmond and Philadelphia to pass on the word about the new TeleLens. And after that, Germany, England and France. We are scheduling gatherings such as this, where we can discuss all the many factors involved in cataract diagnosis and treatment. So, with no further delay, let me introduce my esteemed colleague," Dr. Connor looked over his shoulder. "Dr. Dieter von Fricke."

Lauren smiled as he approached the podium. When he spoke, she always found herself intrigued by his accent, as if it added sophistication to mundane words.

"Velcome, velcome," he said. "I would like to begin today's discussion by adding my recommendation to Dr. Connor's. I, too, have been using the TeleLens for almost a year. It is a wonderful product, no doubt. I think you will all agree after the first implant. I do not doubt that.

"The TeleLens is like no other. It is the thinnest lens available. When folded, it goes through a 2.0 millimeter incision. Patients can be back to work the same day.

"It is also the most flexible lens, fitting along the back capsule like a woman's glove. Once on, the patient can focus like a twenty-year-old. As they move the internal muscles of the eye, they can focus both distant and near, like natural bifocal vision.

"All this, and they are the cheapest lens on the market. From what Brett tells me, Teleplunkt is offering a reward system. For every ten lenses a doctor uses, they earn credits towards new equipment for the office."

A young doctor in the row in front of Lauren turned around. He winked and looked at her name tag.

"Bethesda, huh? Long drive. Have you used this new lens?" he asked.

She nodded. "Yes."

"Dr. von Fricke is pushing it hard. He must be getting a lucrative consulting fee," he said.

"I doubt that," she said.

He laughed. "And why's that?"

"Because I've known the doctor for a long time," she said. "Money has no meaning to him. Only medicine."

The young doctor shrugged. "We'll see."

He turned back around and Lauren listened to Dr. von Fricke again.

"To begin," he said. "I would like to open a discussion on surgical complications of cataract surgery as it pertains to different types of lens implants. I've asked Dr. Evans from Washington to come up and start us off."

Dr. von Fricke finished introducing Dr. Evans. Before he left the podium, he glanced back at Lauren. His thin lips cracked into a smile and he nodded. She smiled back, and then glanced at Connor. He was shaking his head.

After the symposium, Lauren mingled her way through an informal reception. Off to one side were refreshments. Trays of food rested on tables covered with white linen. She grabbed a small plate of cubed melons and reentered the crowd.

She made small talk with a few doctors she recognized from her time at the Wilmer Eye Institute. As she made her way toward Dr. Connor, she nearly ran into her friend, Melanie.

Melanie had changed since the last time Lauren saw her. Back at Hopkins, she had always worn a lab coat and had her hair pulled back. Now, her blonde hair was down, wisps falling over one eye. She wore a tight red business suite which flattered the curves of her figure.

"Lauren," she said. "I didn't know you were coming today."

"I had a free day and thought I'd come up," Lauren answered. "How are you?"

"Good," Melanie said. "And you?"

"Great."

"How's the practice?"

Lauren smiled. "I really like it. It's nice to observe the same people over time. You get to know them as more than just patients."

Melanie laughed. "That's great until they start calling you in the middle of the night."

Lauren nodded. "I've been lucky so far. What are you up to?"

"I'm sure you've heard I've completed a cataract and laser surgery fellowship under Dr. Platt and Dr. Connor. It's been a great experience. As you know, they are terrific teachers with a lot of clinical experience. I really improved my surgical techniques."

When her friend said that, Lauren felt a surge of jealousy. She had known that Melanie took the position Dr. Connor had offered to her. Lauren hid her reaction behind a yawn.

"I'm really happy for you," she said. "Dr. Connor is certainly world renowned."

"Yeah," Melanie said. "I'm surprised Dr. von Fricke invited Dr. Connor to share in this great opportunity with the TeleLens since they are such competitive rivals on the world stage."

"So that's still going on?" Lauren asked.

"Even more," Melanie said. "We were racing to get a paper out on the TeleLens and von Fricke beat us to it. I've never seen Dr. Connor so upset."

"That's a surprise," Lauren said. "I've never known Dr. von Fricke to be so supportive of commercial ventures."

"He loves these lenses, I guess." Melanie's lips parted in an evil smile. "Word is he's well paid as a consultant. You would think our prestigious professors get paid enough for their outside lectures."

Lauren smiled but did not respond.

"Who knows?" Melanie looked over Lauren's shoulder then waved at someone. "I have to go. Call me when you'll be in Baltimore, okay?"

"Sure," Lauren said.

They hugged and Melanie crossed the room to talk with the young doctor who had spoken to Lauren during the symposium. She snorted and looked around for Dr. Connor. To her surprise, he was standing right in front of her.

"Hello, Lauren," he said. "It's been too long."

"Hello, chief," she said, shaking his hand. "How are you?"

"Good," he said, "Although I don't love being the spokesman for that salesman."

"You did great. So those lenses are the best?"

He nodded. "You haven't used them yet?"

"I have, but I do less surgery than others," she said. "None of the TeleLens reps have visited my practice yet."

"Ah, your practice, how is it?"

Lauren heard the insincerity in his voice. "Fine."

"Good," Dr. Connor smiled. "And your father? How's his health."

She arched an eyebrow. "Good, I assume. Thanks for asking."

"Excellent. I should be . . ."

Lauren surprised herself by interrupting him. "Can I ask you something first?"

He forced a half smile. "Of course."

"Last month, I had an influx of patients with rapidly developing cataracts. It struck me so I checked the stats and found an anomaly. There seems to be a significant increase of the incidence of cataracts in the Washington metro area."

"Hmmm, interesting," he said.

"I thought so," she continued. "I started to try to figure out what could be the cause. Dr. Connor, do you think this is also occurring in Baltimore?"

"I haven't observed it, but we get referrals from all over the country."

"Should I pursue this and go to places like HCFA to look for actual numbers?"

"Probably a waste of your time," he said. "I would attend to your practice and come to do real research with us. I'm sorry, dear, but I really have to go," he said. "It's great seeing you."

Dr. Connor walked away, disappearing into the milling crowd. Lauren stood still for a second, staring. Then she slowly walked toward the exit, talking to herself.

"Just like Ignaz Semmelweis."

"Excuse me?" someone said behind her. She turned to see Dr. von Fricke.

"Oh, nothing."

Dr. von Fricke arched an eyebrow. "Did you say something about Semmelweis the 19th century obstetrician, a fellow Austrian?"

"I did," she said. "I was just remembering how no one believed him when he said that doctors washing their hands reduced the rate of maternal deaths during delivery."

Von Fricke smiled. "He was shunned by his peers. Are you feeling that way?"

She laughed. "I guess not."

"Glad you could come," he said. "I thought I'd see you at the symposium in Washington next month."

"I'll be there, too," she said. "Do you think I could be on the panel? I'd love to speak on alternate treatment of cataracts through supplements. I've had some success recently with multi-vitamins in people of the same age group. As you are aware, Vitamins A, C, E and lutein have all been associated with a reduced risk of developing cataracts that require surgery and, of course, wearing sunglasses is still the best protector of the lens and the entire eye."

Dr. von Fricke waved his hand. "I appreciate your candor and your insights but I don't think that would be all together appropriate. This is sponsored by an independent company."

"Oh," Lauren said, taken aback.

"I'm sure you understand."

Dr. von Fricke walked away without saying anything else. Lauren walked out, her intuition telling her something was not right.

Once outside, Lauren took a deep breath of the crisp, fresh air. She pulled out her BlackBerry and dialed.

Mark picked up. "Hey, Lauren."

"Hi," she said. "How are you?"

"Fine, but how are you?" he asked. "Was it a worthwhile meeting?"

"All right, I guess." She shrugged. "The meeting was educational and I met my former chief, as anticipated. I told him what I'd found about the increased incidences of cataracts. He and Dr. Fricke were dismissive."

"Are you kidding?" Mark asked. "For someone as distinguished in the field, you would think he'd have some reaction, whether he took note or called you a nut.

She nodded, and then cradled the phone on her shoulder as she paid the parking attendant. "I've known him for a long time. He acted strange. But so did the other doctor I told you about."

"How so?"

"He's coming to Washington to hold a symposium on cataract treatment. It's sponsored by this lens company. I asked him if I could speak. Normally, he'd have no problem. He's always given me the opportunity to offer a counterpoint to surgery, you know, my normal mantra. This time he said, 'no.'"

"Really?"

"Yes," she said. "It just wasn't like him."

"Hmmm." Mark was silent for a second. "What now?"

"I don't know," Lauren said. "I think I need to head back to Bethesda, think this through."

"But what about the cataracts?"

"What about them?" she asked.

"You're just going to let more people get sick?"

She frowned, thinking about her Hippocratic Oath. "Of course not. Maybe I didn't find out anything. Maybe that's why I got dismissed by Dr. Connor. Maybe he didn't have the heart to tell me I'm a fruit cake."

Mark's tone was serious. "You really believe that?"

"Of course not," she said. "But the next time I talk to either of them, I am going to be better prepared."

"That's what I thought," Mark said. "You know you can't just ignore it."

"No," she said. "I never intended to."

"So what's next?" Mark asked.

"I don't know. I need to get back, get settled, then I'll think about it."

But her mind was already planning a trip to the National Institute of Health to visit the statistics and epidemiology departments.

FRANKFURT, GERMANY 2009

Becker sat in his car on *Hochstrasse* looking out at the *Alte Oper*. Just down from the Stock Exchange, the façade harkened back to the heyday of Italian Renaissance with its arched windows and carved friezes. Before burning down during World War II, it had been an opera house. Now rebuilt, it was used as a conference centre. In Becker's opinion, a fine example of the future devouring the past.

Through his open window, he could hear the flowing fountain outside the building. Tourists milled about, taking pictures laughing. All in all, it was a mundane scene, as it should be.

Becker had been waiting there for half an hour. Having tailed von Müller for a week, he knew the man would leave his office on *Bleichstrasse* in the next few minutes. He would drive his Mercedes along *Hochstrasse* to where it became *Neue Mainzer Strasse*. He would cross over the Main River and head to the prostitute's apartment south of the city. She would be waiting for him right at that moment, Becker was sure of it.

He did not have to wait much longer. A minute passed and the silver Mercedes rolled past. Becker could clearly see von Müller in the driver's seat. He wore expensive sunglasses, his gray hair greased back, and a BlueTooth glowing faintly in his ear.

Becker eased out of his spot a car behind von Müller. He followed behind for a block before pulling up to the back corner of von Müller's car.

For that day Becker drove a car that was stolen at gunpoint from a tourist the day before. The report claimed a heroin addict had stopped the family in traffic on the eastern side of the city. Other reports had come into the authorities concerning the car driving erratically. Soon, they would find it on the side of the road in Wiesbaden, the addict OD'd behind the wheel.

For today, it had a different task. Becker knew the guardrail on the bridge across the Main was damaged. It was one of the accidents called in earlier that day involving the vehicle he drove. As von Müller's car neared the spot, Becker sped up. He came abreast of von Müller and looked over. The man paid him no attention.

The two cars reached the damaged portion of the guardrail. Becker yanked the wheel to the right. His car slammed into von Müller, cutting in front of him as it did. Von Müller's Mercedes hit the guardrail which gave way. The car tumbled off the side of the bridge as Becker drove off.

Five minutes later, Becker pulled up to an apartment building off *Walte-Kolb Strasse*. He was careful to position the car so that the damaged front end was obscured by a newspaper vending machine. The sun was setting and down the street, he could see the brilliant oranges and reds reflecting off the surface of the Main. Sirens blared in the distance.

Becker hurried into the apartment building. When he reached the third floor, he found Apartment 304. Without hesitating, he picked the lock and walked inside.

"Gunter, is that you?" a woman asked from the bedroom area.

Becker found her reclined on a chaise lounge wearing a sheer robe and lingerie. When she turned and saw him, her mouth opened to scream. He was on her in a flash, covering her mouth and slamming her to the ground.

"This will not go well for you, *fraulein*, if you do not tell me the truth."

Her muffled screams rose from under his clenched hand. The skin on her cheeks was pressed white, and her eyes were so wide they looked like they might pop right out of her skull.

"Who are you working for?" he asked.

She thrashed around. Becker pulled his polished Luger out and pressed the silencer attached to the barrel against one of her protruding eyes. She winced. He lifted his hand away from her mouth.

"Who?"

"I don't know."

Becker smiled. He moved the gun. Turning it sideways, he pressed it against the side of her nose and fired. Her left nostril exploded and blood sprayed out, peppering the white-washed walls.

His hand covered her mouth when she screamed again. Blood made his grip slip, so he jammed the gun into her mouth instead.

The woman whimpered. He leaned closer.

"Who are you working for?"

She mumbled something. He removed the gun.

"I don't know," she stammered. "He takes the pictures and finds out who the men are. I just do my part. That's all. I promise."

"Who is he?"

"I don't . . ."

He shot her in the arm next. She tried to scream but the blood pouring out of her nose caused it to come out more as a gurgling sound.

"Name," he said.

She was crying. He pressed his gun against her stomach.

"Name."

"Jontz," she said. "Eric Jontz."

"Thank you," Becker said.

He shot her between the eyes and walked out of the apartment. Other than the blood on the palm of his hand, his clothes and shoes where clean. It did not matter, though. No one would care about a dead prostitute.

Outside he called Kugler.

"What did you find?" his boss asked.

"A two-bit operation, they got lucky. Von Müller must have spouted at the mouth to the girl. It must have put her pimp onto something at Teleplunkt. Random from as far as I can tell."

"Have you taken care of von Müller?"

"Yes, he is in the river."

"And the girl?"

"Yes. There is one more loose end, Eric Jontz. Once he's dead, I will ditch the car."

"Excellent," Kugler said. "This makes up for that mess in the States."

Becker did not say anything. The States had been a debacle. He blamed himself for that. But he also blamed Kugler for having to kill his best man, Walter, in order to leave no loose ends.

"Just kill this Jontz and ditch the car," Kugler said.

Becker hung up. One more killing and his day's work would be done.

BETHESDA, MARYLAND 2009

Lauren watched her father's driver pull up in front of her practice. It was in an exclusive two-story medical building, her predecessor having purchased it ten years before. Behind her, a plaque on the door read: Chandler Ophthalmic Consultants. From the front stoop, she could see the steady current of tourists heading down into the Metro stop, a fifteen minute ride to the many attractions in D.C. One of her patients, the manager of a local crab house waved to her from across the street. She waved back and stepped up to meet her mother and father.

The black Lincoln rolled to a stop beside the curb. The back door opened and Senator Chandler climbed out. He wore his usual dark suit and red tie. Reaching back, he helped her mother out. She was dressed impeccably in a red suit and matching Molonoblanics.

"Hi, mom, dad," Lauren said.

"Hi sweetie," her mom said, giving her a big hug. Lauren breathed in her mother's scent, a perfume she had worn for twenty years.

The Senator nodded. "You look well."

Lauren hugged her father, too. "You do, too."

"So, this is your office?"

She nodded and led them inside. The office was on the first floor, well planned considering many of her patients were elderly. Stenciled on the window, it read: Chandler Ophthalmic Consultants, Comprehensive Eye Care. The waiting room was still crowded, mostly with loved ones waiting for the last few patients of the day to come back out. Lauren looked at her parents.

"Come on in," she said. "You can wait in my office while I finish up the last few patients."

Her mom smiled. Her father checked his watch.

Lauren poked her head into the office fifteen minutes later. "Dad, you want to go first?"

She led him back to one of her three exam rooms. She chose the largest one but even so, once he stepped into the room, it felt too small.

"Have a seat," Lauren said. "I'll check your prescription first."

"Don't you have a tech that does that?" he asked.

"Dad," she protested. "I do, but, oh, just forget it."

After checking his eyes with the chart and putting drops in his eye, Lauren pulled the phoropter around.

After having drops in the eye, the slit lamp narrow beam could look deeply into the eye detecting cataracts easily. She placed a handheld Volk Lens into the beam, providing a clear view of the retina. This magnified view could detect the presence of diabetes, cholesterol deposits, blood diseases and some cancers. Checking her parents always made Lauren nervous, dreading what she might find.

With a professional's calm, she finished up the exam. Fortunately everything looked perfect.

"Dad?" she asked, finishing up.

"Yes."

"Have you noticed more people having eye trouble?" she asked.

"In the U.S., or world wide. Developing countries?"

"No," she interrupted. "I mean in Washington."

"Well, we are a bunch of old guys," he said with a laugh.

She rolled her eyes. "That's what you said last time. Seriously, have you noticed anything?"

"I guess," he said. "Come to think of it, my colleague heading up Senate operations mentioned something to me the other day. He said our deductibles might be going up due to a large influx of surgery."

"What kind of surgery? Cataracts?"

"No idea," he said. "But considering I sent three guys your way, I would not be surprised."

Suddenly, Lauren's chest tightened. Something was definitely going on and she felt a sudden worry for her father.

"Make sure you keep taking those supplements."

"You saw them when you were over last time," he said.

"I know that. But just because you have them, doesn't mean you're taking them."

He nodded. "I have been. Regardless of what you may think, I know you're a great doctor."

Lauren blushed again. Her hazel eyes twinkled. "Something's not right. I checked some preliminary statistics at HCFA and found an increase in incidence in the metro area compared to previous years' data. I was starting to think it was all in my head. But I know I'm right. I know I found something."

"I'm sure you did," her father said.

Her chest swelled with pride and determination. Regardless of her mentor's reaction, she had to learn more.

"But sweetie," her father added. "It's not what you know; it's what you do about it."

"That's true," she said.

"So, what are you going to do about it?"

"I'm not sure," she said. "I was thinking about going to investigate at the National Institute of Health where I trained. I can collect the HCFA data, providing actual diagnosis and cataract surgeries within a month's time. Doctors have to bill by diagnosis, all of which is compiled by HCFA."

"Ask for Padma Patel, Ph.D. in their Department of Statistics," he said. "Tell her who you are and that I suggested you contact her. She'll give you everything you'll need."

Lauren's mouth opened. She stared at her dad for a second.

"Thanks," she said.

"No problem." He stood up. "She owes me a favor."

"No," Lauren said. "Thanks for taking me seriously."

Senator Chandler arched an eyebrow. "Why wouldn't I?"

Lauren walked him back to her office and collected her mother. Her exam went well, too. When she was finished, Lauren asked her if they could stay for dinner.

"Maybe your father can, sweetie," she said. "I'm heading back to Danbury in about an hour."

Lauren arched an eyebrow. "You are? You've been heading up there a lot, haven't you?"

"Busy, as always," she answered without looking at her husband.

Back at Lauren's office, she noticed something was off. Her mother and father stood too far apart and failed to look at each other.

"Everything okay?" she asked.

The Senator smiled. "Great, but we need to be going."

"Okay," Lauren said.

She walked them out, feeling confused. After waving them off, Lauren returned to her office. She sat there, alone, for an hour, thinking, only half of the time about cataracts.

A day later, after seeing patients, Lauren was sitting in her repaired Acura. Crossing town, she merged onto Rockville Pike, heading for the National Institute of Health campus.

For the past year, Lauren had made the drive from her office to the campus hundreds of times. Her fellowship, where she was studying the effect of diet on macular degeneration in lab rats, took place in the Clinical Center, the main building on campus. Brick with classical white columns, it was not her destination this time.

When she pulled up to security, she showed her ID to the guard.

"You don't have any tobacco products on you?" he asked.

Lauren shook her head.

"Not allowed on campus as of yesterday," the guard said.

She laughed. "I'll remember that."

He grunted and waved her in. Although she had never gone to the building before, she drove directly to the National Library of Medicine. Unlike the Clinical Center, the Library was a concrete slab with two thin, glass high rises on either end. After searching for a parking spot for ten minutes, she walked about a half mile to get to the entrance. Once inside, she approached the receptionist.

"Hi," she said. "I'm looking for Dr. Padma Patel."

The receptionist stared at her. "Is she expecting you?"

Lauren paused. "Tell her Senator Chandler sent me over to speak with her."

The receptionist reached over. She picked up the phone and rang Dr. Patel. She whispered something just softly enough for Lauren not to hear it. A minute later, a tall woman with flowing black hair and dark skin hurried down the hallway toward them.

"Dr. Chandler?" Padma asked. She had a beautiful, Eastern accent.

Lauren blinked. "Yes, how'd you know?"

"Your father called yesterday," she said.

"He did?" Lauren asked.

Padma tilted her head. "Yes. He said you were looking for some information on cataract incidence. I've been pulling the Medicare records if you want to follow me."

Lauren nodded in shock that her father called ahead. When they reached Padma's office, a closet sized space deep within the library, she pulled a seat over to the desk for Lauren.

"So, may I ask what it is you're looking for?" Padma asked.

"Definitely." Lauren slid her chair closer. "About a month ago, I noticed an odd statistical anomaly when I was researching some data over at the Clinical Center. I thought I found a significant increase in cataract incidence in the D.C. metro area."

"Hmmm," Padma said. "No one over here has mentioned it. Let's see though. I just downloaded all of the HCFA Medicare claims for the city."

"Can you also search by procedure such as cataract surgery?" she asked.

"Procedure, not diagnosis?" Padma asked.

Lauren nodded. "I figure they both should correlate . . . and I'd be interested to see what the numbers are."

Padma picked at her keyboard and hit enter. Numbers scrolled across the blue screen.

"Here's the surgery claims for the past three months."

"Can you compare that with the same data from five years ago?" Lauren asked.

"Sure."

More clicking and more numbers, Padma leaned forward, the light from the monitor reflecting off her dark eyes.

"Wow, look at this." Padma tapped the monitor. "Quadrupled. How come no one found this before?"

Lauren shrugged. "I think because the incidence is rising nationwide due to greater solar exposure and fast food habituation, not to mention the baby boomers. Can you run the same numbers countrywide?"

"Good idea," Padma said. "There's an increase, but nothing like quadrupling. Looks more like about a twenty-five percent increase."

Lauren's eyes widened. "Twenty-five compared to four hundred. That's significant."

"Sure is."

"What about three years ago?" Lauren asked.

Padma checked. "About the same as five years ago."

"Two years?" she asked.

"Here we go," Padma said. "This one is about twice the number compared to the five year number."

"So it started about two years ago," Lauren said, twisting a strand of hair around her finger. "Let's look at the cataract surgery claims, and YAG Laser claims. What could have changed?"

"Excuse me but what are YAG Lasers?"

"A laser is simply fortified light coming from an electrical or crystal source. YAG stands for Yttrium Aluminum Garnet which is a combination of crystals that emit a very precise ten-sixty-six nanometer wave length. This type of laser is capable of cutting open the posterior capsule which has remained in place from the cataract surgical procedure. The intraocular implant is nestled in the capsular bag like a letter in an envelope. Over the ensuing months, residual cells can grow across the capsule creating a haze which reduces vision. The YAG Laser can focus the specific wavelength of light to open the capsule without doing much damage to the intraocular lens.

"I wonder if laser procedures have a higher incidence as well," she said, since she had been doing more herself.

"I know we haven't seen anything," Padma answered.

Lauren stared at the screen. "I would appreciate you running through a list of searches. If we find more data to support this, we need to publish, together, as soon as possible. Other ophthalmologists and the general public need to know this information."

Padma looked excited. "Sounds great. This is something different for a statistician."

"Good," Lauren said. "Let's run the same searches, say three years ago compared to now, for every major metropolitan area in the U.S. Maybe look at other countries on the same latitude to see if we can find other increases."

Padma took notes as Lauren continued.

"Then, maybe, we can look for contributing factors. Maybe check some other conditions such as: macular degeneration, glaucoma, cornea dystrophy, and procedures such as glaucoma and LASIK in addition to cataract and laser surgery. For that matter, let's cross-reference the cataract patients with Lasik surgeries; see if there is some correlation there. How long do you think it'll take you?"

"I'll get on it," Padma said.

"Perfect," Lauren said. "Call me once you have something."

"Definitely."

"Thank you so much," Lauren said.

"No problem," Padma said. "I'm so glad your father suggested me to you."

Lauren smiled. "Me, too."

And she meant it.

BETHESDA, MARYLAND 2009

A week after she returned, Lauren's secretary rang through to her with a phone call. She was with a patient but something made her take note. Excusing herself, she glanced at the incoming number. It was from the National Institute of Health. She stepped out of the exam room.

"Hello."

"Dr. Chandler, this is Padma from the NIH."

"Hi Padma," Lauren said. "I was hoping to hear from you. Did you find anything?"

Padma sounded excited. "Maybe. I have to show it to you. When can you come over?"

"I'm booked with patients this afternoon and have surgery in the morning. Can you stay until after five tonight?"

"Sure," Padma said.

"Is it good?"

"I don't know if it's good," Padma said. "But I think you're on to something."

A rush ran through Lauren's body. "Great."

"See you after five?"

"I'll be there," Lauren said.

She hung up and returned to her patient. She found it difficult to concentrate. Afterwards, she sped through her schedule. All the while, she was writing an article in her head: "Unexplainable Spike in Cataract Surgeries in Washington Metro Area." Not only was it sure to get published, but Lauren was already thinking ahead. She would run that data against the patients in her own practice who were taking the prophylactic vitamin supplement. The follow-up article: "The Effect of Able-Eyes Among Washington, D.C. Residents During Known Spike in Cataract Surgeries." That way, she could evaluate the effect of Able-Eyes and other supplements on the incidence of cataracts in that same area over the past two years.

All Lauren had to do was prove a statistically significant difference comparing her patients to the general population of the city. Having recently checked out her father and many other elderly patients, she had a great feeling. With these two articles, no one could ignore the importance of diet and supplementation. Perhaps her theories would finally become accepted practice across the country.

Excited and in a rush, Lauren threw open the private back door of her practice only to find Mark standing there. With wide, surprised eyes, he held out a bouquet of lilies, Lauren's favorites. Her heart missed a beat. At the same time, she could not be late.

"Hey," she said. "You surprised me."

"You, too," he said, smiling. "I almost fell down the stoop."

"What are you doing here?" Lauren asked.

Mark looked hurt. "I, uh . . ."

"I didn't mean it that way," she said. "It's great to see you."

"You look like you're heading out," he said. "I guess I should have called. I just wanted to surprise you, maybe get dinner."

"You came all the way here just to have dinner?" she asked.

Lauren could feel her cheeks warming. Mark held out the bouquet. His eyebrows curled up in a look of total innocence. Lauren felt the urge to reach out and touch him.

"Here," he said.

Lauren took the flowers. "Thanks."

"Maybe I can walk you to wherever you're heading," he said.

Lauren thought for a second. "Why don't you just come along? Yeah. I'm just going to the National Institute of Health. I'm taking the Metro since it's rush hour. I don't think I'll be all evening. We can have dinner after."

Mark smiled. "Sounds great to me."

On impulse, Lauren wrapped her arm around his elbow and let him lead her down the stoop toward the Metro station.

"Did you drive?" she asked.

He shook his head. "Took the Metro."

"You were in D.C. again?"

Mark blinked. "Yeah. I got a job there, security for the Smithsonian. I'm thinking of renting a little place down by Foggy Bottom."

Lauren was about to follow up on her question. She had no idea he was working in D.C. Thinking about it, she realized she always called him on his cell phone. She had assumed he was busy in Baltimore working private security, but maybe not.

"What?" he asked.

"Just didn't know you were thinking of moving to the city," she said.

"I thought I told you," he said.

"Nope," she said. "Typical man, short on words."

Mark stopped. He looked her in the eye. "You calling me a brute?"

Crunching his brow, he grunted like a caveman. He picked Lauren up clear off the street and spun her around. Lauren barked out a surprised scream and was back on the ground before she could protest.

"Whoa," she said, laughing. "Where'd that come from?"

Mark grunted. "Me like girl."

Lauren laughed. "Come on, my Neanderthal, or we'll be late."

He grunted again and shuffled along beside her. It made her laugh.

They walked into the National Library of Medicine. After showing her ID and Mark signing in as a guest, the receptionist waved Lauren and Mark back and led them down the long hallway to Padma's office. The door was open and she was sitting behind her computer. Lauren knocked on the doorjamb.

Padma looked up. "Hi, Lauren."

Lauren saw her glance at Mark.

"Hi, Padma," she said. "This is my friend, Mark Bartholomew."

"Nice to meet you, Mark," she said.

Mark strode into the room and shook her hand. "I hear you've been doing some research."

"I sure have been," she said. "I haven't stopped since Lauren left the other day. It was intriguing to say the least."

"I'm dying to see what you found out," Lauren said.

"Come on in and take a seat." Padma handed her a folder. "Inside is all the raw data for your article."

"Our article, you mean."

Padma smiled. "Our article. I can tell you the interesting part in a nutshell. See, I was following your request. I checked every metropolitan area over 100,000 people in the U.S. None of them showed anywhere near the same increase. The highest I could find, Miami, had a thirty-five percent increase. But that increase was gradual over the five years and may be related to demographic changes with the influx of snowbirds."

"That's high, but not even close to what we found in D.C.," Lauren said.

"I know," Padma said. "However, I found that LASIK surgeries were flat and actually declining because of the recession. So there is no correlation with the incidence of LASIK procedures, so it isn't the cause. I did do the latitude search. That took the bulk of my time. It's a good thing I don't have much on my plate so I was free to do this immediately."

"Did you find anything?" Lauren asked.

"I sure did."

"Tell me."

Padma smiled. "There was an almost identical increase somewhere else."

"Where?"

"Bonn, Germany," she said.

Lauren's brow furrowed. She looked at Mark. He was leaning back, half paying attention. She turned back to Padma.

"Bonn?"

"Yes, 300 percent increase in cataract and 250 percent increase in cataract surgery over two years," Padma said.

"But what do Bonn and D.C. have in common?" Lauren asked.

"They're both capitals," Mark said.

"Huh?" Lauren had not expected him to say anything.

"Bonn is the capital of Germany," he said. "At least it used to be before the wall came down. After that, it was moved to Berlin, but some of the government is still there."

"Hmmm," Lauren said. "But what does that have to do with cataract surgery?"

He shrugged. "That's your expertise."

Lauren looked at Padma. "Any ideas?"

"None," Padma said. "But I'd think the data alone would make a compelling article. Very strange, only two areas of a spike in cataract incidence."

Lauren cradled the folder to her chest. "No doubt about that."

At dinner that night, Lauren could not get what Padma said out of her head. She sat across a square table from Mark. A large sheet of white paper covered the surface. There was a hole in the middle of the wood and a silver bucket hung suspended inside it. An entire roll of paper towels rested inside the bucket.

Their waiter approached. Lauren looked up and noticed the young man's eyes did not move in sync. His right lagged behind, barely moving at all. She knew immediately he had a glass eye.

Mark spoke to the waiter, ordering two dozen jumbo crabs. He looked at Lauren and arched an eyebrow.

"What do you want to drink?" he asked.

"Whatever you're having," she said.

He smirked. "Great, two Bud drafts."

The waiter walked away. Mark gave Lauren googly eyes. She smacked him on the arm.

"Stop it," she said.

"What?"

"You know what."

He shrugged. "You look preoccupied," he said.

"Just thinking."

"About what Dr. Patel found out today?"

"Yeah," she said. "It doesn't make a lot of sense."

He shrugged. "You'd know better than I."

"D.C. and Bonn," she said.

Mark stared at her for a second. She got the feeling he was assessing something, but she was not sure what.

"Maybe you could check with your father?"

Lauren frowned. "What?"

"He works in D.C., doesn't he?" Mark asked.

"Yeah," she said. "And it is odd. Maybe he knows someone in Bonn I can talk to. He really helped me so far."

"He did?" Mark asked.

"Yes. He was really encouraging when I told him about it. He gave me Padma's name."

Mark looked surprised. "I thought you and he didn't get along that great."

She shook her head. "We've definitely had our moments. But, I don't know. He was the first person that took me seriously about this."

Mark cleared his throat.

"Oh," she said. "After you, I mean."

He smiled and touched her hand. "That's better."

The crabs arrived. Twenty-four burning ocean bugs with liberal mounds of Old Bay covering their perfectly steamed shells.

"Mmmm, mmm." Mark rubbed his hands together. "Nothing like 'em."

Lauren grabbed her first crab and went to work. After pulling the claws off, she flipped it over. She found the sword shaped latch on its belly. Prying it up, she pulled, exposing the back fin. Digging out the inedible portions, she picked out the sweet chunks of meat. Using her fingers, she popped it into her mouth, savoring the taste. She followed that with a swig of beer from a frosty mug.

When she looked up, Mark was busy on his first crab. He smashed the small wooden mallet into the claw.

"Don't do that," she said, laughing.

"What?"

"You can't smash it," she said. "You have to crack it, then pull the meat out."

"Oh."

Mark looked sheepish as he cracked the second claw. He pulled out a nice blade of pearly white meat from the shell. He smiled at her.

"Didn't know you were such an expert," he said.

"I have to admit, crabs and beer are my guilty pleasures."

He laughed. "Not too good for the eyes, huh?"

"Not particularly." She looked into his eyes. "Maybe that's what happened to our waiter."

Mark laughed. He looked so at peace, so happy. She told him so. He blushed. It gave her a tingle down her spine.

"I really think I'm going to take that apartment," he said between bites.

"In Foggy Bottom?"

"Yeah," he said. "I'd like to be closer to you." He looked down at the table. "Maybe see you more often."

She leaned closer. "I think I'd like that."

After a few beers and too many crabs, they walked arm in arm toward the Metro stop. The last train was in ten minutes. When they reached the platform, it was nearly empty. They stood under a poster for the Smithsonian and spoke softly to each other.

"Must be an omen," he said.

"What?"

He pointed at the sign. She laughed.

"Must be," she said.

The rumble of a train brought on a pang of sadness for Lauren. She stepped closer to Mark, wrapping her arms around his waist.

"I wish you didn't have to go," she whispered.

"Me, too," he said. "But everything in its time."

She turned her head, resting it on his chest. He felt strong, solid under her touch. She felt safe.

"I hope you take that apartment," she said.

He leaned back a little so he could see her face. She looked up at him. Their bodies were closer than they ever had been before. Her head tilted slightly.

"I already have," he whispered. "They just don't know it yet."

He made the first move. She felt his arms guiding her up to her tip toes. At the same time, his mouth met hers. They kissed. It was innocent and far too quick.

The train rumbled to a stop, the hydraulic brakes hissing loudly. Mark kissed her on the forehead.

"If I don't leave now, I won't ever," he said. His voice was low, husky.

Lauren looked up at him. "Would that be such a bad thing?"

"Not at all," he said. "But I can't. I want to do this right."

She shook her head. "Once a cop, always a cop."

He laughed. "Chivalry's not dead."

Lauren hugged him, her body pressing against his. He sighed, and then she pushed away.

"Get going," she said. "And call me tomorrow."

"I will," he said, backing toward the Metro. "And good luck with your dad."

Her brow lowered.

"With calling him about what you found out," he clarified.

"Oh," she said. Some of the electricity of the moment seemed to fade. "Thanks."

He stepped into the train. The doors rattled.

"Call you tomorrow," he said.

Then they were closed. Lauren waved as the train rumbled back the way it had come. Alone, she climbed the steps. With a final glance back, she hugged herself against the chill in the air, her lips parting in a content smile.

Bethesda, Maryland 2009

The next Saturday, Lauren sat at the table in her breakfast nook, looking out at the center of Bethesda. She was scheduled to meet with Padma downtown at an internet cafe in an hour. She had finished the first draft of their article late the night before and sent her a text message. Padma had responded at 2 a.m. saying she would see her at nine o'clock the next morning.

Lauren touched the top page of the cataract spike article. She felt great about it. In her opinion it was one of the best things she had ever written. And she had no doubt people would take notice.

At the same time, so many follow up ideas sprang to mind. She wanted to do more research of incidence of surgery besides cataracts, look at the economics of this apparent epidemic, and see if there are class or gender distinctions. She wondered if there were correlations between different diseases, such as; diabetes, heart disease or cancer. Even more enticing, she planned to look at her own patient stats compared to those of her predecessor in regard to both the incidence and the rapidity of cataract development.

Although Lauren preferred prevention, she was a very accomplished surgeon, not knife happy, like some of her colleagues. All of it made her want to go speak with the Greater D.C. Ophthalmology Society, discuss her findings and get her fellow physicians' impressions.

While her mind continued to race, one thing continued to itch at her. One piece of evidence in the report troubled her.

Sipping at her Earl Gray tea, she reached across to the marble counter and picked up her BlackBerry and phoned her father. He was in Connecticut for a Veterans Day parade and then on the road back to D.C. for a committee meeting. When he answered the phone, she could already tell he was distracted.

"Hi, dad," she said.

"Lauren, what's up?"

"Do you have a second to talk?" she asked.

"A second," he said. "I'm due inside soon."

"I just wanted to ask you something," she said. "I thought you might be interested."

"What is it?"

"Remember the thing I talked to you about when you came in? I did what you said and went to the NIH and met with Padma Patel. She's great, by the way."

"Great," he said. "I'm happy to hear that."

"Well, we found something odd."

"Oh, yeah?"

She could almost see her father on the other end of the phone, mouthing to someone that he would be right there. In the past she would just get off. But he had shown such an interest in what she said, she bulled through the feeling.

"Yeah." Her confidence built. "Padma looked at every city in the country to see if there was another spike like the one in D.C. There wasn't in the U.S., but she found one in Europe."

"Europe?" he asked.

She had his full attention now. "In Bonn."

There was a long pause. She waited for her father to say something. She took the silence to mean she had lost him again, until she heard his voice when he replied.

"Bonn? Are you sure?"

She stood up. "Yes."

"But why?"

"What do you mean?" she asked.

"Listen," he said. "Does anyone else know?"

She frowned. "Padma does. Why?"

When she answered, she had not meant to leave Mark off the list. After she realized she had, though, she had no intention of mentioning him. Her father did not know the depth of their budding relationship.

"I don't know," he said. "Something doesn't add up."

"We've written it up. I have the first draft in my hand."

"An article?" he asked.

"Yeah," she said. "I was planning to submit it to the American Journal of Ophthalmology. Dad? Is something wrong? Do you want me to hold off?"

"No," he said. "You figured all this out. Go for it." There was a pause. "Could you submit without mentioning the Bonn connection?"

Lauren closed her eyes. "I guess. It wouldn't be as powerful, but . . ."

"Great, sweetie," Senator Chandler said. "Sounds good."

Lauren's stomach turned. Somehow, she had expected her father's reaction. She guessed that was why she had held off calling him. At the same time, she could not stop the itch of curiosity that drove her to find more answers.

"Do you know anyone in Bonn?" she asked.

He sounded surprised. "What?"

"I was wondering if you knew anyone in Bonn that I might be able to talk to," she said. "I'd like to try to find some correlation that explains all this."

She could almost hear her father thinking through his answer.

"Not an ophthalmologist," he said.

"No, I could find a doctor to talk to through a colleague at Harvard. I'm more looking for a government official, like the equivalent to the NIH over there."

"Oh," he said. "Sure. I'll get a name for you when I get back. Listen, I really have to go."

"Okay," she said, her voice losing its conviction.

"One more thing," he paused. "I'm proud of you."

Lauren's eyes were teary. "Thanks, dad."

She ended the call and sat back down. She had half an hour to get ready but she did not move. Instead, she savored the feeling inside her chest.

The internet café buzzed with activity. Lauren opened the door and stopped, scanning the tables and booths that covered the floor of the shop. They were all taken, but luckily she saw Padma at one near the back. She hurried over.

"I can't wait to read it," Padma said.

Lauren sat before she said anything.

"I need to make a change," she began. "I'm going to take the Bonn reference out. Maybe we'll include it in a later draft when you and I get more data."

Padma looked confused. "Really?"

"Just for now," Lauren said.

"Okay. Your call."

Padma flipped through the pages of the draft article, asking questions as she went. Lauren answered but her mind wandered. Her father had been odd on the phone. Something had definitely changed when she mentioned Bonn.

Lauren knew her father was very interested in foreign affairs. He was Chair of the Senate Armed Services Committee. How could he not? What Lauren wanted to find out was why.

"Are you okay?" Padma asked.

The question interrupted Lauren's thoughts. She looked at Padma.

"What? Yeah, fine."

"I was asking you how long do you think it will take to make the changes?"

Lauren bit the inside of her lip. "Not long. Maybe a day."

"The rest of it reads great," Padma said.

"Thanks for everything."

"No problem," Padma said. "I'm so excited. Do you think they'll publish it?"

Lauren nodded. She really had no doubt. Not only was the data compelling, but Dr. Connor sat on the editorial committee of the journal but she was not going to tell Padma that.

"I'll finish it up and submit it by the end of the week," she said instead. "I figure we'll hear in a month or two."

"Oh, I can't wait," Padma said.

"Me, neither," Lauren responded. But her mind was wandering again.

WASHINGTON, D.C. 2009

Two weeks after submitting the article to the American Journal of Ophthalmology, Lauren attended her second symposium held by Dr. von Fricke. She could not forget his response to her request to be on the panel. At first she had been frustrated. Lauren had thought about calling Dr. Connor and asking him the same question.

Later, her feelings changed to embarrassment. She had questioned even attending the conference. Her absence would be missed so she swallowed the uneasiness and showed up bright and early. Sitting toward the front this time, she sat through the opening remarks feeling a not unexpected sense of déjà vu.

After a discussion on challenges in cataract therapy lead by von Fricke, Lauren raised her hand.

"Ah, Dr. Chandler," he said. "Good to see you this morning."

Lauren stood. "Great to be here." She glanced at Dr. Connor. He was staring from the other side of the room. "I wanted to mention that we've been seeing some real positive results from the use of the Able Eyes eye supplement."

"Yes," Dr. von Fricke said. "I read your article in Investigative Ophthalmology."

"I'm expecting to follow up with another soon," she said.

She thought about mentioning the spike in the incidence of cataracts and cataract surgery in Washington but did not. She still had not heard back from the American Journal of Ophthalmology, which was not odd. It usually took months for them to respond. Nevertheless, it was never a good idea to talk about unpublished ideas in front of a room full of her competition and skeptics.

She continued. "I wanted to mention that we've seen a significant reduction in required surgery at my practice. So far the results are promising."

Lauren heard the murmur in the audience. Whenever she discussed alternative approaches, it generally led to a lively conversation. She waited for it but before anyone could respond, Dr. Connor stood up.

"Great to hear, Dr. Chandler," Connor said, not making eye contact with her. "But I think our discussion today should be more focused on supporting improved surgical techniques and the TeleLens."

The murmur in the audience quieted. Lauren, still standing, felt her throat tighten. Dr. von Fricke shook his head but said nothing. She stared up at Connor for a second, and then found her voice.

"An ounce of prevention is worth a pound of cure," she said, sitting down to preserve her dignity.

There were a few laughs behind her as she took her seat. Dr. von Fricke turned the discussion to a success story concerning a high risk case made easy by the TeleLens. While more case reports were shared, Lauren sat back in her chair and tried to pretend she was paying attention.

At the first session break, Lauren wandered out to the refreshment area. Her intention had been to slip out and return to work when someone touched her shoulder. She turned. It was Dr. Connor.

"Hello, Lauren," he said good naturedly.

"Dr. Connor," she said.

"Are you upset?" he asked.

He had a smirk on his face. She had seen the same expression on his face many times. It was not necessarily condescending, at least not any more so than usual. It was more like a man amused by his precocious granddaughter.

"No at all," she lied. "What would make you think that?"

He shook his head. "I fear I am the bearer of unfortunate news."

Lauren felt off balance by the entire conversation. To hide it, she glanced past her mentor at the crowd milling around the lobby.

"That's doesn't sound fun," she said as nonchalantly as she could.

"Yes," he said. "I was at an editorial meeting of the Journal yesterday afternoon. Although I fought for you, your article has been rejected."

Lauren blinked, trying to keep her composure. She could not believe it, any more than she could believe Dr. Connor had used the word "rejected." She did not know what to say. Thinking of how disappointed Padma would be, she was incensed. She would just have to take her article to one of the bi-monthly journals, who would jump at the opportunity to publish it.

"That is unfortunate," she said.

"It is," he agreed. "The writing was spot on. But the board felt that although the data told a compelling story it did not provide enough scientific information to explain the significance."

Lauren smiled. "I understand. The good news is that from what I can tell, the story is coming together. Maybe I'll resubmit in a few weeks elsewhere, as we put together more data."

Dr. Connor looked away. For the first time in her experience, he seemed agitated.

"It would take a good bit more, I fear," he said.

She nodded.

"The good news, as I see it," he smirked again, "is that according to your findings it is a fortunate time to be an ophthalmologist."

Lauren frowned. "I guess you could see it that way. I'm disappointed in you, Professor Connor. I thought you were a true scientist who encouraged research and epidemiology. It appears that you are now on the payroll of a company which years ago you would have despised. That is the real unfortunate news."

"I'm sorry that you feel that way," he said, looking across the crowd. "Excuse me, I have to discuss something with Dr. Stonebridge."

Lauren watched, her eyes wide, as Dr. Connor crossed the room and approached her friend Melanie. She felt slighted, but there was something worse. As she stared at them, she had an undeniable sense that they were talking about her.

Lauren could not get out of the symposium fast enough. She barely got two steps, however, when she heard someone calling her. She knew immediately who it was from the accent.

"Dr. von Fricke," she said. "Great to see you again."

"Ah, fraulein, how are you?"

"Good," she said.

He raised an eyebrow. "I think not."

"What do you mean?"

"I saw you speaking with that pompous windbag."

"Dr. Connor?" she asked, surprised.

"Don't you look so surprised," he said. "I know you idolize the man. But he is what he is."

She smiled. "You're never one to mince words, are you Doctor? But you couldn't be further from the truth."

"Not if I can help it."

Emboldened by Dr. von Fricke's honesty, Lauren spoke before thinking.

"Do you have colleagues in Bonn?" she asked.

He appeared taken back by the question.

"Of course I do," he said. "Why would you ask?"

Lauren told Dr. von Fricke about what she had found.

Von Fricke was curious but cold. "You realize I am a paid consultant for the Teleplunkt Corporation. It does not behoove me to have a conversation like this while wearing that hat. Come to Boston some time. Maybe we can talk more there."

"Maybe," she said. "Thank you for the offer. I have to go. I have patients in an hour."

When the words left her mouth, she immediately regretted lying for the second time that morning. It was out of character for her and she could not fully understand why she was doing it. She knew, however, that she had to get out of there.

"Dr. von Fricke, Lauren," someone said.

She looked up to see Melanie approaching. Lauren's stomach rolled.

Dr. von Fricke looked at Melanie like he had never seen her before. "Hello, Dr . . ."

"Stonebridge," Melanie said, nonplussed. "I'm at Hopkins."

"Ahh," Dr. von Fricke said from deep in his throat. "I must be going. Take care, Dr. Chandler."

"I will, Doctor," she said. "Can I call you?"

"Anytime my sweet little girl," he said.

Lauren looked him in the eye. "I'm not a girl, and you may find I'm not always so sweet."

Von Fricke smiled, walking away without acknowledging Melanie.

"Lauren," Melanie said, ignoring the slight. "I was just talking to Dr. Connor. He wanted me to approach you with an idea. I'm working on an article on the successful application of the TeleLens. He wanted me to ask you if you'd be interested in participating in it."

Lauren stared at her friend. "What?"

"An article on . . ."

"No, I heard you," Lauren interrupted." But why?"

Melanie looked confused. "Why wouldn't you? Connor would encourage its publication in the Journal as soon as we finished. It's a great opportunity."

Lauren shook her head. "No thanks."

Feeling totally in shock, she turned to leave. Melanie grabbed her shoulder.

"Not a good idea," Melanie whispered.

"Huh?"

"You need to rethink your career," her friend said. "I applaud your interest in holistic, nonconventional medicine, it helps you stand out. But, alternative style, although intellectually stimulating, is neither germane in managing a busy practice and won't stand you in good sted with academic ophthalmology. If you are thinking of merging clinical practice and an academic appointment in the future, you're skating on some thin ice."

Lauren spun around. "What the hell are you talking about?"

Melanie took a step back. "Just remember what I said. I like you, Lauren. I don't want to see you get in over your head."

Melanie turned and walked away. Now she was pissed off. She had received accolades in college and in medical school and knew she was appreciated in some academic circles, although, apparently not around Baltimore.

Once through the door, she checked her watch. It was getting later than she thought.

"Mark," she said when he answered.

"You okay?" he asked.

"I'm mad."

"Dogs get mad, Lauren."

"Oh, funny. No, I am so sick of everyone around here. They're so narrow minded. Sometimes I wonder if all they care about is money."

"Maybe we should get away," he said.

"You know what," Lauren said. "I really want to go to Turks and Caicos. I just finished reading an article about the island in National Geographic."

"Sounds good to me," Mark said. "When do we leave?"

Lauren smiled. "I'll call my agent."

Five days later, they were in a plane flying over the Atlantic.

TURKS AND CAICOS 2009

As the sun rose over the water, casting its colorful shadows atop the sparkling water, Lauren ran. Barefoot, she jogged along the beach, trying to stay on the perfect sand, not too wet but still firm. Her pace was fast and her breathing perfectly rhythmic. She felt like she could run all day.

They had arrived on the island in the middle of the night. When they staggered into their room, they had each fallen on their beds, there were two, and fell fast asleep without a word. Lauren woke early and sneaked out for a run leaving Mark behind sleeping quietly in the dark.

As she neared their hotel, Lauren slowed to a walk. Quietly she slipped into the room. Mark was still asleep so she stood on the balcony staring out at the water. The soft turquoise water rolled onto the beach, lapping against the shining white sand. Two boats with brightly colored sails raced along the horizon. She could hear a small child laughing somewhere below her.

Bed sheets rustled. A moment later, Mark joined her on the balcony. He was wearing a T shirt and pajama pants.

"Some place," he said.

She wrapped an arm around his back. "Thanks for coming."

"Thanks for the idea," he said.

Impulsively, Lauren rose to her tiptoes and kissed Mark. Surprised, he hesitated and then kissed her back. Her body was hungry. It surprised her but she did not stop. She pulled him closer.

He pulled back. She rested her head on his chest and sighed.

"You okay?" he asked.

"Yeah. Are you?"

He nodded. "I just . . ."

Tilting her head, she looked up into his eyes. "You think too much."

She kissed him again. They stood on the balcony, entangled. Lauren's hand slipped under the back of Mark's T shirt. He pressed himself against her, hard. The phone rang.

Lauren laughed. Shaking his head, Mark stepped back into the room and picked up the receiver.

"Hello. Right now?" He looked at Lauren and shrugged. "Sure."

Mark hung up and turned to her.

"We need to get down to the pool."

"Why?" she breathed.

"I guess you signed me up for scuba lessons."

Lauren laughed. "Damn me."

Lauren changed into her bikini in the bathroom. When she came out, Mark was in his suit. He stared at her for a minute and she blushed.

"What?" she asked.

"You look great," he said.

"You, too," she said.

Mark stepped forward and took her into his arms. Lauren could feel the exposed skin of her belly touching his. It sent a crackle of excitement down to her toes.

"We're going to be late," she whispered.

"For what?" he asked, smiling.

"You're mine later."

His hand ran down her back. "Gladly."

Blushing, Lauren wrapped a sarong around her waist and they left the room. Holding hands, they navigated through the lush resort. Palms and eucalyptus lined the meandering walks while colorful birds fluttered over their heads.

When they reached the pool, their instructor waited on the deck, fiddling with two scuba tanks. His name was Philippe. He looked near seventy with the most wrinkled face she had ever seen, but a wiry body that belied his years. His long fingers moved with a deft expertise. Mark glanced at Lauren, arching an eyebrow. She smiled back at him.

As soon as Lauren neared, she smiled at the man.

"I won't need a tank," she said.

The man looked confused.

"I don't need a lesson," she said, speaking slowly.

The man nodded. "Just him," he said with a thick accent.

She nodded.

"You, come," the man said to Mark.

Mark looked at her again. For the first time since she had met him, he looked frightened. She laughed.

"Go ahead," she said. "You'll be fine."

Still holding her hand, he took a step toward the instructor. The old man moved faster than either expected. He stood, lifting a tank with one hand. With the other, he pried their hands apart.

"Come, come," the man said.

He led Mark toward the pool. Philippe showed him how to wear the Mae West, the regulator and use the depth gage and oxygen meter. He explained all of the appendages on his apparatus including how to inflate and deflate his Mae West in order to maintain buoyancy. He made Mark spit in his face mask and wash it out. Working quickly, the old man had the tank strapped to Mark's back in a matter of seconds and was busy showing him how to wear the mask.

While they were occupied, Lauren looked around. They were at a smaller, satellite pool. Over the hedge, she could hear people splashing in the main pool, a giant lagoon with a floating bar and rocky waterfalls. This one was nearly empty. There was one other couple sitting in the far corner under an umbrella. The man was asleep and the woman was reading a magazine.

As she waited for Mark to be ready, she wandered toward a small path lined with palms that led to the main pool. She saw someone already on the path, standing off to the side, partially hidden in shadows. Whoever it was walked quickly away as she approached.

"Lauren," Mark called.

She turned and found him in the pool.

"You're not leaving," he said.

She smiled. "Never."

Unwrapping her sarong, Lauren dove into the pool. Her body cut through the water as she did a butterfly kick, crossing almost the entire length of the pool under water. She came up for air inches away from Mark and the instructor.

"Hey," he said.

"How's it going?" she asked.

"Good." He appeared much calmer. "Philippe, here, is deft."

"No doubt," she said.

"Listen," Philippe said in his terse, thick accent. "We must improve your ability to clear the water from your face mask. You must remember to breath slowly and regularly at all times. You dive tomorrow."

"Okay," Mark said, smiling.

Lauren had her PADI certification which allowed her to dive without supervision. Since Mark had never scuba dived before, she thought they could take the resort's "fun" course, an hour of instruction and then a soft-core, shallow dive with an instructor.

Lauren swam around, half listening as Philippe rapidly delivered pointers about ascending and descending, and buoyancy. In the end, Mark came up looking lost and Lauren laughed.

"Thanks," he said as Philippe peeled the equipment off his back.

"Don't worry," Lauren whispered when the instructor was out of earshot. "The dive will be fun tomorrow. We're not going deep and we'll all be together. Nothing can happen."

"Famous last words," he said.

Lauren hugged him.

From Mark's lesson, they wandered over to the main pool and spent most of the day relaxing. By the time they noticed, there was only another hour of sunlight so they had a few drinks and then headed up to shower and got dressed for dinner. They ate at a sushi restaurant on the resort. It looked like the type of upscale place that would be found in New York City except that the outer walls were glass doors, all thrown open to the soft night breezes of the island.

After a bottle of sake and a colorful array of rolls and sashimi, they sat at their posh but modern booth, leaning across the table and speaking in soft voices. Occasionally they picked at the remaining rolls scattered on the wooden tray between them.

"I'm glad you came," she said.

"Me, too."

"Do you ever think about how random it is that we met?" she asked.

Mark's eyes widened. "What?"

"Think about it," she said. "I went to the beach once since I started my internship. And it just happened to have been when you were there."

Mark took a drink of his sake. "I guess I should get shot more often."

"Come on." She placed her hand atop his. "If I hadn't met you down there, I never would have."

"We might have run into each other," he said.

She squinted at Mark. He looked uncomfortable.

"Sorry," she said.

"No, not at all," he said. "I just don't like to think about that kind of stuff. The 'what ifs.'"

"I can understand that," she said.

"I'm glad we met, though," he said. "And I'm glad we came down here."

"Yeah, it's nice to get away from work. It's so busy."

"That's good, right?" he asked.

"Definitely," she said. "But I had no idea. I guess I got the practice at the exact right time. It's been great, and fun, but it's still nice to get away."

"I'll second that."

Lauren took sip of her drink and leaned back. "Did you enjoy your lesson?"

"I enjoyed the pool," he said.

"Not Philippe?"

Mark smiled. "He scared me, a little."

Lauren laughed.

"You look great, by the way," Mark said.

Lauren glanced down at her dress. It was one her mother bought while on a trip to Paris. She had packed it for a night just like this one.

"Oh, this," she said. "Thanks."

"You want to get going?" he asked.

She took a final sip of her sake. The rice wine warmed her throat. She looked into Mark's eyes. He stared back at her. His hand caressed hers.

"Sounds good," she said with a wicked smile.

After signing the meal to their room, they walked hand and hand to the elevator. Another couple got off when they got on. Otherwise they were alone.

Once the doors closed, Lauren wrapped herself around Mark. She pushed him back against the wall and her lips met his. The sake fueled her passion, giving her an abandon she had never felt before. Her tongue pushed into his mouth as her hand slipped under the waistband of his jeans.

Mark exhaled, pushing her away to arms length. Her hungry mouth would not close. She pushed back, her face sliding past his.

"Just go with it," she whispered into his ear. Then she bit the lobe.

When the door opened to their floor, an older gentleman wearing a camel hair jacket stared. Lauren pulled her hand out of Mark's jeans and pulled him off the wall. Giggling, she took his hand and led him out of the carriage.

Lauren felt some of the emotion that possessed her slip away as she reached the door to their room. She had one second to rethink her impulsive behavior before Mark wrapped his arms around her. She felt him pushing against her from behind. She looked over her shoulder. His hand turned her face and he kissed her passionately.

Without looking, she fumbled with the key card. The door would not open. Laughing into Mark's mouth, she disentangled herself and opened the door.

Before she could take a step, Mark swept her off her feet. He carried her into the room as they kissed passionately. When he reached the bed, Mark gently put her down. Lauren looked up at him. She felt waves of passion crashing over a tide of fear. Never before had she felt that out of control.

"Promise," she whispered.

"What?" he asked.

He touched her thigh. His hand eased higher, under her skirt. Lauren breathed out, trying to concentrate, as Mark knelt over her on the bed.

"Promise me this is real," she said.

Mark looked into her eye. She caught something there, a hint of hesitation, but his words belied that.

"I promise. No matter what, this is real," he said.

He touched her and all caution vanished in a spark of electricity. Her hips rose, hungry for his caress, as her fingers laced into his hair. She pulled him down to her and she moaned as they kissed.

With her other hand, Lauren unbuttoned his jeans. At the same time, Mark pulled her dress up, sliding it over her head. Pushing himself up, he tore off his own shirt as she tugged at his pants. She used her feet to kick them off to the floor. He eased down on top of her, his skin warm against hers.

"I love you," she whispered.

"I love you," he said.

They made love. Lauren fell asleep in Mark's arms.

Turks And Caicos 2009

While Lauren and Mark had sat on the plane the day before, Steinmetz boarded. It was the first time he saw Lauren Chandler up close. He had looked at a picture, but it was not the same. Even then, in that first moment, the tingle of something dark and animalistic tickled his gut.

Walking down the aisle, he tried not to stare. The man sitting next to her looked at him. He was not sure they were together, but he knew he had to be more careful. He took his seat toward the back of the plane and waited.

During the flight, whenever Lauren moved, turning her head, showing the side of her face, or standing up to let the old woman in the window seat use the bathroom for the fifth time, he watched her. He had never seen a woman like her before. Sure she was different from the women of Germany, with their blunt features, but there was something about her fine bones and defined muscles that enthralled him. He found it difficult not to stare.

Over time he became aware that the man was with her. Steinmetz watched him carefully from behind. He was tall, fit, and when he stood up, he moved with the practiced grace of someone very in control of his body. From years of experience, Steinmetz pegged him as danger right from the start. He would watch the man very carefully.

When they landed on the island, Steinmetz sat back, watching Lauren Chandler as she collected her carry-on bag. By the way she moved, he knew she was athletic. He had watched her run. Too bad he hadn't been given the go ahead by Becker before. Hefting her bag, he could tell she was strong, too, a formidable adversary for a woman, an excellent fighter in bed.

His phone rang as Lauren and the man shuffled up the aisle toward the exit. He checked the number. It was Becker.

"Hello."

"Steinmetz?"

"Yes," he said.

"It's Becker. Was she on the flight?"

"Yes."

"Have you landed?"

"Yes."

"Excellent," Becker said. "Our newest board member has convinced Kugler to give us the green light."

Steinmetz stared at Lauren. "He has?"

"Yes. Seems the doctor is poking around, researching increases in cataract surgery. She must be silenced, permanently. It must look like an accident."

"Definitely. She has someone with her. May I include him?" Steinmetz asked.

"The man?"

"Yes."

"Do you know who he is?"

"No."

"The green light is for Chandler only. If at all possible, make sure it looks like an accident. If he gets in the way, that is another matter."

"Understood," Steinmetz said.

The line went dead. Steinmetz followed Lauren off the plane.

Later that same day, Steinmetz, known as Miller by the hotel, stood on a shaded path off the main pool. He watched Lauren and the man talking with a grizzled old scuba instructor. Seeing the air tanks, a better plan formed in his mind.

He watched the man get into the pool. Chandler followed him in but did not take part in the lesson. Steinmetz figured she was certified.

Although he should have left them there and began preparations, he did not. Instead, he watched Chandler in the pool. She wore a red bikini, athletic but revealing enough to make his blood boil. He watched her for far too long, so engrossed that he barely noticed when she started in his direction.

Startled, he ducked further into the shadows. She paused, looking in his direction. He backed away, angry at himself. When the man she was with called to her, Lauren looked back. Steinmetz took the opportunity to escape.

Cursing under his breath, he headed straight for the concierge. "Does the hotel sponsor beginner scuba tours?" he asked.

"Yes, sir. We have a couple diving tomorrow morning. Would you like to join them?"

"No," Steinmetz said. "I would like to rent some equipment. Is there a shop?" he asked.

"Certainly, sir. There is a place a hundred yards down the beach. Would you walk, or should I call you a cab?"

"Thank you. I'll walk"

Steinmetz followed the man out the back entrance.

The scuba rental shop was nothing more than a glorified lean-to right on the beach. Inside were masks, wet suits, snorkels, flippers, everything a diver might need. Steinmetz's eyes immediately found the rows of tanks by the small table used for checkout. Behind them, he saw three rows of large oxygen tanks and two rows of smaller tanks usually used by women.

Steinmetz strode to the front of the shop and approached the keeper, an American with long dread-locked hair and a deep tan. A trip to a locale on the less developed side of the island had prepared him.

Without pausing, Steinmetz pulled a hyperdermic needle out of his pocket. The man saw it and sensed something was wrong. He put his arm up defensively but Steinmetz swatted it down.

The shopkeeper tried to stumble away. Steinmetz grabbed him by the dreadlocks and pulled him back, slamming the man's head on the counter. He let go of the hair and grabbed the man's chin, pulling back.

He struck. With the practiced control of an assassin, he lashed out with the needle. It punctured the man's skin, then his jugular. He depressed the plunger. Heroin streamed into the shopkeeper's system and the fight went out of his body immediately.

Steinmetz left the needle there and guided the man's body to the ground. Casually, he took one of the man's hands and wrapped it around the needle. It might not look exactly like an OD, but he didn't care all that much. All he could think about in that moment was Lauren Chandler.

Glancing out the front of the shop, he saw no one approaching. Steinmetz went to work. He took a small tank, the ones used by women, and let three-quarters of the oxygen out. Then, using the tank of nitrogen used to make a Nitrox mixture, he filled the three-quarters of the tank back up. Capping it, he walked out of the shop with it. He shut the door and put the 'closed' sign up.

At 5 a.m. next morning, Steinmetz carried the tank to the docks. There were two trawlers, one clearly outfitted for a fishing excursion. On the other, the captain of the boat was busy laying out equipment. There were already two scuba tanks on deck, one large, one small. The captain placed a bundle down in front of the smaller tank, a woman's wet suit on top.

Steinmetz stashed his tank behind a bench before approaching the captain.

"Captain," Steinmetz called out.

"Yes?" the man said. Steinmetz recognized him as the instructor from the day before.

"Do you provide lessons?" Steinmetz asked.

"I do," the captain said.

"Do you schedule them in advance?" he asked.

"I can, but my book is up at the hotel. Once I'm done, I can meet you there."

"After your dive?" Steinmetz asked.

"No, before," the captain said. "I need to fetch my customers."

"Sounds good," Steinmetz said. "I'll meet you up there."

Steinmetz walked to the end of the dock. Instead of returning to the hotel, he wandered down the beach and found a place to sit. He waited, watching the path back to the hotel. Within ten minutes, the captain hurried along it and out of sight.

Casually, Steinmetz strolled back to the dock. As he passed, he picked up the tank he had stashed by the bench. With a glance around to make sure no one was watching, he switched out the small tank with the one he had specially prepared. He lowered the original tank to the water's surface and then let go. The tank sank to the bottom of the harbor.

Steinmetz walked away smiling.

Turks And Caicos 2009

The morning after, Lauren awoke to a knocking on the door. Disoriented for a second, she reached out and touched Mark's chest. He was still asleep. She rose to get the door, took two steps and realized she was not wearing any clothes.

Smiling, she found a white terrycloth robe in the closet. Putting it on, she cracked open the door.

"Ms. Chandler," the concierge said.

"Yes?"

"Philippe is waiting down stairs."

Lauren whirled around and looked at the clock. It was one in the afternoon.

"Oh," she said. "We'll be right there."

Shutting the door, she ran to the bed. She jumped on top of Mark. When he opened his eyes, she kissed him.

"We're late," she whispered.

"You're late?" he asked.

She laughed. "No, we are, for our dive."

"But that's at one," he said.

She gently turned his head so he could see the clock.

"Whoa," he said.

"I know."

"You kept me up too late," he said with a smile.

"Thanks," she said, smiling back.

They hurried into their swimsuits, no longer caring about privacy. When they reached the lobby, hand in hand, Philippe smiled knowingly at them.

"It's in the water," he said.

Lauren was not sure what he meant, but she blushed nonetheless.

The boat cast off from the dock. Sitting on the back bench, Lauren watched the turquoise water part as the bow cut through the harbor. A salty breeze blew hair across her face so she tied it back with a hair band. She glanced at Mark, who looked pale.

"What's up?" she asked.

"Nothing," he said.

"Nervous?"

He nodded. She smiled and hugged him.

"Just wait," she said. "You're going to love it."

Holding each other, she watched the beauty of the island withdraw as they headed further out of the harbor.

When the boat slowed, Philippe turned to them.

"The reef is below us," he said. "Are you ready?"

"Definitely," Lauren said.

She squeezed Mark's arm. Together, they approached the gear laid out on the deck. While Lauren was pulling on her wet suit, she glanced at the tanks.

"I have the big one," she said.

Philippe nodded.

"Usually, we give the smaller tank to the woman," Philippe said.

Lauren shook her head. "I say we switch it up this time. It will be easier for Mark to maintain buoyancy with the lighter weight. We won't need that much oxygen since we won't be down long."

Philippe looked away as if offended. "Fine by me."

Lauren strapped on the larger tank and helped Mark with his. By the time they were ready, Philippe was already sitting on the edge of the boat.

"Ease off the boat, like me," he said.

Philippe put on his mask and, holding his mask with one hand and supporting his tank with the other, disappeared backwards over the side.

"Some teacher," Mark said.

"I think I offended his machismo."

Mark laughed.

"I'll look after you," Lauren continued.

She led him to the edge. Together, they fell softly into the turquoise waters.

To Lauren, the reef was average. She had seen far more impressive sights, including the dangerous Great Blue Hole. But for a first dive, it was perfect.

The ocean floor was covered in brightly colored corals. There was maze coral that from a distance looked like a green brain. Down a small rise, there was gray lettuce coral and long red sea whips. She noticed sea snails and prickly sea urchins. Through the textures of the bottom, small fish darted in and out of the light. There were black and white-striped longfin bannerfish and translucent yellow milletseed butterflyfish.

Lauren turned to look at Mark, trying to see his expression. The diving mask hid his face so she swam closer. As she approached, she saw a yellow and blue angel fish following closely behind Mark. Smiling, she reached his side.

An experienced diver, Lauren had near perfect buoyancy. She expected Mark to be a little clumsy. When she came to a stop beside him, though, his arms and legs moved in slow, haphazard flails. He pivoted, turning sideways. She tried to move so that she could see his face but his body continued to spin.

Something was wrong. Lauren could tell. Grabbing him by the shoulder, she spun Mark around. His eyes were open but lidded, and looked right past her.

Lauren tapped on the glass of Mark's mask. He blinked. For a second, she thought she had his attention. But he started to pivot again and the regulator dropped from his open mouth while he was slipping out of her grasp. A column of bubbles exploded upwards.

Thinking quickly, Lauren unhooked her reserve regulator and shoved it into Mark's mouth. Initially he was unresponsive and his eyes rolled back.

She knew she had to get him to the surface. Holding Mark, she made to swim upwards and realized that in the panic of the moment, she had lost her orientation. Fighting to keep a hold of Mark, she looked around, trying to find the light of the sun. It was no use. Her mask was fogged.

Lauren pulled the regulator from her lips. The air bubbles rose up and around his body. She watched them, reorienting herself. Grabbing Mark, she pushed up with everything she had, following the bubbles to the surface.

Halfway up, she felt a hand touch her shoulder. She turned to see Philippe. Lauren, the lack of oxygen burning her chest now, frantically pointed up and then at Mark. Philippe nodded. He grabbed Mark under one arm.

When they started to rise, Lauren grabbed her flailing regulator. She took one breath from it and then held the mouthpiece to Mark's lips. The bubbles poured out of his open mouth. He was not breathing.

Lauren let go of Mark's arm, leaving him to Philippe. Holding the piece to his mouth, she reached her arm around Mark's torso. Her hand found his solar plexus and compressed his lungs. When she let go, he breathed the air in.

Philippe pulled Mark toward the surface and Lauren continued to compress his chest. When they crested, she let go of the mouthpiece and switched to a lifeguard hold, supporting Mark's torso on her own and keeping his head above water. She continued to press his solar plexus as Philippe scrambled onto the boat. Once aboard, he reached down and grabbed Mark. He pulled as Lauren pushed. Mark flopped over the rail and landed with a thud on the deck of the boat.

Lauren threw herself onto the boat. Pulling off her gloves, she bent down, ready to do CPR. At the same time, she checked his pulse. His heart was beating fast. She paused. His eyes opened and he coughed out a mouthful of sea water.

"Mark," she said.

He blinked.

"Are you okay?"

Mark coughed again. After a pause, he nodded.

"What happened?" she asked.

"Got tired," he said.

"Tired?"

He nodded. "I think I passed out."

Lauren looked at Philippe. He shrugged. She rolled Mark slightly and took of his tank. She checked the gauge. It read full. Philippe approached.

"I double checked them before . . ."

He stared at Mark's tank. His eyebrow rose. He looked at Lauren.

"Did you bring this tank?" he asked.

"No," she said.

"It is not my tank," he said.

Lauren looked at it again. Slowly, she brought the piece to her mouth. After three breaths she felt lightheaded. She took it away.

"It's CO_2 or Nitrox" she said. "I'm sure of it."

Philippe said, "I filled the tanks myself yesterday. But that is not my tank."

"What do you mean?"

"I mean, I've never seen that tank before."

Lauren looked at Mark. He was looking much better.

"Do you think someone switched out the tanks? Could that have happened?" she asked.

Philippe thought for a moment. "It could have. I left them here when I went to get you."

Lauren stared.

He continued. "And someone was asking about them earlier."

"What?"

"A man," he said. "Had a German accent."

"He asked about the tanks?" Lauren said.

"Yes," Philippe said. "Wanted to know if I scheduled lessons. He said he'd meet me at the hotel, but he never showed up."

Mark sat up. "What did he look like?"

"Tall man, clean shaven, fancy clothes. I took him to be a guest of the hotel but I had never seen him before."

"Anything else?" Mark asked, his voice raspy.

"A scar on his lip," Philippe said as if just remembering.

Mark's eyes narrowed. Lauren looked at him, confused.

"What's going on?" she asked. "What are you saying? You think someone tried to kill you?"

Mark looked at the tank but did not say anything. The truth suddenly dawned on Lauren.

"We switched the tanks," she whispered. "Someone was trying to kill me."

"Let me handle it, okay?" Mark said.

"But he was trying to kill me," Lauren countered.

They were back in their room. Mark had taken a shower and felt fully recovered. Lauren had been on her way to the front desk to ask questions about the man with the scarred lip. Mark stopped her.

"You wouldn't want me to do surgery on someone's eyes, would you?" he asked.

"What does that have to do with?"

"Well, maybe I should be doing the police work," he interrupted.

Lauren sighed. "Fine, but hurry."

Mark left the room.

Not ten minutes later, someone knocked on the door. A bolt of fear ran down Lauren's spine before Philippe announced himself. Taking a deep breath, she opened the door.

"I found where the tank is from. Beach Hoppers."

"Where?" she asked.

"The shop on the beach, an American place."

"Far from here?" she asked.

"No," Philippe said. "Hundred yards south. Right on the beach."

"Huh," she said.

"I'm going to the police," Philippe said.

"Okay," Lauren answered, but she wasn't really paying attention.

Alone, disregarding Mark's admonition, Lauren walked down the beach. Even at midday, it was so peaceful. She could only see a handful of people enjoying the perfect weather. When she saw the dive shop, her pace quickened.

As she approached, she noticed the door of the lean-to was closed. Although totally understandable, something about it struck her as odd since it was still the afternoon. She slowed, approaching cautiously.

The inside of the shop was masked in shadow. Standing at the threshold, Lauren called out.

"Hello!"

There was no answer. She inched forward. That was when she saw the foot, just the sole sticking out through the open doorway.

Lauren rushed inside. She found the shopkeeper on his back. A display of umbrellas had fallen on top of him. When she cleared them away, she saw dried vomit caking his face. His hand clutched a needle sticking into his neck. Lauren tried to find a pulse but couldn't.

Standing up, she backed out of the shop. She felt someone watching her. Her eyes scanned the shadows but she saw nothing. Once her feet touched the sand, she bolted for the hotel.

Mark was in the room when she returned. He was frantic. "Where were you?"

Lauren, shaken from her experience, did not answer right away. Mark seemed to sense it and took her into his arms.

"Are you okay?"

"Yeah," she whispered. "He was dead."

Mark pulled back. "Who?"

"The shopkeeper," Lauren said. "Philippe came by. He told me where the tank came from. I went to check it out and I found him. Looked like he OD'd. I felt like someone was there, though. Watching me."

"You shouldn't have gone out alone," Mark said.

Lauren glared at him. "You did!"

"I know, but,"

"But what? I'm a girl? Is that what you were going to say?"

"No," he said. "I just . . . He was dead?"

"Yes," Lauren said.

"The concierge corroborated Philippe's description. We need to go to the police."

Lauren nodded.

The station was a small white bungalow just off the beach. Once inside, Mark did all the talking. Lauren was thankful for it. He really knew what he was doing.

They were led into a back office. A half hour later, the commandant arrived. He showed them to seats and took one across the table. He carried a large three-ringed binder.

"My man found the body," he said. "And we already spoke to Philippe. Otherwise, I would have to detain you. As is, we have clear descriptions of the suspect. Look here."

The commandant opened the binder. Inside was page after page of passport photos. Lauren remembered customs copying hers when she arrived. When the man reached the back of the book, she saw her picture, then Mark's. He flipped one more page and stopped.

"There," the commandant said.

He pointed at a picture. The scar on the man's lip jumped out at Lauren. She looked at Mark.

"That's him," Mark said.

The commandant nodded. "He left the island an hour ago. We've contacted the American officials. They should be picking him up when he arrives in New York."

"Excellent," Mark said. "Can I get a copy of the picture?"

The commandant frowned. "Of course not. This is official business."

Mark glanced at Lauren. "Can you excuse us?"

Her eyes widened. "What?"

"I just need a minute," Mark said. His voice sounded different, more stern than she was used to.

"Okay," Lauren said.

She left the room and waited in the lobby of the station. A minute later, Mark walked out. A picture of the man was in his hand.

"His name is Miller," Mark said. "But I doubt that's real."

"Well," she said. "At least he'll be in custody when he lands."

"Yeah," Mark said.

But for some reason, Lauren could tell he didn't really mean it.

Washington, D.C. 2009

Senator Chandler sat alone in his office. It was late on a Monday night. Isaac was down the street picking up some dinner. Most of the floor had already left and the building was unusually quiet.

Picking up his phone, he called Lauren's house. It rang five times before her voice mail picked it up. He hung up without leaving a message, forgetting that she had said something about going away for a long weekend.

Papers spread across his desk. The largest pile was documents prepared by his secretary for his review. Right on top sat the committee agenda for later in the week.

Looking at the list of bills on the docket, Chandler's mind returned to the last meeting. He could not forget the look on Kerrington's face afterwards. It was like someone waking up from sleepwalking.

As if in response to his thoughts, the phone rang. Chandler thought to ignore it but glanced at the incoming number first. It was someone inside the building.

"Hello."

"Benjamin," Senator Brown said. "Do you have a moment to talk?"

Rolling his eyes, he looked at the docket. "I'm a little busy. Maybe . . ."

"It will only take a minute," Brown said.

"I . . ."

Brown hung up. Chandler sat for a moment, taking a deep breath. When he stood up to leave, he was interrupted by his office door opening. Senator Brown poked his head inside, a cell phone to his ear and a smug smile on his face.

Without waiting to be invited, Brown walked inside. He took a seat on the couch.

"What do you want?" Chandler asked icily.

"Just a second of your time to discuss SR 2401."

Chandler tented his hands, hiding a scowl. "What about it?"

"I'd like it on the agenda for next week," he said. While he spoke, he slowly turned the shining American flag pinned to his lapel.

"No," Chandler said.

"Don't be so hasty. You might want to reconsider."

"Why would I want to do that?" Chandler asked.

Brown smiled, but stopped turning the pin. "Because I'm sure there are some things you'd like kept quiet."

"What do you mean by that?"

"Some indiscretions on your part," Brown said.

Chandler's eyes widened. Brown noticed before he could hide the reaction. His colleague smiled triumphantly.

"Are you threatening me?" Chandler asked.

"Of course I am," Brown answered.

Chandler paused, thinking. "If I do, no one is going to vote for it."

"That's fine," Brown said.

"Whatever mumbo jumbo you did last time only got you three votes. It won't be enough, Brown."

"Then you have no reason to test me," Brown said.

Anger boiled up inside Chandler. "If you want to throw down, Richard, we can. I'll take you apart."

Brown smiled. "Not before your wife learns the truth. And that daughter of yours."

Chandler froze.

Brown pounced on the chance. "It isn't worth it. She'd be devastated. Makes me wonder what the hell you were thinking."

"Shut up," Chandler hissed.

"Fine," Brown said, getting up. "Just make sure my bill is on the docket. See ya around, Benji."

Brown walked out of the office. When the door closed, Chandler hung his head in his hands. A second later, the phone rang again. Chandler yanked it up, ready to rip into someone. He froze when he heard his daughter's voice.

"Dad?"

"Lauren, are you okay?"

"Are you?"

"Not really," he said.

"What happened?"

"Just work stuff. Are you all right?"

"Nothing else happened?" she asked.

"No. What's going on? How was your vacation?"

Lauren paused. "Something happened. I think someone tried to kill me."

"What?" Isaac walked into the room and Chandler grabbed him. "Someone tried to hurt you?"

Isaac's eyes widened. A second later, the FBI agent assigned to tail Chandler since the van incident walked into the office.

"I think so," she said.

"Are you okay?"

"Yeah," she said. "Nothing happened to me. But someone switched out one of the tanks when we went diving. Filled it with nitrogen."

"Do you know who?"

"A man named Miller," she said. "He's supposed to be taken into custody when he lands in New York."

"Are you there alone?" he asked. "Who's we?"

"No," Lauren said.

"Who's with you?"

Lauren paused. "My friend, Mark. I told you about him."

Chandler frowned. He looked at Isaac and then at the agent.

"Get back to the States, okay?"

"We are," Lauren said. "I'll call when we land."

"Be careful, sweetie," he said.

When they hung up, he turned to the agent.

"There's been another attempt. This time on my daughter," he said.

"I just heard," the agent said.

"Don't you have someone on her?" Chandler asked.

"He should have been there. We will investigate immediately," the agent said.

"You boys need to figure a better system, here."

"We will," the agent said.

"You better hurry. If something happens to my daughter, there'll be hell to pay."

FRANKFURT, GERMANY 2009

Kugler sat in his office chair. An LCD screen on the far wall murmured with the morning news. He paid little attention, instead staring at a report from his U.S. sales team.

"More unrest in Bonn this morning," the television reporter said.

Kugler looked up.

"A group of young men attacked a Turkish mosque on Veingarter Street, killing three. Eye witnesses claim that the assailants wore paramilitary uniforms."

Kugler smiled.

"When the police arrived, a mob impeded their access to the scene, allegedly causing one of the deaths. The mob originated at the government offices where a movement is gaining ground to push United States troops and foreigners out of Germany."

Listening, he rubbed his hands together. Everything was coming together nicely. The current recession was exposing the tenuous nature of Europe's unified arrangement. This was indeed the time for Germany to break away.

He flipped open his calendar. In ten minutes, he had a meeting with Dr. Kim to discuss making TeleLenses without additive. Enough people were now affected so there was no longer the need of producing implants with the additive, especially due to the increased scrutiny in Washington.

As he stood up, the phone on his desk rang. It was his private line.

"Hello."

"There is a problem."

"Becker?"

"Yes, Steinmetz failed us."

Kugler sat down in his high-backed leather chair. "What?"

"His attempt to take the obstacle out failed. He believes his cover has been compromised."

"Was he captured?"

"No," Becker said. "He hired a private plane and bribed a customs agent at a small airport."

"Do they know who he is? Who he works for?"

Becker laughed. "Of course not. They think his name is Miller. He is still in the U.S. Should I call him back?"

"Did the target see him?" Kugler asked.

"No," Becker said.

"What happened? Who saved her?"

Becker cleared his throat. "There was a mix-up in the scuba tanks. She had a companion, but she ended up saving him. This is what happens when we try to be too subtle."

"Next time," Kugler snapped. "You can put a bullet in her head then."

"Gladly."

"What does this mean for us?"

"Who knows," Becker said. "I assume not much. She knows someone tried to kill her, though."

"Put people on her and the father."

"Done."

"We need to be ready. We have come too far to fail now." Kugler looked out the window. "Make arrangements for an emergency situation. If one of them figures out too much, we need to know everything we can about them every bit of dirt."

"Understood," Becker said.

"Good. Should we deal with Steinmetz?"

"No," Becker said. "Not yet. I still need him over there."

"If he slips up again," Kugler said. "That will be the end of it."

"Yes."

Becker hung up. Kugler held the receiver above the cradle for a moment. He hung it up and lifted it again quickly. He dialed a number in the U.S.

"Senator Brown's office," a young woman said.

"Is he in?"

There was a pause. "May I ask who's calling?"

"Tell him a friend from overseas."

"Uh, hold please."

A minute later, the senator was on the phone.

"You should not be calling here," he said.

Kugler smiled. "Relax. You must hurry your plan."

"I don't know if we have the votes," the senator said. "Committee is no problem. Three more just had cataract surgery last month. But to pass the Senate and the House, I'm not sure."

"Get your side done," Kugler said. "Our side will do the rest. With your resolution and the interest we have stirred in Bonn, it will be enough."

"I don't know," Brown said.

"I do," Kugler said. "Just fulfill your responsibilities. Understand?"

Brown did not respond right away. When he did, it was in a whisper.

"Don't forget who you are speaking with."

Kugler stood up. "Don't you forget. When this is over, you will be answering to me. All of Germany will."

There was another pause.

"This is what sank us the last time," Brown said.

"What?"

"Hubris," Brown answered. "This is not about you. It is about our country. Don't let your role go to your head."

Kugler's face reddened. The knuckles of his hand turned white as they squeezed the receiver.

"Enough. You will not speak to me about hubris. You will do as I say. If you chose otherwise, then do not be surprised when your country learns more about Reichart Braun than you want them to know. There will be nothing your father could do about it then."

Kugler stared at the phone, waiting. Brown cleared his throat.

"I will do what I can," he said.

"Good," Kugler responded. "Good."

Bethesda, Maryland 2009

Lauren ran across a small, rounded bridge spanning a narrow creek. Her shoes pounded rhythmically across the warped planks until she stepped onto the dirt trail on the far side. From there, the path wound into a patch of thick pines and towering leafless oaks. It was late and long shadows darkened into an oppressive gloom.

In the past her runs had been the perfect escape. Night, day, even some of the grimy inner-city streets had never taken that from her. As her stride took her deeper into the darkness, she slowed.

From the gray trunks and the tangled underbrush, she felt eyes watching her. She sensed movement from every direction. Her heart monitor beeped, her rate rising above 160 beats-per-minute.

Lauren pushed through it. Her pace quickened again and she focused on breathing. Although her speed increased, the alarm shut off. With renewed determination, she stared back at the shadows, undaunted.

After a mile, the landscape opened up again. The path merged with a paved trail, then the access road to the park. Cars passed her, their lights shining brightly in the dusk. A familiar face passed, a man whose running schedule often intersected with hers. She nodded and he waved. Then she was on Grant Street heading toward the familiar lights of Suburban Hospital and the National Institute of Health.

Seeing the Institute, she thought of Padma. Since hearing back from Dr. Connor on the article's rejection, she had decided to submit it to a bi-monthly journal. She had to call Padma and discuss the plan. As if in response, her phone rang. Lauren slowed to a jog and fished it out of the utility pocket of her Marmot jacket. It was Mark.

"Where are you?" he asked.

She heard the anxious tone of his voice. Since the islands, especially after they learned the man with the scarred lip had eluded authorities in New York and was still at large, he never seemed to like her being out of his sight.

"Where are you?" she asked.

"At your place."

"Did the key work all right?" she asked.

The tension in his voice eased a little. "Yeah. It felt good. Are you sure you want me messing up your house. It's so clean all the time."

"I'll train you," she said, laughing. "Did you bring your stuff with you?"

"A couple of boxes," he said.

"Not that ratty purple chair?" she said.

"Maybe."

Lauren frowned. "You promised you'd throw that thing out."

"I know," he said. "But it's my baby."

"Not anymore," she said.

Mark paused. "Are you running?"

"Yeah."

"I thought you said you'd go at lunch."

"Things got busy," she answered.

"It's dark, Lauren," he said.

"I'm a big girl, Mark."

"I don't doubt that," he said. "But you can't act like what happened didn't happen."

"I'm not acting like anything," she said.

"You are. Until we figure out what's going on, you need to be more careful."

"I'm not putting myself in prison," she said.

"I'm not saying that. But you have to be realistic about this. I know you think you're untouchable, but that guy, he was a professional. This thing is bigger than you want to admit."

"Maybe, maybe not," she said. Lauren thought back to when she and her father had almost been hit by that van. She had never told Mark about that. If she did now, she was sure he would lock her away in some ivory tower. "It might have been some random thing."

"It wasn't," he said firmly.

"Okay, I don't want to fight. Not today. It's not every day some guy moves into my house." She laughed.

"You're right. I already ordered Thai. Get home as soon as you can. Okay?"

"Yeah," she said.

There was a pause. "Great." Mark's voice sped up. "I love you."

Then he hung up. Lauren stopped dead in her tracks. She held the phone to her ear listening to nothing but dead air. A smile spread across her face. When she finally pulled the phone away, she stared at it for another minute. Then she ran to her car, the smile never leaving her face.

Lauren walked into her house and felt the change immediately. It was not that Mark's stuff took over. He had been very neat; the five boxes were stacked in a corner of her room. There was a new smell, however, a subtle hint of spice under toning the stronger aroma of Pad Thai. This new scent made her think of testosterone.

"Dinner's ready," Mark called from the kitchen.

Lauren unzipped her jacket. When Mark saw her, he stared. She glanced down, noticing how her running suit clung to her body.

"We could always reheat it," she whispered.

Mark stood, covering the distance between them in three steps. He picked Lauren up and kissed her passionately. She fell into his embrace, wearing the safety like she did her running jacket.

When her feet touched the ground again, they backed toward her bedroom—their bedroom now. Easing her to the bed, Mark undressed her, slowly. She looked up into his eyes and she could see the love there. Something inside Lauren opened up. She let Mark in, utterly and forever.

The next day, Lauren felt revitalized. She left a message for Padma, telling her the plan to submit to a bi-monthly. Also, she wanted to schedule time to expand on the article, to build in the German data.

On the way to her office, she received a text message. Hoping it was Padma, she read it while driving. Instead, the note was from Melanie.

"Lunch today?"

At a light, Lauren texted back.

"Full schedule."

Immediately, Melanie's response came.

"It's important."

Lauren read the message, her eyebrows lowering. She tapped the keyboard of her BlackBerry and glanced out the window. A man across the street caught her eye. He had been looking at her. Her spine tingled and her damp palm slid off the wheel. She stared at the man, trying to see his lip. Was there a scar?

Just as her panic hit a crescendo, the man waved at someone. A well dressed woman scurried up to them and they hugged. At the same moment, the light turned green. Lauren hit the gas, shaking her head.

When she reached the office, she checked with her scheduler.

"How are we today?"

"Booked solid, except one cancelation at ten. You have a full book for surgery tomorrow, too, four lasers and a half dozen cataracts. Luckily, we got another shipment of TeleLenses in."

"Another?"

"Yeah," the woman said. "We are burning through them."

Lauren thought about it. Even with her vacation, she had been doing a ton of surgeries. She wondered how many other practices, ones that didn't focus on more holistic approaches, must be doing.

Curious, and a bit uneasy, she texted Melanie back offering coffee, but in Bethesda. When Melanie responded immediately saying that she would be there, Lauren felt that tingle down her spine again.

Lauren arrived at the Starbucks downtown at 10:03. Melanie was sitting in the back almost invisible behind a jutting wall and a display case of whole-bean coffee. When she saw Lauren, she waved her over.

"Hi," Lauren said.

Melanie's eyes darted around the store. Even with her friend's uncharacteristic behavior, Lauren had wanted to tell Melanie all about Mark moving in. It was really the only thing Lauren felt like talking about, but after one look at her friend, she just sat down.

"How are you?" Melanie asked.

"Good. How are you?"

"Good."

There was a pause. Lauren felt guarded but she was not going to sit there and play games.

"What do you want?" she asked.

Melanie blinked. "What do you mean?"

"Something's up. What is it?"

"Oh." Melanie looked away. "How's your article?"

"My article?"

"Yeah," Melanie said.

"It's fine. In fact, Ophthalmology Times is publishing it next month."

"I heard the American Journal rejected it."

"How'd you hear that?" Lauren said, incensed.

"Doesn't matter." Melanie made eye contact. There was a sneer to her mouth. "I warned you at that symposium. I told you to drop it."

"Drop what?" Lauren said.

"That research you're doing."

"Are you kidding? Have you read it? This is the strangest thing. You're close to people at Hopkins. Isn't anyone worried about this, thinking about it?"

Melanie frowned. "Let me do you a favor. This is not your business. All these stories about people trying to kill you, I'm not sure if they are real or not, but I think it's time to take a much lower profile."

Lauren froze, looking at her friend. Something about what Melanie said froze the blood in her veins but she remained as calm as she could.

"I'll research what I want, Melanie," she said.

"I didn't want it to come to this, Lauren. We were friends. But there are people around in the TeleLens community who have actually alluded to an affair your father is having. They will make it public if you don't back down."

Lauren reeled. "What? Are you kidding?"

"No, I'm not," Melanie said. She leaned forward and her voice softened. "Look, girl, I'm trying to be your friend, here. Just back down and everything will be fine. Okay?"

Without a word, Lauren stood. She stared directly into Melanie's eyes for a moment, and then walked away. She was back at her office before her next appointment had been processed. She had to finish her day. No matter how hard she tried, though, she could not suppress Melanie's words.

Her father was having an affair. The words rang too true. Lauren remembered visiting his townhouse. He had said her mom was in Connecticut. But there had been a wine glass with lipstick on the rim in the sink.

Regardless, there was something else that Melanie had said that troubled Lauren far more deeply. Although she had controlled her reaction, when the words left her friend's mouth, Lauren's heart had missed a beat. She could still hear the words ringing in her ear.

"All these stories about people trying to kill you," Melanie had said.

Lauren was sure she had never mentioned either incident to Melanie.

WASHINGTON, D.C. 2009

Lauren took a deep breath and then knocked on the door. She heard footsteps approaching from inside. They were heavy and immediately recognizable. Her heart beating quickly, she looked up at the ornate light post. When the door opened, she closed her eyes.

"Lauren," her father said. "What are you doing here? You okay?"

She looked at him. "Can I come in?"

"Sure," he said, taking her arm and guiding her across the threshold.

She let him lead the way to his formal living room. Sitting heavily in an overstuffed leather seat, she looked at him for the first time. She could see the worry on his face.

"Did something happen?" he asked.

She was taken by surprise, thinking he knew why she was there. Then it dawned on Lauren. He was worried about what happened on the island.

"Nothing like that," she said.

"You're okay?"

"Yeah." She frowned. "Kind of."

"What is it?"

She had come to confront him, to learn the truth. Now she could not find the words.

"What happened?" he asked again.

She took a deep breath. "You're having an affair."

Her father blinked. He did not move. There was no surprise, no anger, nothing. He just stared at her.

Lauren said nothing, too. She stared back, a tear pulling free and trailing down her cheek.

"I'm sorry," he said.

"Why?" she whispered.

"I don't know," he said. "It just happened. Your mom never really liked it here. She's away a lot. And you know what it's like for me. I'm a celebrity here. People are always coming up to me, saying complimentary things. I was weak."

The tears dried up and Lauren found herself feeling strangely calm.

"Does mom know?"

"No," he said.

"Is it still going on?" she asked.

"No. It became too consuming for the woman. She came onto me from the start. What do you want me to do?"

She shrugged. "That's up to you. I'm not telling mom. It would kill her."

"Okay."

They looked at each other for a moment.

"Are we okay?" he asked.

She nodded. "I guess."

"How'd you find out?" he asked.

There was something behind his eyes, a look of relief mingled with intense fear.

"My friend told me," she said.

He looked surprised. "She did?"

"Yeah, but it was, like, a threat."

"A threat!?"

"Yeah," she said. "I don't get it. She was talking about my article, the one about the cataract spike. She told me to give it up, lay low, or someone was going to make your affair public."

"That doesn't make any sense," her father said. "What do I have to do with your article? If she was going to threaten, you'd think it would be to blackmail me."

"There has to be some kind of connection," she said.

Her father looked thoughtful for a moment. "I don't know."

"Is something weird going on?" Lauren asked.

"Yes, but I doubt it has anything to do with this. There's a Senator, Brown from Montana, who is a real pain in the ass. He's gotten it under his skin to get our troops out of Germany. It makes no sense, really, at least for him to be so interested.

"But recently, things have gotten weird. It's like people are doing whatever he tells them to do, even my buddy, Kerrington. And when I asked him about it, he acted like he couldn't even remember it."

"What do you mean?" she asked, looking skeptical. "Like some kind of mind control."

"Look, I know it sounds farfetched, but if you had been there, you'd see."

"Could that have something to do with my article? With the cataracts?"

He shrugged. "You'd know better than I."

Lauren paused for a second. Then she looked excitedly at her father.

"Do you have another meeting soon?" she asked.

"Yes," he said.

"I have a wireless probe camera at the office. Would you wear it to the meeting? I'll stay back in your office and watch. Maybe I can see something that connects the two."

He shook his head. "This is serious. They tried to kill us, or you. I can't let . . ."

"We have to know, daddy," she said.

He nodded. "But maybe we can get help. I'll talk to my . . ."

"Do this first," she pleaded. "If it looks like something is up, we'll get help. Okay?"

Lauren looked him in the eye. Her expression said it all. He had put her through hell by having an affair. He owed her big.

"Okay," he said. "I still can't believe she told you."

Lauren was confused. "Who?"

"Melanie," he said.

"How'd you know she told me?"

"Who else," he said, looking equally confused.

When the realization struck, Lauren felt like someone punched her in the stomach. She reeled back, the tears coming again.

"You mean," she whispered. "It was with Melanie?"

Her father's eyes widened. "I thought you knew."

"Oh, dad," she said. "How could you?"

"I'm sorry, sweetie. I am."

He took her into his arms. She cried, too tired to hate.

WASHINGTON, D.C. 2009

Benjamin Chandler sat behind the large hearing desk, gavel in hand. Although he tried to focus on the meeting at hand, all he could think about was his daughter.

All his adult life, he had built up the perfect career. Everything he had done, every decision, every stroke of luck, had brought him to the pinnacle of success.

Now, when he closed his eyes, he saw his daughter. He saw her beautiful auburn hair, her bright, hazel eyes. In the end, that was his greatest success. And all those years, he had forgotten that. He had hurt her, but in that moment, he vowed to make it up to her if it took the rest of his life.

For the time being, however, he had to focus. They were nearing the end of their last committee meeting of the year. He could feel Brown's eyes on him. He touched the small camera hidden in a pin on his lapel. His daughter already knew, and she was watching. He wanted to laugh.

"If that is all, we'll adjourn until next . . ."

"There is one more item on the agenda," Senator Brown spoke out.

"Excuse me?" Chandler said.

"SR 2401 is on the agenda for today," Brown said.

"It is not. And you are talking out of turn again, sir."

"Check your agenda," Brown said. "Your staff must have left it off, probably on purpose."

"Of course they did not," Chandler said.

"I doubt that. I call for a vote to open discussion on SRR 2401, as it was *accidentally* left off the docket."

Chandler took a deep breath. He hated Brown more in that moment than ever before. Looking around, he tried to make eye contact with all the other members. He knew they could read his expression. If any one of them dared second Brown's motion, they would never see a bill through his committee again.

No one said anything. Chandler smiled.

"Do I hear a second?" he asked.

Brown coughed so loud that everyone looked at him. Chandler noticed the pin again, the one Brown wore the last time things had gotten strange. As everyone stared, Brown touched the pin, turning the stripes horizontal.

"There is a second," Brown said.

Chandler wanted to explode. He fought to keep his voice even keeled.

"Don't be a fool. You can't second your own . . ."

"Second," Senator Kerrington interrupted.

"Second," another member said. Then another and another.

Chandler slammed his gavel down. "This is absurd."

"There is a second," Brown said with a smile. "More than one, actually. Call the vote."

"Call the vote," Kerrington said.

Chandler looked around at his committee. They were all lost. Someone should be stepping up, calling out Brown for this charade. But no one did.

Isaac touched his shoulder. Chandler looked up and his aide nodded.

"All in favor?" Chandler whispered.

Two-thirds of the committee members raised their hands.

"SR 2401 is up for discussion," Chandler said, his eyes closed.

"I call for a vote," Brown said, turning the pin again.

"Fine," Chandler said. "All in favor?"

The same two-thirds raised their hand.

"Opposed," Chandler said. He, and three others, including Senator Carter who had seen his daughter and was taking the vitamin supplements, raised his hand. "SR 2401 can be considered passed by this committee and sent to the Senate for consideration. This meeting is adjourned."

The other members milled about, cordial as if nothing had happened. Chandler pushed past them, ignoring Kerrington's wave, and left the chamber, Isaac close behind.

Lauren was waiting for him in his office.

"It's the pin," she said. "I'm sure of it."

Chandler nodded. "It's gotten worse. Last time, it was only a few votes. This time, a majority."

"I hate to say it, but it must be some kind of mind control," she said.

"Is that even possible?" he asked.

"Theoretically, yes. I had a neuroscience professor at Wesleyan who specialized in it."

"This is just too much. We need to call someone in," he said.

Lauren shook her head. "They'll never believe you."

"They will," he said. "Think about it. People are trying to kill you. This is serious."

"But you're claiming your rival is using mind control to get bills passed."

"Passed through the Armed Services Committee, Lauren. This is no joke."

"I know," she said. "But they won't buy it. I'll go visit my professor, see what I can dig up. If we can get some idea of how they are doing it, we might have more of a case."

Chandler shook his head. "I don't like it. I'm worried about you."

"I'll be fine," she said.

"Well, take your friend with you. Mark."

Lauren blushed. "Why? Okay. No problem. I'll call you from there."

She took the lapel camera off and put it in her pocketbook and gave him a hug and rushed from the office. Chandler looked at Isaac, who stood in the corner shaking his head.

"What the hell just happened?" the Senator asked.

"I have no idea," Isaac said.

"Is that agent here?" Chandler asked.

"He's down stairs."

"Get him up here," Chandler said. "They need to look into this."

Bethesda, Maryland 2009

Steinmetz glanced down the street. A middle-aged woman talking on a BlueTooth rushed by. Once she was past, he stepped into the narrow alley between the two homes.

Hidden in the growing shadows, he waited for a couple to pass. He could hear their conversation, something benign about a movie or something. Once in the clear, he went to work on the window. Using a passing truck to hide the noise, he slid a thin bar between the panes. One brisk strike with his fist pried the window open. Steinmetz climbed inside.

The house was empty. He took a deep breath. He could smell her, and something else, something masculine. He thought about the man she had been with, the one he had almost killed. A flush ran up his neck, coloring his cheeks.

Ever since returning from Turks and Caicos, Steinmetz had followed her. Every step she took, every date they had, he had been there, watching. Each morning he awoke to a burning need to find her. He could no longer wait for the order from Becker.

She was beautiful, yes. And there was a strength to her that excited him. But there was something more. She had gotten away, the first of his victims to do that. Ever since, it was as if she had taken a piece of his manhood. And he needed it back.

Walking through the study, he entered the foyer. He found a picture of her with her father. Picking it up, he stared at it for a moment before moving on.

Steinmetz walked quietly up the stairs. He found her bedroom. When he saw a pair of men's pants on the floor, anger bubbled through his chest. His eyes narrowed as he approached the chest-of-drawers. He opened the top and his hand caressed the garments inside. He pulled out a pair of black stockings. At that exact moment, his phone rang. He quickly yanked it from his pocket and checked the number. It was Becker.

Steinmetz stared at the phone for a second. He had already ignored two calls from his boss since getting back. He knew that he walked on thin ice. Once more, and Becker might send someone after him. His boss had a notorious dislike of loose ends.

Taking a deep breath, he answered.

"Where are you?" Becker demanded. Steinmetz could hear the anger.

"I'm in Washington," he said.

"Are you trailing the girl?"

"Yes."

"I asked you to contact the Senator's little friend, Melanie. I had to do it myself. I'm beginning to wonder if something happened to you down there on the island."

Beads of sweat appeared on Steinmetz's forehead. "She got away. I am going to finish the job."

"On whose authority?" Becker snapped.

"You gave me the green light," he whispered.

The conversation paused. Steinmetz fidgeted, his feet shuffling on the carpeted floor.

"You are not right," Becker said. "I'm going to . . ."

"I'm in her house," he blurted out. "I'm taking her and the boyfriend out, today."

"You are, are you?" Becker said.

"Yes." Steinmetz swallowed hard. "Then I will come to Germany. You can assign someone else to this mess."

Static crackled on the line. Steinmetz strained to hear Becker's response. When it came, it sent chills down his spine.

"I already have."

BETHESDA, MARYLAND 2009

Walking back from the Metro stop, Lauren spoke to her old neuroscience professor's secretary, Anna.

"Dr. Peterhagen is out of town until Tuesday," Anna said.

"Does he have time then?" Lauren asked.

"I usually keep his first day back free. He gets worn out by travel lately," she said.

"This is really important," Lauren said.

"Okay, I'll see what I can do."

"Thanks."

She hung up the phone just as she reached her front walk. At the door, she paused. It was late and eerily silent. Immediately she sensed something was wrong. When she stepped inside and reached over to flick the light switch, nothing happened. The air caught in her lungs as she stood frozen in place.

"Mark?" she whispered.

As she stood at the foot of the stairway, looking into the gloom of the second floor, fabric rustled in the study to her left. She backed away, her eyes wide. They ached with pressure as she tried to cut through the darkness, to make sense of the shadows. She caught a hint of movement and her heart missed a beat.

Her phone rang. She startled, and then frantically yanked it out of her bag.

"Lauren," Mark said from the other side of the line.

"Mark," she whispered. "Someone's in the house."

"Get out of there," he snapped. "I'm three blocks away. I'll meet you at the corner. Go!"

Lauren moved. She turned and bolted out to the street, not slowing until she was a few houses away. Before she even reached the corner, she heard an engine roaring toward it.

It was Mark driving her Acura. He slammed to a stop in the middle of the road and jumped out.

"Are you okay?"

"I'm fine," she said. "But let's go."

"What?" he asked.

"We need to hurry before they get away," she said.

Mark laughed. Someone laid on his horn. Lauren turned to see cars lined up behind the Acura.

Mark jogged back and parked the car. Together they approached the house carefully. Mark insisted that Lauren get behind him. To her surprise, he drew a handgun from a holster under his jacket. It was the first time she had ever seen him with a gun in his hand. As they neared the door, she could not take her eyes off it.

Inside, Mark tried the lights. They were still dark. He motioned for Lauren to stay on the stoop as he inched inside. She ignored him and followed close behind. When he glanced back at her, his expression stern, she pointed to the study. Shaking his head, he went in.

The study was empty. As Mark cleared the room, Lauren saw the shade by the window blow outward. She walked over and checked the window. It was open.

"Did you leave this open?" she whispered.

"I don't think so," he said. "I never do."

Mark checked it out. He traced the framed of the window with a finger. He checked the locking mechanism. From what Lauren could see, it appeared untouched.

"Could someone have broken in?" she asked.

Mark shrugged. "I need you out of here, Lauren. I don't want to scare you, but if someone did break in, they might have left something behind."

"What do you mean?" she asked.

"I mean, considering everything that is going on, I doubt some thief just happened to break into our house."

Lauren noticed his use of the word "our." With everything going on, it seemed childish. But she did. She smiled but Mark seemed not to notice.

He continued. "I might be over reacting but we should be careful. Just wait outside, stay around people. I'll check the house and then meet you out there."

Lauren started to protest but Mark stopped her with a look. It was dangerous and unquestionable; the kind of look only a cop can give. She shook her head but went to wait on the sidewalk outside.

Bethesda, Maryland 2009

From her bedroom, Steinmetz heard her talking to her boyfriend. When she had come into the house, his body had tingled with anticipation. His mind pictured what he would do in vivid colors and stark sounds.

But something had gone wrong. As he quivered with excitement upstairs, she had stopped. Somehow, she had known he was there. When she left the house, he had crept down the stairs and checked the window. He left it open.

His own carelessness troubled Steinmetz. It was out of character, he knew. But there was nothing he could do about it.

Through the window, he saw her half a block down the street talking on her phone. Then the boyfriend had arrived.

Having moved back upstairs, he waited. The minutes ticked by. When he heard the boyfriend tell her to stay where she was, he reached behind his back and pulled the nine millimeter out of its holster. The grip felt warm in his hand.

From the bedroom, Steinmetz could see down the stairway to a small section of the foyer. He watched the boyfriend enter the house. Immediately, his trained eye picked up something. The man moved like a highly experienced soldier, clearing each room before moving on.

Suddenly, everything changed. The desire inside him that burned to take the girl faltered and his own experience took hold. He realized this was not the time, that the boyfriend was something more than he had appeared.

He backed across the room without making a sound. Carefully, he opened the window and eased himself out. There was a canopy covering a small patio right below the window. He stepped onto it and then dropped to the ground, gun still drawn, aiming at the back windows of the first floor.

After a moment, he moved. The gun still leveled, he backed quickly across the yard and through to the neighbor's. As he reached the street around the corner from her house, he heard the sirens. He holstered his gun and stepped onto the sidewalk, joining the other pedestrians. As a professional, he knew well enough to never run.

It wasn't until he had walked a few blocks that he realized he had taken something from her house. He looked down at his hand. It held the pair of her black stockings like a starving hunter might hold a fresh kill.

Bethesda, Maryland 2009

Five minutes later, Mark emerged from inside the dark house. He took Lauren by the hand and led her back to the Acura. As she was getting in, confused, she heard the roar of sirens. They came from everywhere at once. Before Mark had the car started, a large black van careened into sight. It slammed to a stop outside their house. Officers in padded uniforms stormed out the back and began to cordon off the road.

One of them approached the Acura. For a second, Lauren was sure they were going nowhere. Then the officer nodded at Mark, who nodded back. With a wave, the officer made room and Mark drove off. As they passed the van, Lauren saw the words "Bomb Disposal Unit" stenciled on the side.

Lauren did not say a word as Mark wove through traffic, cutting across D.C. like a cab driver. She could not believe that a bomb was in her house. It was just too farfetched. At the same time, she doubted the bomb squad responded unless the threat was real.

"This is big, isn't it?" she whispered as Mark drove past the White House.

He looked at her. She could read the concern in his eyes.

"I'm not sure. But whoever is behind all this, whatever it is they really want, they have some real heavyweights working for them. The thing on the island, this, it reeks of a professional, or more than one. And that makes me nervous for you."

"You called the police?" she asked.

"Yeah," he said. "I had to. I know you want to figure all this out yourself, but we're taking an awfully big chance. We should hand it over to professionals."

"Maybe," she said, looking out the window. "Where are we going?"

"I was going to surprise you," he said, "before all this drama started."

She looked at him. "You were?"

"Yeah," he said. "I got a room for us at the Hay Adams and reservations at the Red Sage. Downstairs this time."

Lauren smiled. "You did? Why?"

"Just figured I would take you out on the town," he said, his eye twinkling with mischief.

"The town, huh?" she said.

He winked.

The clerk at the Hay Adams looked askew. He was a tall man with a pressed shirt and womanish glasses. His head tilted back slightly as he spoke.

"Your luggage?" he asked.

Lauren blushed. She looked around the hotel. The Hay Adams, named after two of the properties renowned past owners: John Hay, former Secretary of State, and Henry Adams, descendent of the two presidents, was one of Washington's, if not the world's, most distinguished hotels. Walnut wainscoting lined the thick columns of the lobby and the ceiling was adorned with an intricate Tudor motif. She had never stayed there but she heard the rooms were fabulous.

When Lauren turned back around, Mark put a hand on the counter.

"None today," he answered the clerk with a smile.

"Of course," The clerk handed a small envelope with gold leaf lettering over the counter. "Room 312. The elevators are to your right."

"Thanks," Mark said.

Lauren took his hand and hurried him away from the desk.

"I feel so tawdry," she said.

Mark kissed her.

When they got on the elevator, she ran her hand through his hair. But as the door shut, the reality of what had happened at her house crept back into her mind. She felt the tension rising up her spine. Moving her hand away, she glanced at her watch.

"I have clinic at the hospital," she said.

Mark took her into his arms. "You need a massage."

"What?"

The door opened to the third floor. Mark swept her off her feet and carried her off the carriage. Lauren squirmed for a second, then laughed. She heard one of the room doors rattle as they passed and she guessed someone was spying at them through a peep hole, wondering what all the commotion was.

The thought made Lauren laugh even more. When Mark fumbled to unlock the door while still cradling her in his arms, she choked.

Once inside, Mark lowered her gently to the bed. Lauren felt the lush fabric of the linens on her exposed calves and her head sank down into impossibly plush pillows. She sighed.

"This is beautiful," she whispered.

"Not as beautiful as you," he said.

Lauren barked out a laugh. "Cheeseball."

"What?" Mark mocked offense.

"Just take your clothes off," she said in a husky voice.

Mark took a step back, surprised by Lauren's candor. She reached out with her legs and wrapped them around his waist, pulling him closer.

Lauren stared into his eyes. A tingle ran through her body as she reached out and unbuttoned his jeans.

"Wow," Mark whispered.

Lauren barely heard him. Her mind returned to her house, the stress of the moment, the fear and the excitement. She unwrapped her legs and looked into his eyes. Then she pulled at his zipper and yanked his pants down. Her hand slid under his boxer briefs.

Mark moaned and lowered himself on top of her. His hands pulled at her shirt. Her mouth found his and she bit his lower lip. He squeezed her waist and his hand ran up her stomach under her shirt.

Lauren's hands wrapped around his lower back, pulling him hard against her body. She felt him against her and her breathing quickened. She arched her back and tore her pants off.

Mark lifted his arms, and she pulled his shirt off, then her own. She savored the feeling of her bare skin touching his.

Mark groaned. At that moment, Lauren pulled away, twisting her hips slightly, barring his advance. She bit his lip again and pulled back. When she let it go, she smiled. Mark looked wildly down at her, need painted across his face.

"Not yet," she whispered.

"Why?" he moaned.

"Promise me."

"What?"

"You'll help me figure this thing out," she said.

Mark's eyes widened. Lauren reached for him, tugging him closer to her.

"Promise," she hissed.

"Okay," he said. "Okay."

With a gasp of pleasure, she guided Mark into her. Their sighs of ecstasy mingled into a single, vibrating crescendo. Lauren clawed down Mark's back at the final moment. Then they crashed back to earth and laid motionless, intertwined, exhausted.

When Mark finally stirred, Lauren looked away. He kissed her on the forehead and slipped off the bed and into the bathroom. She laid there for a second, staring at the ceiling.

As she listened to the soft sound of the running shower, she closed her eyes. Shaking her head, she wondered what had come over her. Sure she wanted to figure out what was going on. Maybe it was ego, or just curiosity, but she wanted to be the one that figured this whole thing out. But there was something more.

She had never felt so alive, so passionate before. The mingling of danger and lust had sent her to a level her sheltered, intellectual upbringing had never dreamed of. And she still felt the stirring inside her, like a door had opened that could never be closed again.

With Mark still in the bathroom, she got up and walked over to the window. Naked, she pulled open the curtains. It was dark outside and no lights were on in the room. Still, her skin itched with excitement as she watched the city lights below.

Still feeling somehow detached from herself, she opened the balcony door and stepped outside. The cool night air surrounded her. She let it chill her body as she stared at the nation's capital.

Suddenly, arms were wrapped around her. At first, she was startled, the adrenaline coursing through her veins again. Then she recognized the strong, warm hands. She turned to find Mark standing behind her, still wet from the shower, and as naked as she was.

"This is interesting," he said.

"I'm sorry about . . ."

"What?" he asked, surprised.

"How I was, earlier."

He laughed. "You can be like that all the time."

She smiled. "I meant what I said, though."

"And what was that?" he asked, looking guilty.

"I intend to figure this thing out."

"I know," he whispered.

"And I need your help," she said.

Mark nodded. "I promised, didn't I?"

"So what's next," she said.

Mark pulled her in close. "You mean after you cancel all your appointments for tomorrow?"

She pulled back. "I can't."

"Oh," he said, smirking. "Then I guess I can't get you access to the FBI database."

"Are you kidding?" she said.

"No, but it seems you're too busy."

Lauren pushed him back into the room. She closed the curtain and rushed over to her discarded clothes. Finding her BlackBerry, she emailed her receptionist.

"This might cost me some patients," she said.

Mark smiled. "It's your choice."

She smiled back. "I'm not so sure about that."

WASHINGTON, D.C. 2009

In the morning Lauren and Mark left the hotel. They walked across Lafayette Square, directly in front of the White House, until they reached Pennsylvania Avenue.

"It's about ten blocks," Mark said. "You want to take a cab?"

"No, we can walk," she said. "Where are we heading?"

"You'll see."

They strolled down Pennsylvania Avenue, passing the Willard Hotel and the Grand Theater. They cut across Freedom Plaza, walking over the stone depiction of L'Enfant's utopist plan for Washington, D.C.

Four blocks more and Mark slowed down. Lauren looked up and immediately recognized where they were.

"This is the FBI Building," she said.

Mark nodded. She looked up at the authoritative façade with its dark, recessed windows and the massive overhang on one side.

"This isn't . . ."

"It is," he said.

"But we can't go in there," she said.

"We can, actually," he said. "A friend owes me a favor. Trust me, okay?"

Something about the way he said that caught Lauren's attention. She looked into his eyes for a moment, assessing what it was she sensed. He looked away.

"Are you sure about this?" she asked.

"Definitely," he said in a more confident tone. "Let's go."

Mark led the way up to the front entrance. When they walked in, an elaborate security checkpoint took up most of the lobby area. Mark walked a little ahead of her. He approached one of the guards, an older man wearing a pressed black suit. Mark whispered something to the man and then motioned Lauren to stay where she was. The two talked quietly for a time and then the older man called someone on his radio.

A moment later, Mark motioned for her to follow. The guard led them through the checkpoint and toward a side elevator. To Lauren's surprise, he did not follow them into the carriage. Instead, Mark hit the button for the fourth floor. The doors closed.

When they reached their floor and exited the elevator, the hallway was empty. She could hear the soft sounds of industry surrounding her but she did not see a single person.

Mark paid it no mind. He led her to the first office they came across. A man in his mid-forties with glasses and a graying goatee sat at a small table with a computer. He nodded to Mark.

"This is Agent Francis, a friend of mine. This is Lauren Chandler."

The agent said hello. Lauren waved. She felt ill-at-ease being in the FBI building.

"So," Agent Francis said, "what are we looking for?"

Unintentionally, Lauren looked over her shoulder, as if to make sure no one was listening. Her skin tingled with excitement as the reality of the situation dawned on her.

"Um. Can you check up on Senator Brown of Montana?"

The agent looked at her askew, but then typed into the drab, DOS based database, nothing like the colorful, illustrated ones she'd seen on detective TV shows. Green text scrolled across a black background. Mark leaned forward.

"Huh," he said. "That's interesting."

"What?" she asked.

"Brown. He wasn't born in this country."

"He wasn't," she said, shocked. "How could he be a senator?"

"That's the president." Mark winked at her. "Isn't your dad a senator?"

"I never paid much attention to politics," she said with a smile.

"So much has changed," he said.

Agent Francis entered a new page. "Whoa. Check this out. His name is really Braun. Reichart Braun. He was born in Munich."

"Germany?"

"Yeah."

Lauren bent over to look at the screen. "Are you kidding me? That can't just be a coincidence, can it?"

"I doubt it," Mark said.

"There must be some tie in here. Let's think about this. We know there was an increase in cataracts in D.C. and in Bonn. We know Brown, or Braun, or whatever his name is, is interested in the withdrawal of U.S. troops from Germany. Now we know that he was born in Germany, same country as the other spike. Somehow the cataracts must have something to do with what's going on with my dad. But what?"

"Well, it has something to do with Germany, that's for sure. But it'll be hard to figure out what until we figure out who is behind it all."

Lauren's eyes widened. "That might be it."

"What?" Mark asked.

"The TeleLens," Lauren said. "It's a new lens used for cataract surgery. This lens company called Teleplunkt was not in this business until five years ago. I never heard of them before and never even thought of learning where the lenses are manufactured. The sales, at least here, have been through the roof. Maybe this is all about money. Maybe the company that manufactures the TeleLens found a way to induce cataracts."

"But how?" Mark asked.

"I need to think. What causes cataracts? The sun, age, trauma, vitamin deficiencies, drug side effects." She paused, thinking. "Can you search the database by keyword?"

"Sure," the agent said. "At least in the case files I can."

"Let's do that."

Agent Francis tapped at the keyboard. More text flashed on the screen. He scanned page after page before stopping.

"Look at this."

Lauren leaned forward again. She read over Agent Francis's shoulder. The subject of the file was a fire in Delaware. At first it had been classified as the standard unsolved murder case. But the medical examiner in Delaware found the remains of lab animals and a myriad of chemical residue. Fearing a terrorist plot, they called in the FBI.

The agents in the FBI collected samples, including the animal remains: rats, rabbits and even monkeys. That's where they got the hit on the keyword "cataracts." As Lauren read, she couldn't believe her eyes.

The animal remains provided the clue.

"They found signs of cataracts in every autopsied cadaver," she said. "Obviously sunlight and age are not the factor here, especially when a chemical residue was found."

"And an unidentified chemical chain," Mark said.

"Can you put the formula on the screen?"

"I think so," Agent Francis said.

He fussed around for a second and then the chain appeared.

"It looks like some kind of drug," Lauren said.

"Can you make out what kind?" he asked.

"No," she said. "Can you print it out?"

"Sure," the agent said.

He hit a button and the printer began to run off. Lauren watched the paper, thinking.

"Wait a second," Mark said, "look at that."

"What?" she asked.

"The explosive used on the warehouse. It was Semtex. That was the same trace found when that van nearly hit you and your father."

"Are you sure?" she asked.

"Definitely."

"This is more serious than I even thought," she said.

"So what's next?" Mark asked.

Lauren frowned. "First I want to check up on that chemical we found. Then, I think we need to go talk an analyst at the pharmaceutical company that man worked for."

"We better hurry," Mark said, glancing at Agent Francis.

"Why?"

"Because," he said. "If they find out what we know."

Lauren shivered. "We might get ourselves blown up."

WILMINGTON, DELAWARE 2009

Lauren and Mark drove up to Wilmington, Delaware, that afternoon. Agent Francis had put them in contact with the head of security for Pharmoletia. The security chief had agreed to meet with them and bring one of their scientists with him.

After getting off of I95 and taking Route 202 north, they found the office complex quickly. The security officer was waiting for them. He ushered them inside to a small conference room and waited in silence for another man to arrive. This one was dressed to the nines in a crisp brown suit and Italian shoes.

"Hello," the man said. "My name's Arnie Jenkins. I'm the head council for the company."

Lauren frowned. She had expected to be meeting with a scientist. Mark, however, stood up and shook the man's hand.

Arnie took a seat and started the conversation. "I hear you all are looking for information on one of our ex employees."

"Somewhat," Lauren said. "We're more interested in this.

She pushed a copy of the chemical chain across the table to Arnie, who took it. With barely a glance, he put it down and cleared his throat.

"Uh hmmm," he said. "I'm familiar with part of that. But you have to understand that it has been tampered with."

"What was it?" Lauren asked.

"Off the record, it was a failed drug. We developed it thinking it would be a groundbreaking cholesterol med. In trials, it was more effective than the top three combined, but there was a problem."

Lauren smiled. "It caused a side effect, didn't it?"

Arnie nodded. "Cataracts. They were slow to form, so we didn't see them for some time."

"Could someone have learned about the side effect?" she asked.

"Sure," he said. "We published on the drug and then had to add a disclaimer when we found out."

"Was the man they found in the fire working on it?" Mark asked.

Arnie shook his head. "No, Harvey was a tech for our erectile dysfunction meds group."

Lauren looked away, stifling a laugh. Mark continued.

"How'd he end up mixed up in all this?"

"Disgruntled, a little mentally unstable. Whoever was behind all this must have found him. From what we can tell, and we have sufficient circumstantial evidence mind you, he stole the formula and took it off campus."

"What about the part that was added on? Any idea?" Lauren asked.

"I'm not at liberty . . ."

Mark cut the man off. "Can we step outside for a second?"

"Uh, sure."

Mark led Arnie out into the hallway. They were gone for a moment. When they came back in, Arnie's cheeks were flushed.

"The side chain looks like something that would compound the side effects of the drug. It most likely would cause rapid growth cataracts in a high percentage of patients."

Mark nodded to Arnie who continued.

"And, it looks like it was adapted for wide distribution."

"What does that mean?" she asked.

Arnie looked down at the table. "Harvey made our drug into a biological weapon."

MIDDLETOWN, CONNECTICUT 2009

On the road to Connecticut to see her collegiate advisor, Lauren asked Mark about their meeting in Delaware.

"What was that about?" she said. "I thought we would meet with a scientist, not a lawyer."

Mark shook his head. "They're worried. And I guess they should be. Their drug was used, in essence, as a weapon of mass destruction. At least that's what it seems now."

"We've found so much so fast, I can't process it all yet," she said.

"Does your father know Senator Brown well?" Mark asked.

Lauren shrugged. "I know he doesn't like him. I guess they've been running into each other for years, from what I can tell."

"Hmmm," Mark said. "Maybe I'll have some buddies of mine dig into his past a little."

"Why?" Lauren asked.

"You amaze me. I've never seen anyone react to having their life threatened quite like you. It's like it never happened. I can't be calm. If whatever is happening with your father is related to whoever is after you, this Brown might be the key. I'm going to find out."

"Come on, Mark," Lauren said. "I'll admit I'm a little curious, but what are the odds of this stuff being related. That would be pretty random."

"Would it?"

"Of course it would."

Mark smiled. "Then why are we driving to Connecticut?"

"We, well . . ." She laughed. "Guess you got me. But that doesn't mean I'm going to let whoever is behind all of this stop me. If I do that, they win. Besides that, my father and maybe even you might be in danger, too."

"So you are going to bring them down single-handed?"

"No," she said, touching his hand. "I have you with me."

Mark laughed.

Lauren felt a pang of nostalgia as she approached Wesleyan. She parked her Acura behind the Exley Science Center. Getting out of the car, she stared up at the massive building with its concrete frame and dark, recessed windows. Remembering long hours of study and frequent visits to the Pi Café for coffee made her feel as if she had returned home.

Next door to Exley and behind the Science Library sat Shanklin Labs. A more classical building with arched windows lining the first story, it always seemed more collegiate to her. Pausing at the bottom of the steps leading up to the entrance, she watched the students walking along Church Street. They were so young.

"Has it been that long?" she whispered.

"What?" Mark asked?

"Oh, nothing," she said. "We better get up. I don't want to keep Dr. Peterhagen waiting."

Together they climbed the steps and entered the labs. Familiar smells, formaldehyde, sulfur and others, intensified her nostalgia. Although she had not set foot in the building for nearly ten years, she had no trouble finding the stairwell and Dr. Peterhagen's office on the second floor. When she knocked, his voice carried through the door, giving her a slight chill down her back.

"Come in," he said.

She opened the door halfway. "Dr. Peterhagen. It's me, Lauren Chandler."

She saw him rise from behind the desk. He had aged since the last time she saw him. His eyebrows were bushier and his glasses a little thicker. Otherwise, he was the professor she remembered.

"It's been a long time, my star student," he said, giving her a hug.

She hugged him back.

"Oh," he said, seeing Mark.

"This is my friend, Mark Bartholomew. Mark, this is Dr. Peterhagen."

"Nice to meet you," Mark said, extending a hand.

Dr. Peterhagen nodded and returned to his chair. Lauren took a seat and Mark settled against the wall, partially hidden in the shadows. As she watched her old professor settle into a plush leather desk chair, picking at the front of his collared shirt, the years since she had attended Wesleyan struck her with a jarring force. She thought through her time at Hopkins and the start of her practice. Her life had been set to full speed since starting medical school. Now, with everything that was going on, it seemed to reach a break-neck speed.

"I need to ask you about something," she said. "It might seem odd, but bear with me."

"To a man who has spent his entire life studying the brain, nothing sounds odd."

She laughed. "Something's happened," She paused. "Well, I'm looking for information on mind control."

Dr. Peterhagen's eyes opened wider under his unruly gray brows. He leaned forward.

"Mind control?"

Lauren nodded.

"What is it you want to know?" he asked. "Are you talking early history? The Chinese were very active during the war. And Margaret Singer published some very important studies involving her conditions of mind control."

"Conditions of mind control?"

"Sure," he said. "She posited conditions that required no violence, such as keeping the subject unaware of the conditioning goal, control the subjects psychological and physical environment, create a sense of powerlessness, and so on."

"I'm thinking more recent advancements," she interrupted. "Something that might cause the brain to be open to control."

"Oh, there has been incredible work lately on brain wave controlled devices for the handicapped."

Lauren nodded. "More like that."

"Interestingly enough, that work originated in the mid 1900s. A man named Dr. Jose Delgado. In the fifties he invented a device known as the *stimoreceiver*. It stimulated brain waves while the subject was connected to an EEG. He found the device could cause the subject to emote, and could even control behavior."

"He could control behavior?" Lauren asked.

"According to him," Dr. Peterhagen said with a smile, "just by directing radio frequencies at the subject. His most intriguing work involved using these frequencies to stop the brain from producing certain brain signals."

Lauren interrupted him again. "Could it control behavior?"

"There was a famous incident," he said with a laugh. "Dr. Delgado got into a ring with a bull fitted with a *stimoreceiver*. The bull charged him and he used a remote controlled device to activate the implant. The bull, it seemed, stopped in its tracks before crushing the doctor."

Lauren leaned closer. "Really?"

"Sadly, no," he said. "It was found later that the experiment was a fraud, a matter of trick photography."

She sighed. "What about now? Is there work being done on controlling behavior?"

"Definitely," he answered. "Yet I'm not sure how trusted it is. In the 1980s an official committee of the American Psychological Association submitted a comprehensive report on brainwashing to the board. The board rejected it, claiming insufficient data to make an informed ruling. There still remains strong differences between clinical and research psychologists. Although many professionals are split, there is much skepticism concerning the entire field of study."

"But you said there has been a great deal of advancement on mind control lately," she said.

"I did, and there is. Most of the work is outside the field of psychology. Neuroscience is the wave of the future. I've been working with the U.S. Army on creating a helmet that would allow troops to be commanded by thought, using brain waves transmitted by their commanding officer."

"The purpose of this work is to avoid soldiers mind chatter during the course of battle. Through this type of neuro-sensory influence, they can be receiving surveillance information about the enemy and about the terrain from overhead drones, et cetera. This study was not meant to be brainwashing but rather to improve efficiency as well as safety for our men and women in combat. Fascinating stuff, really."

"That's more what I am looking for," she said. "How does it work?"

"Each helmet contains over a hundred sensors that pick up speech related brain waves," he said.

"One hundred sensors?" she asked, disappointed.

"Yes."

"Is there anyway that would be more conspicuous?" she asked.

He arched an eyebrow. "Conspicuous? I doubt it since this technology does not look to be viable for another ten years."

"Oh," she said.

He looked directly into her eyes. "Maybe you can give me a hint as to what you are looking for, Lauren."

She stared back for a moment. Taking a deep breath, she told him about what they had learned. He hung on every word like a child listening to a fascinating fairytale. In the end he leaned back and nodded.

"Sounds more like hypnosis to me," he said.

"Hypnosis? I had always thought that was just a parlor trick."

"It is," Dr. Peterhagen said, "in less knowing hands. In the hands of a neuro-scientist, that's a different story. I've heard, nothing official, that some amazing work has been done in Asia. They have always been far more open to this topic than here in the States. Nevertheless, nothing is on the market."

"Could there be something more covert?" she asked.

"Definitely," he said. "In fact, I would venture to guess where it came from."

"Where?"

"North Korea," he said. "They have been working on visual-stim suggestive hypnosis for a few years now."

"Visual-stim?" she asked.

"Yes. The eye has a deep level of influence on brain function. And brain function, ultimately, has total control over behavior. Consider the Stroop Effect."

"I remember that from your class. It was the color and word experiment, right."

"Exactly," he said, pointing over his shoulder. "There on the wall."

Lauren looked at the poster behind Dr. Peterhagen. On it, two groups of words were printed in different colors. The top two rows were printed in the same color as their names and read:

GREEN RED BLUE RED
YELLOW BLUE YELLOW BLACK

The bottom two rows were printed in different colors and read:

BLUE YELLOW RED WHITE
GREEN YELLOW GREEN BLACK

"Yeah," she said.

She read the first two rows perfectly. When she read the second, she finished much slower and with a couple of errors.

"See," he said. "Your brain is overpowered by the sight stimulus of the colors and it is far more difficult to read the second set correctly. My point is that this simple experiment shows how the eye can influence normal brain function."

"But how does that relate to hypnosis?" she asked.

"A visual stimulus could, in essence, hypnotize a subject."

"I had always read that subliminal messaging is ineffective. So, I would assume that a subject would know if he or she was hypnotized"

"That is were the Koreans have made great strides. They have created chemical compounds that can stimulate Alpha waves in the brain. In a sense, the effect is similar to a dis-inhibitor. The subject becomes suggestible."

"To the point they might act counter to their beliefs?" she asked.

"I assume so," he answered.

"So maybe the senators have been drugged?"

"Doubtful," he said. "To my knowledge, such chemical compounds would not be effective taken orally."

"What about through the blood?"

"Again, doubtful, and logistically difficult to administer to large groups of people."

"Then how could something like this be administered?" she asked.

He smiled. "You should know."

"What?"

He pointed at his eye. "Through the window to the soul, of course."

Lauren walked slowly back to the car. Mark matched her stride, glancing at her from time to time. She finally looked at him.

"What?"

He smiled. "You guys lost me in there. It was like I wasn't even present."

"Sorry," she said. "Did you hear what he said, though?"

"Which part?" he asked.

Lauren stopped. "He said that mind control, if that's what this is, can come through the eyes."

"So?" he said.

"So, I have a bad feeling," she said. "We need to get back to D.C."

Washington, D.C. 2009

Benjamin Chandler's phone rang. He was sitting in his office alone. He answered it quickly thinking it was Lauren. It wasn't.

"Senator, this is Hans Krauss."

"Hello, Hans. What's new in Bonn?"

There was a pause. "Not good."

"What is it?" Chandler asked.

"Have you seen the Reuters reports? There has been a string of violent attacks across the northern sector of the city. Mostly Turks and Jews were the targets but other immigrants as well have been harassed."

"I read something about it in the Post."

Hans took a deep breath. "It is easy to think this kind of violence happens here on occasion, but this is different. What the reports have not said is that these attacks have been well organized. The assailants are well organized. They even wear dark uniforms. And they have been waving anti-American slogans."

Chandler leaned forward. "Do you think this has something to do with the movement to remove U.S. troops?"

"I'm not sure," Hans said. "If someone wanted the U.S. out, I would think starting trouble would be the last thing they would do."

"So they aren't related," Chandler said.

"I did not say that. I have a feeling they are. But what frightens me the most is that an action like this would only come from someone who has already won."

"What do you mean?" Chandler asked.

"I think these attacks are a vanguard to what will come once the U.S. is gone. I . . ."

"What?"

Hans paused again. "When I was a kid, my grandfather used to talk to me about the time before the war. He always spoke of an emotional surge that helped a man like Hitler to rise to power. It was as if someone stirred the population into a frenzy of hatred. The Beer Hall Putsch, Night of the Long Knives, and Kristallnacht."

"When I see how some people are reacting to these attacks, I am worried. It's a small number of these people who hate. But they are loud and overbearing. I fear that given enough time and enough freedom, history could repeat itself."

Chandler's eyes narrowed. "What are you saying? You think Germany could have another Hitler?"

"No," Hans whispered. Then his voice rose. "Not exactly. What I am saying is that Germany could revert to an isolated state. Germans are getting tired of being weighed down by the European Union especially after we've had to absorb the debt of East Germany.

"We have already made moves in that direction. Last month the government refused to support the European Union request for a fiscal package to forestall a recession. Our budget is balanced and our borrowing costs are low. We are in the best place to help out. But we balked at doing our part to support the union. Couple that with the growing sentiment for U.S. withdrawal and increased racial tensions, this could be bigger than we Christian Democrats thought."

"But why?" Chandler asked. "It doesn't make sense. What would someone gain by going through all this? In my experience, everything is done for money. I just don't see the rationale."

"You have to understand, there is still a sentiment here that goes deeper than money. There are some who wish to finish what their fathers started. Look at your Iraq war. We are not so different."

"Some would say that war was about money," Chandler said.

"Others might say it had something to do with a son making his father proud."

"That's childish," Chandler said.

"So is anger," Hans retorted.

Chandler thought for a moment. "So you're saying that there might be those in Germany who want us out simply because their fathers failed to keep us out in the first place."

"It is more than that," Hans said. "But yes."

"This is too much," Chandler said, standing up. "The Armed Services Committee has already voted to withdraw troops. I have to get back before it reaches the floor of the Senate. I will not allow this to happen on my watch. It's one thing if there was a logical reason to move forward with withdrawal. But what you're telling me is that once the U.S. is out, innocent people living in your country won't be safe. I can't stand by and let that happen."

"What can you do?" Hans asked.

"I'm coming over," Chandler said "to learn more from you and your colleagues. And maybe exert some influence back home."

"To Germany?"

"Yes. Can you get me time to speak to the commission over there? I can arrive by Tuesday."

Hans sounded excited. "I'll see what I can do."

Chandler hung up the phone and then picked it right back up. He paged his secretary.

"Get me tickets to Bonn for Monday."

"How many?" she asked.

"Just me."

He hung up.

Washington, D.C. 2009

When Lauren returned from Connecticut, the first thing she did was visit her father's office Monday morning before patient hours. She wanted to tell him what she had learned about Senator Brown and about her suspicions concerning mind control.

She rushed through the hall of the Dirksen Building. Arriving at his office, she approached his receptionist.

"Hi Lauren," the woman said. "I'm surprised to see you."

"Hi, is my dad in?"

The receptionist frowned. "No, he didn't tell you? He left for Germany about three hours ago."

Lauren's heart sank. She took a step backwards.

"Why'd he go?" she asked.

"I really don't know," the woman said. "It was spur of the moment."

"Who went with him?"

"No one."

Lauren shook her head walking back toward the hallway.

"Are you okay?" the receptionist asked.

"Uh, yeah, sure," Lauren said.

Lauren took the Metro back to her house. Sitting toward the back of the car, she could see the door to the next one behind her. As she thought about everything that had happened so far, a shadow blocked out the light from that door. When she looked up, it disappeared.

At her stop, she hurried off the train. She was the only one that got off her car. As she headed for the escalator up to the street, she heard footsteps behind her. Whirling around, she saw no one.

Lauren hurried down the street to her house looking over her shoulder every few steps. When she made it to her house, Mark was there reading the paper. She was about to tell him about it when she noticed he was sweating and a little out of breath. He spoke first before she could ask about it.

"Did you see this?" he asked.

"What?"

She leaned over and looked at the article at which he pointed. The headline read: UNREST IN GERMANY—Angry Mobs Deface Mosque in Potsdam, Kills Two Turks in Cologne.

"Oh, God," she whispered.

"Do you think it's related?" Mark asked. Then he looked over his shoulder at her. "What's wrong?"

"My dad," she stammered. "He just went over there. Alone."

"Are you kidding?"

"No," she said. "I tried his cell but he didn't answer. I left him a message to call me back, immediately."

Mark stood up. "I have to call someone."

Lauren looked confused. "Who?"

This time, Mark stammered. "Uh, work stuff. I'll be right back."

Lauren watched him walk out the front door. Through the window she could see him pulling out his phone and dialing a number. His abrupt departure shocked her. He had never acted so uninterested. For a second she thought about listening in, but she couldn't. Instead, she walked upstairs upset with him and worried about her father.

Lauren had patients in less than half an hour. Totally distracted, she dressed quickly. She could not find the shirt she wanted. Frustrated, she knocked the rod that held up all her hangers. Her clothes tumbled to the ground in a wrinkled mess.

"Shit!"

She glanced at her watch. She had ten minutes to reach the office. Grabbing the top shirt on the pile, she hurried back down stairs, throwing it over her head on the way down.

Mark still stood on the sidewalk when she rushed out the door. He hung up his phone and looked at her. His expression was full of guilt.

"Hey. You okay?"

"I have to go," she said briskly.

"Wait. I want to talk about your dad," he called after her.

"Later," she said over her shoulder.

Lauren jumped in her Acura and took off down the street.

Her receptionist stared when she walked into the office through the rear entrance.

"What?" Lauren said. "I'm not too late."

"Uh, no. You're fine. Mr. Smith is prepped in room five and Mrs. Andrews is being worked up in six."

"What's wrong then?" she asked.

The receptionist didn't say anything, but Lauren noticed she was staring at her shirt. She looked down and for the first time noticed what she had put on. It was a shirt her dad had bought her for Christmas one year. He had notoriously bad taste and this shirt did not prove it wrong. It was red and white vertical stripes. She had never worn it before but had felt too guilty to throw it out.

"Oh, wow," Lauren whispered.

The receptionist laughed. "Get dressed in the dark?"

"Kind of," she answered.

"Just don't move to fast. You might hypnotize your patients."

Lauren barked out a laugh on the way to exam room five. She grabbed the chart out of a plastic sleeve hung outside the room. When she opened the door, Mr. Smith was sitting in the high-backed exam chair, squinting despite the bright light and trying to read Newsweek.

"How are you?" she said, glancing through his chart.

"Not too good," Mr. Smith said. "Can't see a damn thing lately."

Lauren hesitated, reading the work-up history more carefully. The tech noticed the formation of a severe cataract in both his eyes. She flipped the page and noticed he had been in the office six months prior and nothing had been present at the time.

"Did you ever take the supplements I prescribed?" she asked.

"I forgot," he mumbled.

Lauren went through her exam and then rolled her chair away from him.

"I hate to say this, but you need surgery," she said.

She brought out a model of the eye and explained the cataract and the procedure. While he reacted, the back of her mind returned to the fact there had been nothing out of the ordinary at Mr. Smith's last exam.

"We'll schedule you when you're ready. You'll need a pre-op counseling along with measuring of the eye. For that, no one has to be with you. But someone has to drive you on the day of surgery," she said. "Everything will be all right."

She walked out of the room, her mind rolling. She needed to get everything straight. What had she learned so far? There was an increase in rapidly forming cataracts. There was odd behavior among her father's colleagues. No matter how farfetched it seemed, after talking with Dr. Peterhagen, it appeared some kind of mind control might be the reason. Lastly, there was a fire at a strange lab experimenting on animals with cataracts and traces of an unusual statin compound had been found. Lastly, traces of the same explosive had been found at the warehouse and the van that had nearly killed her and her father.

Her train of thought paused when she reached exam room six. She grabbed the file and read through it half-heartedly before entering. The patient was a post-op follow-up.

She opened the door. Mrs. Andrews looked up at her. Her mind still distracted, Lauren accidentally dropped the chart. She bent down quickly to grab it. When she straightened, Mrs. Andrews' eyes were locked onto her shirt.

"Oh, great," Lauren thought. "Another fashion critic."

"How are you feeling Mrs. Andrews? Good?" she asked.

"Good?" Mrs. Andrews said.

Lauren noticed the strange tone of her voice as if her answer had been a question. She ignored it.

"Can you lean forward so I can have a look?" she asked.

Mrs. Brown leaned forward even before Lauren had swung the chinrest into place. She stared at her patient. The woman looked like she was in a trance. Lauren remembered what her receptionist had said moments earlier.

"Don't move too fast," she had said. "You might hypnotize your patients."

Suddenly the comment took on an eerie quality. Lauren stared at the woman for a moment.

"Lift your right arm," she whispered.

Mrs. Andrews lifted her right arm.

"Slap your face," she said a little louder.

The woman did. Lauren startled and then felt bad. But she could not believe what she was seeing.

"Say 'yes,'" she said.

"Yes," Mrs. Andrews said.

Lauren shot to her feet. "Stay here."

She left the exam room and went to a nearby closet. Inside was a lab coat. She put it on over her shirt, buttoning it up as high as she could. She returned to the room.

Mrs. Andrews smiled when Lauren walked in.

"Hi, Dr. Chandler," she said.

Lauren blinked. "Did I see you already today?"

The woman laughed. "No, of course not."

Lauren felt a rush of adrenaline, the kernel of an epiphany rising in her mind. She reached for the woman's file. Scanning quickly, she found what she was looking for. She had implanted a lens in the woman's eye not three weeks before. It was a TeleLens.

BONN, GERMANY 2009

Kugler walked along the streets of Bonn. He could smell the energy in the air. Everything was moving along as planned. He knew that Germany was awakening from a long, silent dormancy. And he was responsible; he was the catalyst. He walked with a light foot befitting someone without a heavy conscious.

"See how far we have come, father," he whispered. "You were always right. Our people have been waiting for the right time. Just as I thought, American's economy has crashed. They have festered under bad government. Soon we will rise from under the weakness of the west and a new era of dominance will begin."

Bonn had a two hundred year history at the heart of the Rhine valley. It was always one of Germany's cultural centers. It was the birthplace of Beethoven, the seat of the *Max-Planck Institut fur Mathemetik,* and the former seat of the West German government.

As he neared the government building, he passed a man hawking newspapers. He read the headline: "More Unrest, More Violence." He smiled. Finally, they would take back what was theirs and do away with impurities that infected Germany like a plague.

Kugler entered the *Regierungsviertel.* Walking down the street, he took in the changes. Once, decades before, this was the hub of power for one of the most powerful countries in Europe. In 1991 two years after the wall finally came down, the government of the unified Germany was moved to Berlin. Although a few ministries, particularly the Office of Foreign Affairs, still remained in city, the *Regierungsviertel* was a shell of what it once was.

Fitting, he thought, that it would come to this, that the final push would occur in a city that most closely portrayed the true Germany. The country, like Bonn, had become a shell of what it could be. Kugler knew, though, that he stood on the cusp of a great victory. He would get the Americans out of his country. And using the TeleLens, he would control the government of Germany. From there it was only a matter of time before she would return to prominence atop the backs of their weaker people.

When Kugler reached the Bundestag building, Becker was waiting on the front steps.

"Are we ready?" Kugler asked.

"Everything is going as planned. The vote will be held at noon today."

"Did you contact the press?"

Becker nodded.

"Does the Minister have the full support of the council?"

"Nearly," Becker said. "There is one who is not. He has not had surgery. Healthy bastard."

"One will do no harm," Kugler said. "What of Berlin?"

"Kim is developing more of the statin drug. We will be ready to deposit it into the Spree a hundred miles northwest of the city. We should be ready to strike by early 2010, Berlin first, then other industrial cities to follow."

"Excellent," Kugler said. "Has Kim made the changes to the drug?"

"Yes, he said it is ready. This time, the effect should be almost immediate, weeks until the cataracts form."

Kugler scratched his chin. "I wonder if we might be more targeted this time."

"What do you mean?"

Kugler looked around to make sure no one was nearby. "We should learn from this debacle in the U.S. Although down the road, once things are set in stone, we can sweep the world and we will make billions on the Lens. But for now, such collateral damage just draws attention. Maybe we could cut into the Reichstag's water supply directly."

"Good idea," Becker said. "I'll have a man check the security there."

"Excellent. Let's get inside. I want to be there when the Minister announces the vote."

Kugler led the way up the stairs and into the building. The guard waved them through with a nod to Becker.

They rode the elevator to the top floor. When the doors opened, the lobby area was filled to capacity. Men and women with cameras and microphones pressed forward toward a dais raised in the far corner.

"Good turnout," Kugler said.

Becker smirked.

The two of them pushed forward as far as they could. When they stopped, Kugler could see into the back hallway that led to the Minister's office. What he saw shocked him.

"Becker," he hissed.

"What?"

"That is the American senator," Kugler said, nodding in that direction.

Standing just outside the lobby, partially hidden in the shadow of the doorway, Kugler could see Senator Chandler speaking urgently with the Foreign Relations Minister. There was a man standing beside them that Kugler recognized from Berlin, Hans somebody.

"What is he doing here?" Becker said.

"You need to find out. I would guess he found out about the vote and is here to stop it."

"Could he?"

"I don't know." Kugler looked at Becker. "But you must be ready to do something about him."

As they stared at Chandler, someone approached Kugler. When he turned, he saw Hulger Schmidt, one of his board members, standing there.

"Schmidt," Kugler said. "You look awful."

Schmidt's eyes were red and his hair was disheveled. He looked as if he had been wearing the same clothing for at least a week.

"My wife passed," Schmidt said, his tone cold.

"I'm sorry to hear that," Kugler said. "Take some time off to be with the family. Your son is here with you in Bonn, no?"

Schmidt stared into Kugler's eyes. "She died during the operation."

Kugler sensed something was wrong. "What operation?"

Schmidt stepped even closer. His nose nearly touched Kugler's.

"Cataract surgery," Schmidt hissed.

Kugler took a step back. "I'm sorry," he stammered.

Schmidt's eyes grew distant. He looked around the room as if in a daze. Then he paused. Kugler followed his gaze and saw Schmidt looking at Chandler. Schmidt walked away without saying another word.

As the Minister started to speak, Kugler grabbed Becker by the arm.

"We have trouble," he said.

Becker looked surprised. "I can handle the senator. He has nothing to go on."

"Schmidt," Kugler said. "You must deal with him."

Becker looked askew. "Deal with him?"

"Yes," Kugler hissed.

"Whatever you say," Becker answered.

Kugler heard the Minister make the announcement. The vote would proceed. Barring an overturn from the Parliament, the vote was like gold. But Kugler was too distracted to enjoy it.

Bethesda, Maryland 2009

Lauren sat at her desk, her mind whirling. She opened up her web browser. Her home page was Google. She typed TeleLens into the search function.

The first hit was for a company in Germany, Teleplunkt. They were based in Frankfurt, not Bonn. Why would her father be heading to Bonn? It made no sense.

She dialed her father's office. When the receptionist answered, she asked for Isaac. He picked up the other line immediately.

"Have you heard from your father?" he asked.

"I was hoping you had," she said. "Why did he go to Bonn, Isaac?"

"Did he tell you about Senator Brown?" Isaac asked, obviously careful with his words.

"Yes," she said. "And I know he's a German and that he has something to do with what's going on."

"Well, I just got word that the German Minister of Foreign Relations has called a vote to order the withdrawal of U.S. troops from Germany."

"That's what Senator Brown wanted," Lauren said.

"Exactly."

Lauren paused. "Is the Minister in Bonn?"

"Yes," Isaac said.

"So my dad went there to stop it," she said.

"Most likely."

"You need to get him back here. I think I know what's going on. It'll sound farfetched but I'm pretty sure now. There is a company in Germany, Teleplunkt. They developed this new cataract lens. I think there is an additive in it that causes the patient to become hypnotized with certain visual stimulus. In fact, I think it's vertical stripes."

"Brown's pin," Isaac said.

"I think so," she said. "These people have to be the ones behind the attempts on my life. Think about it. It happened after I wrote the article on the cataract upswing. We found out that there was a statin drug being made illegally in Delaware. It had a strange chain attached to it that caused a side effect of rapid cataract growth. I think that maybe it was what caused the cataracts."

"So this company caused cataracts and then sold a lens that would cure it and brainwash them all?"

"I know, it sounds . . ."

Isaac sounded as if he thought out loud. "It sounds like it all makes sense now. I can't believe your father went there all by himself. He even slipped away from his tail."

Lauren's eyes narrowed. "What was that?"

"What?"

"That part about a shadower?" she asked.

"Your father had a security tail ever since the accident outside his apartment."

"But I thought that after what happened on the island, he'd decided that the attempts were on me, not him."

"He did," Isaac said, the controlled tone returning to his voice.

"Why would he have someone following him then?"

Isaac did not say anything. A horrible thought crept into Lauren's mind.

"Did I have a tail, too, Isaac?"

He still didn't say anything.

"Oh, God, I did," she said. "Was it private?"

"How do you mean?" Isaac asked, his voice gravelly."

"Private security?"

"No."

Lauren closed her eyes. "FBI?"

"Yes."

Lauren's heart missed a beat. Her legs felt numb as a tear rolled down her cheek.

"Get help to my dad," she managed to say before hanging up. She slumped down in her chair and cried.

Bonn, Germany 2009

Benjamin Chandler stood outside the council chamber, speaking quietly with Minister von Weiss the Foreign Relations Minister of Germany.

"You cannot hold this vote today," Chandler implored.

"Why can't I?" von Weiss said. He never made eye contact with Chandler. "Your own committee passed on a similar resolution just this month."

Chandler rolled his eyes. "That's different." He paused. "Has anything strange happened during your meetings? Has the council been acting strange?"

"I have no idea what you're talking about," von Weiss said. "I really must go."

The Minister pushed past Chandler and entered the chamber. Benjamin looked at Hans. He was a small man, bald with thick glasses and a mustache. He wore a turtleneck under a wool jacket. He had ruddy cheeks and a bulbous nose that were particularly pink due to his current anxiety.

"That was unlike him," he said.

Hans nodded. "The Minister has been acting odd of late."

Chandler waited as people ushered into the voting chamber. He scratched his chin. He thought about his own committee meetings.

"I think we should watch," he said.

The two of them shuffled along with the rest of the crowd. While they found a seat, he felt someone staring at him. When he turned around, he saw two men. One was obviously a German business man with an arrow straight back and a haughty tilt to his head. His icy blue eyes did not look away as Chandler stared back. There was something familiar about him but the senator could not place why.

The other man caused Chandler to feel ill at ease. He, too, did not look away. Yet his stare was different. It was like a lion staring at an injured wildebeest. The senator diverted his gaze first, glancing around the room and then at Hans.

"Do you know the men in the corner, the one in the pressed black suit with the man in the overcoat standing next to him?"

Hans glanced over Chandler's shoulder. "Not the one in the overcoat, never seen him before. But the other one looks familiar. He runs a manufacturing business that is doing quite well despite the economy."

Chandler glanced back at the men. They were no longer paying him any attention. Instead they were watching the council take their seats. The Minister stood at the end of the long, polished walnut table.

"Gentlemen, welcome. I would like to yield the floor to Councilor Braun."

The Minister took his seat. His eyes looked glassed over and unfocused. An older, white haired statesman stood up. Chandler took a sharp intake of breath.

"Brown," he whispered.

The man standing looked like an older version of his nemesis on the armed services committee. When the man spoke in German, he realized that man must be Brown's father.

"Today is a historic day," Councilor Braun said.

While he spoke, he spun the sparkling striped pin. It looked very similar to Senator Brown's, but this one was not a U.S. flag. Instead it was simply the stripes, red and white. Braun stopped turning it, leaving it so the stripes were vertical.

"For too long, Germany has wilted under inaction. Well, no longer. With the vote of this council, the first move will be made. Germany will awaken. And together we will rid the country of its dead weight and race toward a future where Germany retakes its rightful role as a world leader.

"Now, vote yes to proclaim the withdrawal of American troops from German soil immediately."

"All in favor," Minister von Weiss said in an empty voice.

"*Ja!*"

The vote was a landslide. Chandler could not blink. His mouth hung open as he watched the men. They looked so much like his own committee had. Finally, he turned to look at the two men. The one still stood still, his face an emotionless mask. The other, however, beamed with pride.

"Let's go," Hans whispered.

Chandler nodded. Hans led him from the room. And the man with the emotionless face followed.

Once outside, Chandler quickly regained his composure.

"We have to go to Berlin," he said.

"Why?" Hans asked.

"To convince Parliament to overturn this."

Hans shook his head. "I fear it will be useless. They have no reason. There is enough sentiment, at the very least enough indifference. No one is going to take the side of the Americans."

"I have to try," Chandler said.

At that moment, a man approached from in front of them. He had a wild, lost look on his face. To Chandler's surprise, Hans stepped forward to greet the man.

"Herr Schmidt," Hans said, reaching out a hand.

"Who is this?" Schmidt asked, pointing at Chandler.

"This is Senator Chandler from the United States. He was here to observe the vote today."

"The vote," Schmidt said, spittle flying from his lips.

Hans looked at Chandler and shrugged. With his attention diverted, Schmidt pushed past Hans and stood nose to nose with Chandler.

"Maybe you can stop their madness," Schmidt said.

Schmidt handed Chandler an envelope and walked away. Chandler watched him for a second and then looked at Hans.

"What the hell was that?"

Hans shrugged. "Not sure. He did not look well. He is a prominent businessman here in Bonn." Hans paused. His eyes widened as if remembering something. "In fact, Herr Schmidt sits on Teleplunkt's board."

"What was he talking about, 'stop the madness'?"

"Something to do with the vote, it seems," Hans said.

Chandler turned around, trying to find Schmidt. But the man had disappeared.

Washington, D.C. 2009

Lauren sat in the dark. She half listened to the traffic rolling at intervals past the house. The headlights stretched odd shadows across the foyer.

"How could I have been so stupid?" she thought.

The past few years of her life filtered through her mind. Every moment with Mark seemed to replay itself in a broken parody of the happiness she had felt.

The door opened. Light slanted across the hardwood floor then a shadowed figure appeared. She watched in silence as a hand reached out to hit the light switch.

The light came on. Mark stood on the threshold. His eyes met hers. He took a step in, a question on his lips, but then came up short.

"Are you okay?" he whispered.

"You're with the FBI, aren't you?" she asked.

Mark's eyes widened.

"I should have realized it. I was so blind. Who can just walk into the FBI building and use a computer like we did." She shook her head. "Maybe I knew all along. Maybe I didn't want to know."

"I can explain," he whispered.

"How long did you think you could pull this off?" she asked, her tone lifeless.

"What do you mean?"

She stood, anger flaring. "Don't you dare play me for the fool anymore! You know what I'm talking about. How long did you think you could lie to me?"

"Lauren, I . . ."

Lauren stood up. She walked right up to Mark.

"You're a liar," she hissed. "Get out."

Mark took a step back. "It wasn't a lie, Lauren."

"What do you call it, then?" she asked.

"I didn't plan it this way. When I met you, it was all real."

"A real job, you mean. I was an assignment to you. I bet you and your little agent buddies had a good laugh about all this. You really *tailed* me, didn't you?" She barked out a sardonic laugh. "My father knew, didn't he? All along."

"I don't know," Mark said.

"I said, get out." She pushed him out the front door. "You can send someone for your stuff."

Once he was clear, she slammed the door in Mark's face. Fighting as hard as she could, she held back the tears until she had made it to her bedroom. Once there, she leaned against the wall and then slid to the ground. Her arms around her knees, she wept.

Later that day, Lauren's cell phone rang. Her heart jumped. When she pulled out her Blackberry, she paused for a second before looking at the number. When she saw it was her father's office, a renewed wave of sadness washed over her.

She took a deep breath, steadying her voice, then answered.

"Lauren?"

"Isaac?"

"Yes," he said.

"Have you heard from my dad?"

"I just got a call from him, yes," he said. "He asked me to call you."

Lauren closed her eyes. "Did he know?"

"Know what?"

"That my, that Mark was with the FBI?"

There was a pause before Isaac answered. "I honestly don't know. We knew you had an agent watching out for you. I don't think he knew who for sure."

She hung her head. "I wish you had told me."

"I'm sorry," Isaac said. "I really am."

She didn't say anything for a while. Neither did Isaac. Finally, he cleared his throat.

"Your father needs your help, Lauren."

She opened her eyes. "Is he in trouble?"

"No, but things are moving. Right before he called, I learned that somehow Senator Brown has pushed his resolution to the entire Senate for this afternoon. If he was able to do that, then there are more people who have been affected by this whole thing than we thought."

Lauren thought for a second. "Odd that you and dad weren't. Were you both taking the supplements I gave him?"

"I was," he said. "And I know your father was, too."

She thought for a second more. In her head, she went through her patient list. Although not scientific, she realized that people who had been taking the supplement had not developed cataracts while so many others had.

"You should get everyone there to start taking it," she said. "I doubt it will do anything for those already with the lenses, but it might forestall even more from getting cataracts."

"I'll do that. That's partially why I called. Your dad said that the same thing is going on in Germany. Some councilor there had a pin almost identical to Senator Brown's. And the Foreign Relations Council just signed a proclamation calling for the withdrawal of U.S. troops."

"The Bonn spike," she said.

"What?"

"Remember my initial research. We found a similar spike in Bonn. Whoever is behind this, I think we have a pretty good idea of what his agenda is. They've gotten a lot of people sick just to get U.S. troops out of Germany."

"I think that it's just the beginning," Isaac said. "Have you seen the news? Unrest is spreading like wildfire over there. I think this is just the first step. And if I'm right, a lot of people are about to get hurt, innocent people."

"People are already getting hurt," she said. "Cataracts are no joke. Just like any other procedure, people can die during surgery. And we've been putting a lens into the eye with some unknown additive. God only knows what that might do over time. And worse, until all those lenses are removed, tens of thousands, maybe hundreds of thousands of people are susceptible to mind control. If that got out, could you imagine what people could do? No one would be safe."

"That's why your father asked me to call," Isaac said. "He wants your help."

"My help?"

"Of course. You know more about what's going on than anyone."

She thought about Mark and the sadness crashed over her again. She pushed it back, though, focusing on Isaac's voice.

"He needs us to keep this Senate vote from going the wrong way this afternoon."

"How bad is it?" she asked. "How many people have had lenses?"

She thought about the numbers. She had already implanted over five hundred lenses in the past two years. Worse, she knew she operated less than any other ophthalmologist in the metro area. And if her theory was right, the supplements had forestalled the cataract development, at least for the time being. As she knew too well, most of her colleagues neither prescribed, nor believed in her methods.

"It's bad," she said. "Do you have any idea?"

Isaac cleared his throat again. "I've poked around. I know that over sixty senators have had surgery."

"Sixty!? How the hell hadn't someone noticed this before?"

Isaac didn't say anything. Lauren thought about it. She remembered something Dr. von Fricke had said to her. "It is a good time to be an ophthalmologist." Doctors were making a killing, Teleplunkt was making a killing. She guessed it was no wonder why no one had thought to question it.

"The pin is the key," she thought out loud. "It is the stimulus that triggers the chemical in the eye. I'm sure of it. It's either the drug that caused the cataracts or the lens. It must have had something to do with the intraocular lens, because the cataract was already washed out. Some of the people that voted against it, like my dad, didn't have cataracts. so no lenses. If we could come up with something that might counteract that stimulus, you'd at least have a fighting chance."

"Can you think of anything?" Isaac asked.

"Mind control isn't my specialty," she said.

Isaac laughed.

"What?" she asked.

"You always underestimate yourself, Lauren."

Her eyes widened as Isaac's words hit home. She had known him for years and never really progressed past pleasantries. But with one short sentence, he had hit deep into her core.

All her life she had underestimated herself. It had affected her confidence, her relationships, everything but her studies. That was what she had clung to her entire life, hard work and determination. But she had never given herself credit for anything else.

His words opened up her mind. Why couldn't she find a way to stop all this? She didn't need Mark, or her father, or a mentor, or a professor. She didn't even need a book. She just needed to think.

Vertical lines, what did they do to the eye? That was the key. But it was not just the lines. She thought about the day in her office. She had moved quickly and that, coupled with her shirt, had triggered her patient. She remembered her father saying that Senator Brown had turned the pin prior to everything turning weird.

So it was moving stripes. She thought about the eye. For normal vision the eye muscles had to move in unison. If one muscle was not working, double vision could occur.

Like the funhouse effect, or a top spinning with a design on the top, the movement of the horizontal lines could distort the brain's perception. She thought about what Dr. Peterhagen had said about the word color test. The pin must act similarly. It must distort the eye-brain connection, thus allowing the specific visual impulse to hypnotize the mind for at least a short time.

The answer lay in how the eye saw the stripes on the pin. What could alter that? Once she thought of it that way, the answer jumped out as if it had been waiting to be found.

"Polarized sunglasses," Lauren said.

"Sunglasses?" Isaac asked.

"That's it. If you can get some of the compromised senators to wear sunglasses for the vote, it might counteract the pin."

"I might be able to do that, but what kind of sunglasses?"

"Anything that is polarized," she said. "It should help the eyes counteract the funhouse effect caused by the stripes. It's that effect which leads to the mind control."

"Where could I . . . ?"

Lauren laughed. "I'll take care of that. You get them to agree to wear them."

"Deal."

Isaac sounded excited. She fed on his response. He trusted her. And she knew she was right. The thrill took the edge off of everything that had happened with Mark.

Feeling invigorated, Lauren hung up the phone. She rushed to her office and entered through the back door. Her office manager was still there. She looked up, surprised to see Lauren.

"I thought you were in clinic?" the office manager asked.

Without slowing down, she called over her shoulder.

"I canceled."

"That's twice in one month," she heard the manager call back.

Lauren reached the supply closet and took out a nondescript white cardboard box. Holding it under her arm, she raced out of the office again. Jumping into her Acura, she sped toward Capitol Hill.

Washington, D.C. 2009

Isaac guided Lauren into the Senate chamber. He found her a seat in the gallery and sat down next to her.

"I think I got enough but it is going to be close. I wish your father were here. We'll miss his vote. Did you bring the glasses?"

Smiling, Lauren showed Isaac the box. "Security made me open it. Gave me a funny look when they saw what was inside."

She reopened the box and pulled one of the glasses out. They were large, black and flimsy, the disposable lenses she gave out after patients had their eyes dilated. Looking at them, Isaac laughed.

"This is going to make the news," he said.

She handed him the box. He got up from his seat and scurried around the chamber. He approached over twenty senators. She could see him hand them the glasses, and the skeptical looks on their faces. But Isaac was persistent. With a pat to their shoulder, he was off to the next senator.

Just as he was heading back, the Senate was called into session. There was some debate on another bill. Lauren half-listened. She had been in the chamber many times and the newness had long ago worn off. Now, the monotony of the debate lulled her into thinking of other things.

Against her will, her mind returned to Mark. She had never felt comfortable with dating and relationships. Up until Mark, she had always been guarded, kept her wall up. She had let Mark in totally. And now she had been betrayed.

When she thought about it, though, it made no sense. Why would he fake a relationship with her? He was FBI. He could have tailed her without her even knowing. Why create such an elaborate lie?

Her heart reached for an explanation. Maybe he had fallen for her. Maybe their relationship had been real.

The hope made the pain all that much worse. Even if that was the case, she could never trust him again. And he hadn't even called her yet. She had to let go, learn from it, and move on. But her heart was broken.

Isaac tapped her on the shoulder, saving Lauren from her own thoughts.

"We're on," he said.

Lauren listened to the conversation. Senator Brown was given the floor. He stood before the Senate of the United States. The smug look on his face turned her stomach.

Before Senator Brown could speak, another senator stood. Lauren recognized him as her father's friend, the one she had treated.

"Senator Kerrington," the Senate Pro Tem acknowledged.

Senator Brown looked about to erupt. Before he could say anything, Senator Kerrington leaned forward and spoke into his microphone.

"It's bright in here, today," he said.

Smiling, Kerrington placed the large, flimsy disposable glasses over his eyes. Some of the senators laughed, but others followed suit. About twenty in all sat at their desks and slid the glasses over their ears, settling them in place.

Lauren watched Senator Brown. She saw his face turning red. The whites of his eyes showed as if foretelling an explosion of rage.

"This is an abomination," Brown roared.

The Senate Pro Tem banged his gavel. He was smiling when he said the floor was Senator Brown's.

Brown shuffled his feet. The smug look was gone, replaced by obvious discomfort. His soft fingers wrapped around the flashing pin on his lapel. He turned it, once, twice. Then he leaned forward to the microphone.

"Vote yes to the resolution."

Brown stood there for a second. Then he walked away. The vote was called. When the roll call reached the first of the senators wearing the absurd glasses, Lauren held her breath.

The senator looked absurd in the massive black glasses. Lauren noticed a ruckus behind her. The CSPAN cameras were jostling for a better view. This vote would surely make the networks.

"No," the senator said.

She looked to Brown, saw the look on his face. His hand lifted slowly and he touched the now useless pin. Then his eyes met hers. She ate his disappointment, his failure. It fueled her.

From there, the scene became comical. Every few votes, a senator wearing the glasses would lean forward and vote "no." In the end, the vote was 56-44. Lauren's heart raced.

"We did it," she said, yanking on Isaac's sleeve excitedly.

He smiled. "You mean, you did it."

Lauren walked out of the Capitol. As her steps took her down the massive stone stairs, her mind crackled like lightning. She had won on her own without anyone's help. And even better, she had not done it to make her father proud or to impress a mentor. She had done it for herself, and more importantly, for all those people made sick by those behind this.

At the same time the last few years of her life weighed down on her sense of accomplishment like a vest of chains. She had given herself to someone, trusted someone fully, only to find it had all been a lie. On top of that, she had thrust herself into an international incident where people had tried to take her life. It was like a new door opened inside her, leading to a world where her life as a doctor and professor had become the mundane.

Before she reached the bottom step, Lauren sensed someone approaching from behind. She tensed.

"Ms. Chandler," a man said behind her.

She turned to see Senator Brown. He stopped to close to her. She could feel his hot breath on her face when he spoke again.

"You've made a terrible mistake," he said.

She stood her ground. "I have no idea what you're talking about."

"Don't play stupid with me, young lady," he said. "I know you're behind what happened inside. What you don't realize is that you can't win. It's too late. Just go away before you get hurt."

"Hurt?" She laughed. "You've tried that already a couple of times. Hasn't worked out so great for you, has it?"

Brown's eyes flashed with rage. He grabbed her by the upper arm. "You have no idea."

Lauren tore her arm away from him. With her other hand, she pushed him away.

"You have no idea!" Her voice rang out. Passers-by paused, staring. "You disgust me. Who do you think you are?"

Brown's voice lowered to a whisper. He glanced around as the crowd started to disperse.

"Why do you care?" he said, obviously off balanced now. "This has nothing to do with you."

"Nothing to do with me?" She shook her head. "I'm a doctor, sir. I made an oath to protect and treat people in need. You've made thousands of people sick. Whatever your reasons are, it doesn't matter. You have to be stopped."

Brown laughed, a snide but not completely confident sound. "Such an idealist. But there are other doctors who feel very differently from you. And they've taken the same oath."

"I don't care about other doctors," she said. "I . . ."

"Oh, I think you're wrong," he interrupted. "You should follow the lead of your betters."

"What's that supposed to mean?"

"I think you know one of those doctors, someone who has been very prominent in our efforts. In fact, I think he's someone you know very well. Maybe you should go talk to him about all this. Then you'll see it a little clearer."

Senator Brown turned and walked quickly back up the steps. Lauren watched him go, her mind reeling.

When her phone rang, she nearly jumped. Distracted by her confrontation with Senator Brown, she answered it without looking at the number.

"Lauren," a gruff voice with a German accent said.

Her heart missed a beat. It was Dr. von Fricke. Everything Brown said returned in a flash. Someone she knew who had helped his cause! She thought back to the TeleLens symposiums. Dr. von Fricke had organized them. He had been Teleplunkt's advisor. How had she not seen it before? "Lauren, are you there?" he asked.

She didn't know what to say. Why would someone as prominent as Dr. von Fricke have totally disregarded his Hippocratic Oath? Money? Power?

"Hello," he said.

Lauren hung up. Her hand shook as she stared at the phone. She suddenly felt very alone. She had always trusted Dr. von Fricke.

She had trusted Mark, too. Anger mixed with her trepidations. She needed to act.

As a strange smile spread across her face, she dialed a number. There was one person who she was sure would love to help her deal with Dr. von Fricke.

"Dr. J. Edgar Connor's office," the receptionist answered.

"Hi Margie, this is Lauren Chandler, is Dr. Connor in?"

"Hold on a second," Marge said. "Let me see if he's available."

Lauren stared up at the Capitol. As she settled in to wait, Dr. Connor picked up the phone.

"Lauren, is that you?"

"Yes, hi, Dr. Connor. I know this is going to sound strange, but I need your help."

"I know all about it," he said.

"You do?" she asked, shocked.

"Yes," he said. "And you are in terrible danger. Can you get to my office?"

"Sure," she said. "I have my car."

"Go, hurry," he said.

"Okay, I . . ."

"Please trust me, Lauren. There isn't time. You must hurry."

Dr. Connor hung up. Lauren held her phone up for a moment, staring off at nothing. Suddenly she felt as if a hundred eyes were watching her. Putting her phone away, she walked quickly toward her car. When she went to put the keys into the ignition, she found her hands were shaking.

Bonn, Germany 2009

Benjamin Chandler stood holding the envelope in his hand. He looked at Hans.

"Teleplunkt?"

"Yes," Hans said. "A mid-sized electronics company in Frankfurt. Recently, they've gotten into the cataract lens business and have been doing . . ."

Chandler's eyebrows shot up. "Did you say cataract?"

"Yes."

The senator fingered the manila envelope in his hand. A board member of a German lens company had just handed him an envelope and disappeared right after the Foreign Minister's proclamation. It could be nothing, he thought. Or it could be exactly what he needed.

Chandler scanned the crowd. He found the man in the crisp black suit. He noted the other man, the dangerous looking one was not with him. He turned back to Hans.

"Hold this," he said.

Chandler handed the envelope to Hans and then pushed his way through the crowd. The man in the business suit saw him approached. The man turned as if looking for his friend, but then stepped forward to meet Chandler.

"Senator Chandler, I believe," the man said. "My name is Gerhardt Kugler."

They shook hands.

"I hear you're in the cataract lens business," Senator Chandler said.

"I am," Kugler answered with a smile. "It has been good to me lately."

Chandler frowned. "I'm sure it has. What brings you here today? Do you have an interest in foreign relations?"

"Everyone should, no?" Kugler said.

"I wonder, have you been to the States lately?"

Kugler shook his head. "Me? No. But I have colleagues there. In fact, one of my board members is a prominent ophthalmologist there. You may know him. His name is Dr. J Edgar Connor."

Chandler's eyes widened in surprise. A sudden jolt of panic shot through his body. In a moment of clarity, he realized his daughter was in great danger.

At the same moment, he felt something hard press against his lower back. He turned to see the other man, Kugler's missing companion, standing close behind him.

"Don't even flinch, Senator," the man hissed in his ears. "When I tell you, wave to your friend. Let him know everything is fine."

Kugler looked into Chandler's eyes.

"This is the last thing I wanted to do," Kugler said. "But we all must sacrifice for the greater good."

"What the?"

Chandler was cut off when the barrel of a gun jammed into his kidney.

"Now, wave and then follow us. Everything will be fine if you stay calm," the man said.

Before Chandler could react, Kugler leaned in closer.

"And if you don't, your daughter will be dead."

Defeated, Chandler motioned to Hans. His friend looked confused but the senator shook him off. With the gun still pressed into his back, and the fear for his daughter's life reaching a crescendo, Senator Benjamin Chandler followed Gerhardt Kugler away from the crowd and out of sight.

Baltimore, Maryland 2009

As Lauren drove down the familiar inner-city streets approaching Johns Hopkins University, she glanced nervously at her rear view mirror. For more than half of the drive, she had been sure someone was following her. She could never nail down the car, for it seemed to stay just out of sight. But as she drove, she had caught familiar movement in the mirror.

The entire drive, she had also struggled with what Dr. Connor had said on the phone. Could her mentor know everything? She recalled telling him about the cataract spike. He had said she was wasting her time.

She could not ignore his offer of help, no matter how suspicious she felt. She had no doubt that von Fricke was working with Teleplunkt and thus with Senator Brown. She also knew that they would never let her get away with fouling their vote in the Senate. If she didn't stop them now, they would surely stop her.

Lauren barreled down Wolfe toward the parking garage. She stopped just before crashing into the gate at the entrance. As the machine beeped at her to take a ticket, she stared out her rear view mirror waiting for whoever had been following her. When no one appeared, she drove into the shadowed belly of the parking garage.

The lot was full. She realized that it was visiting hours for the hospital. There were no open spaces until she reached the roof of the building. Cursing under her breath, she parked and jogged toward the lit exit signs.

Lauren reached the elevator and pushed the button. It did not light up. She hit it again. Nothing.

"Shit," she hissed.

Looking around, she found the stairwell. When she opened the door, however, she knew something was not right. The air had a thick, stagnant feel. With a last glance to the useless elevator, she stepped inside. The heavy door slammed shut behind her.

Lauren lowered her head, focusing on each step as she rushed down. Before she reached the first landing, she heard the sound of footsteps rising up toward her. She froze.

She knew who it was. It was the man that had been in her house, the man she had seen on the island, those dead eyes that stared up at her from the photo in the police office on Turks and Caicos.

And she knew that if he caught her, she would be dead.

A thin film of perspiration clung to Steinmetz forehead. Waiting three landings below, he listed to the sound of her feet on the stairs. His hand slipped into his front pocket. His fingers caressed the black silk stocking.

Excitement rolled up his spine, settling into the base of his brain. He knew it was over now. He would have her this time. If her uncanny ability to escape flared up, Steinmetz was prepared.

Even in America, there were those sympathetic to the cause. Most of them grew from a need to survive prison life, and it had not been hard for him to find them. When he asked them for help in finally snaring his prey, they had been more than willing to do just that.

He could not stop himself. He knew that he should wait for her to get closer, but he could hold back no longer. He climbed the stairs, intent on having Lauren Chandler.

Lauren knew she was in trouble. After returning to her house after the last scare, it had been in a shambles. The police had dug through her private belongings with a callousness that had shocked her.

It had been days later when the real fear struck. She had been getting dressed for a nice dinner with Mark. She was planning on meeting him in the city, a swanky place. This was all before she learned the truth about him.

That evening she had tried to find her best pair of stockings. She looked everywhere, but from the start, had known they were gone. Worse, she knew somehow that the police had not taken them. No, it had been the man who had hunted her for months.

Lauren moved. Surprising herself, she raced down to the next landing. The footsteps below quickened as well. Grunting, Lauren hit the exit door one level below, reentering the parking area. She broke into a run.

Weaving through the parked cars, she knew she had two strengths that had to carry her to safety. First, she was a runner. Her pursuer might be faster for a short time, but she had endurance. She had no doubt about that. Second, she knew this place. She had been there countless times. She had navigated this exact parking lot after going 36 hours without sleep.

Instinctively, she headed for the ramp. A car appeared as she rounded the dark tunnel. Breaks squealed and a horn roared. She veered around it and kept running.

She had two choices. She could stay with the ramp. It would take her to the street. But she would have to run across and down half a block to get to the hospital entrance.

Her other choice was to make a break for the raised skyway on the second level. The entrance was right next to the stairwell. If she could make it, she would be in the hospital, and there would be people everywhere, even on the ramp. She was sure she would be safe.

When she reached the second level, she chose the later. Breaking for it across the parking area, she was about thirty yards away from the skywalk when she saw him. The stairwell door opened and the man stepped out. Their eyes met. And what she saw in that moment frightened her to the core.

Baltimore, Maryland 2009

Steinmetz saw her. He stopped, his eyes widening and his mouth slowly falling open. The corners of his mouth rose, not in a smile, but more like a predator savoring the scent of its prey.

In that instance, his mind embraced the future. He saw himself grabbing her, embracing her like a lover. She would fight. The thought aroused him. He pictured taking her right where she stood, hurting her, devouring her.

An animalistic moan pushed through his parted lips. He took a step closer to her, then another and another. And he found her waiting there for him, as he knew she would.

Lauren stood her ground for a moment mesmerized by the expression on the man's face. Whoever had sent this animal after her had lost control of their tool. It was personal, an obsession, and something more.

For a second, she considered making a break for the skyway. Just as she readied for an all-or-nothing sprint, the man moved. He stepped toward her, and she paused.

She would have to make a run for the street. She knew that he might turn and use the stairwell and beat her to the first level. For a sickening moment, she felt trapped. But she knew beyond anything she had known before, that she could not lose.

Lauren moved. She broke for the ramp again. Just as she reached the downward bend, however, she stopped. Whirling around, she looked to see if the man had turned back to the stairwell.

What she saw made her blood run cold. He was running full speed toward her. His eyes burned with lust and hatred. When he saw her turn, it seemed to fuel his madness, as if he thought she could not bear the thought of leaving him behind.

Lauren ran. She tore down the ramp with everything she had. She could hear him behind her. When she saw the glow of the street ahead of her, her pace somehow quickened.

Adrenaline coursed through her body, not all born on the wings of fear. She was outrunning him. That realization made Lauren feel stronger than she ever had before. Alone, she was winning.

When she reached the street, she let out a triumphant scream. Turning toward the hospital, she knew she would make it there with time to spare. She was . . .

She sensed the movement around her before she saw them. It seemed to surround her, press her away from the hospital.

At first, it did not make sense: two strangers, both young men, both staring at her. Sensing the danger, she veered off.

Another one appeared in front of her. He was about the same age as the other. His head was shaved as well and a swastika had been tattooed to his forehead.

"Hey sweetheart," the one with the tattoo said. "We've been looking for you."

Lauren froze for an instant, shocked. She looked around. The sun had slid behind the surrounding buildings which cast a long shadow across the street. No longer running, she walked briskly across the street toward a small park that the students at the University called the Square.

It was usually bustling with people. When she reached it, however, she found the park frighteningly empty. The three men fanned out behind her.

"I'm talking to you," the man said.

Every muscle in Lauren's body tingled. Her breathing slowed but her heart continued to pound. She had nowhere to go but forward into the shadows of the Square.

The skinheads pushed closer. She could smell alcohol. Glancing back, she saw that the leader had pulled out a switchblade.

The path she followed toward the center of the Square came to a T in front of her. A sturdy bench blocked the way to the slightly overgrown section at the center of the park. She could hear the familiar fountain gurgling behind the brush.

Using her knowledge of the park, she laid out a plan. Slowing, Lauren allowed the men to get closer. Timing it right, she let them get so close that they could almost touch her just as she reached the intersection.

Lauren tilted her head as if about to turn to the right. Then she broke forward, right at the bench. Lifting her foot to the seat of the bench, she vaulted over the back. Landing cleanly, she broke into a sprint. When she hit the grass, though, the small heels of her shoes dug into the ground. Without breaking stride, she pulled the shoes off and ran barefoot through the brush and toward the center of the Square.

Lauren heard the skinheads behind her. When the sounds of pursuit grew closer, she glanced over a shoulder. Although she had easily outrun two of them, the leader was gaining fast.

Lauren banked down one of the narrow side paths. She wove between small trees, her quick movements gaining ground on the man. When she saw the kidney shaped fountain up ahead with a low wall surrounding it, she jumped into it. The man hesitated and then attempted to head her off by running around the outside. Seeing it, Lauren veered at a ninety degree angle and jumped back out of the fountain.

The skinhead stopped on the opposite side. A second later, he jumped into the water and crossed after her. Lauren ran back into the trees. By the time she heard him scrambling out of the fountain, she was deep into the darkest portion of the underbrush.

She was tired of running. She could have gone on forever but something inside her seemed to break in that instant. She would not be chased around; she would not be frightened.

With a quick dodge to the right, she took cover behind a shrub. She heard the man racing toward her. Fortune was with her and the skinhead passed full speed right by her.

Lauren clenched her teeth and struck. Spinning from behind the brush, she lashed out with her forearm. It struck the man's neck, clothes-lining him.

The force of the blow sent both of them off their feet. Lauren sat hard onto the wet grass and then rolled. A branch tore through her cheek; blood clouded her vision. She could just see the man fall onto his back coughing out a loud gag.

Lauren was up in a flash. She broke for the path and ran with everything she had back they way she had come. Breaking out of the underbrush, she hurdled the bench. The other skinheads stood there. Lauren raced past them, the puzzled expression on their face making her laugh, a feral sound full of adrenaline.

She was already on the sidewalk by the time the two skinheads were after her. Not slowing at all, she tore down Monument Street and into the safety of the hospital lobby.

Bonn, Germany 2009

The man with the gun pushed Chandler into a black luxury sedan parked in a dark tunnel under a busy raised highway. It was dark and when he fell into the seat, he felt someone sitting in the other seat. He caught a glimpse of the man who had handed him the envelope, Schmidt, sitting beside him before the door was closed. With the heavily tinted windows, the backseat returned to darkness.

Chandler had a second alone in the car with Schmidt.

"What was in the envelope?" he asked quickly.

Schmidt did not respond.

"Look, I'm not sure if you know just how much trouble we're in here. If there was anything in that envelope that could help us, we might have a chance here. My friend still . . ."

Chandler froze when the front door opened. Light poured into the back seat. He glanced over at Schmidt. That was when he saw the bullet hole in the middle of the man's forehead.

Kugler and his man got into the car. The man turned to look at him. Chandler saw death in those eyes as clearly as he had seen it sitting next to him in the car.

"Should I kill him?" the man said, lifting an antique Luger with a modern silencer screwed to the barrel.

"Not yet," Kugler said. "He may be useful. There is still his daughter to worry about. Have you gotten a hold of your man there?"

The other man shook his head. "I'll try one last time."

"If you don't reach him?" Kugler asked.

The man glanced back at Chandler. Otherwise, they seemed unconcerned with speaking in front of him. That fact chilled Chandler to the core.

"I have a team there tailing him. I'm sending them in to deal with him if he does not pick up this time."

"Excellent."

The man nodded and the car rolled out from under the tunnel and merged onto the autobahn. The man continued to stare at Chandler.

"If anyone hurts my daughter, I'll kill you," he said.

The man laughed. "I doubt that."

BALTIMORE, MARYLAND 2009

Limping toward Dr. Connor's office, she could feel the stares. She must have twisted her knee when she vaulted the bench. Also, blood rolled down the right side of her face, soaking into the collar of her jacket.

Someone approached her. When Lauren looked, it was her old friend Melanie.

"Are you all right?" Melanie asked.

Lauren stared at her. The anger she felt toward the woman reared up.

"Get out of my way," she hissed.

Melanie stepped back. Her eyes widened and her mouth moved, but no sound came out.

"You had an affair with my father," Lauren said. "Why?"

While Melanie fumbled for an answer, other pieces fell into place. Melanie had warned her not to publish the article. She had been there with Dr. von Fricke at the symposium.

But Lauren paused. Melanie had been there, but Dr. von Fricke had dismissed her. Dr. Connor had been at the symposium, too. And she would never forget the look on Melanie's face when she told her that the doctor had given her the position he had first offered to Lauren.

A simple thought crashed into her mind. She was so quick to assume that Dr. von Fricke had something to do with Teleplunkt. He did, but that did not mean he had anything to do with the cataracts. It dawned on Lauren in that instant that if Dr. von Fricke knew the truth, was enmeshed in whatever horrible scheme was behind it all, and had so fully turned his back on his Hippocratic Oath, would he put himself in the limelight?

Yet another betrayal engulfed Lauren. It had not been Dr. von Fricke at all. It had been Dr. Connor.

"Is he in there?" Lauren snapped, interrupting Melanie's sniveling and pointing at Connor's office.

"He is, but Lauren, don't."

Lauren ignored her. She rushed into the reception area for Connor's office. The receptionist desk was empty. Without pausing, she burst into his office.

Dr. Connor was sitting behind his desk. To Lauren's horror, the man hunting her stood beside him.

Steinmetz's phone rang. He barely heard it. Instead, he stared into her eyes. He feasted on the shock and fear.

To his surprise and delight, she lunged across the desk, not at him, but at Connor. Her mouth was open, a scream bubbling up from inside.

He hit her. The blow landed perfectly on the soft spot of her temple. The scream died inside as the girl's eyes rolled back. She fell limp across the top of the desk. Steinmetz's entire body tingled.

"This was ill advised," Dr. Connor said.

Steinmetz barely heard him. He barely heard the phone ringing in his pocket. He reached out to touch the girl but stopped himself. Not there, not in front of that pitiful traitor of a man.

The anticipation boiled up. He savored it, his hand reaching into his front pocket again, finding the stocking. He took a deep breath.

His phone rang again. He ignored it. Dr. Connor picked up his own phone and pressed a button.

"Can you bring up a wheelchair, please?" he asked, and then hung up. He looked at Steinmetz. "We can wheel her out to your car. I'll go with you, that way no one will be suspicious."

"Fine," Steinmetz said.

"Help me get her to the couch," Connor said.

Steinmetz stepped around the desk and picked the girl up. The heat of her body intoxicated him. Her shirt fell open, exposing a hint of her silky bra. He shuddered.

As he placed her lovingly on the couch, his finger traced the jagged gash across her cheek. A mixture of fresh and dried black blood came away. He rubbed it together with his thumb.

An orderly appeared at the open doorway, knocking on the jamb.

"Wheelchair's here, doctor."

"Thank you," Connor said.

The orderly glanced in at the girl on the couch. Steinmetz met the young man's eyes, who cowed under his gaze. The orderly left and he picked the girl up again. The blood on his fingers smeared across her blouse.

Steinmetz placed her in the wheelchair and Dr. Connor led him out of the office. They made it to the elevator without drawing too much attention. From there, it was a straight shot to the skywalk and the parking lot.

Steinmetz barely noticed that Connor followed him across to the garage. He was too busy planning out his next few hours. The girl stirred, which gave him a new thrill, and then something else reached him. It tore through the feelings of lust and anger, reaching his well trained and experienced instincts. He let go of the wheelchair.

There, ahead of him in the shadowed depth of the parking garage, he saw movement. Something about it was familiar. Although it was only a blur, he thought it must have been the girl's boyfriend.

Steinmetz paused for a moment. He glanced at the girl.

"Stay here with her," he barked at the doctor. "Do not let her wake up. Not yet."

When the doctor nodded, Steinmetz eased toward the parking garage, his back against the wall. Silently, he drew his gun, a Glock 9mm, and smiled.

Steinmetz stalked the parking garage. He followed the shadow up toward the higher levels. At one point, as whoever it was slipped into the stairwell and headed up, Steinmetz was almost positive it was the boyfriend. And from what he could tell, he had no idea Steinmetz was behind him.

By the time he slipped into the stairwell behind his prey, it was quiet. The lights had been cut off. Something about that put Steinmetz on edge, but it did not make sense. A professional might do something like that if they planned on ambushing someone. The boyfriend, on the other hand, was looking for them. It must have been just a coincidence.

As he climbed up the stairs, Steinmetz paused. He heard something below him. He was sure the boyfriend had headed up the stairs.

He had one second to consider it before a bullet ricocheted off the cinderblock wall inches away from his face.

Steinmetz dove. He had been standing three steps below a landing. Grabbing the railing, he vaulted over it, landing on the next flight up. Crouching, he peered down the well. He saw someone move and fired.

The sound of his Glock reverberated off the tight, solid walls. Steinmetz crawled up to the next landing. He leaned over again peering down, but saw nothing.

Suddenly the door behind his back swung open. Steinmetz rolled behind it, then kicked out with his foot. The door slammed into someone, who grunted in pain. Steinmetz kicked it again and then reached out with his gun. Without looking, he fired around the door twice. A minute later, blood oozed under the threshold.

Steinmetz did not move for another minute. The blood soaked into his pants. He waited, listening.

When he heard nothing, he cautiously peered around the half closed door. He sensed a corpse lying there but his eyes focused on the parking garage. He saw nothing. Still not looking at the body, he inched out from behind the door and looked down the well. He heard and saw nothing in that direction either.

Steinmetz examined the body. He noticed the two bullet holes, one in the face, one in the neck. They had been lucky hits considering he shot blind. Quickly, he rummaged through pockets. He found a wallet with no ID. Then he found a cell phone. It was locked.

It struck Steinmetz in that moment that things were not what he had assumed. Normal people, boyfriends, they carried ID and did not have locked cell phones. Professionals did that kind of thing, professionals like him.

Steinmetz shuffled back behind the relative cover of the door. Moving quickly but deftly, he pulled his own phone out. He noticed Becker had been trying to call him again. Shaking his head, he thought he understood everything.

He pulled a thin cord out of the back of his phone. It had a USB connection. When he tried it on the victim's phone, it fit. A second later, the phone unlocked. He accessed the most recent received call. Like he thought, it had come from Becker's cell.

Steinmetz rose to his feet. Becker had sent a team after him. That meant there would be another man nearby. He had figured as much. There was no way the man he had fired on below him could have reached the doorway on his flight so fast. But now he knew for sure.

In the silence he heard a door creaking open a flight below him. Steinmetz moved as silently as the assassin he was. He slid out over the corpse. Holding the door so it would not close quickly, he pulled the body out of the threshold and eased the door closed.

Quickly, he pulled off the man's jacket, a thin windbreaker the color of mud. The pants would take too long, so he left them.

Throwing the jacket on over his own, Steinmetz slowly opened the door again. Holding it open, he slid along it until only his shoulder and upper arm, all covered by the jacket, showed. He waited, not moving.

It only took a minute.

"Clear?" a man's voice came from below.

Steinmetz reached out with his arm and used the trained silent signal for a friendly to approach, a terse forward wave. He heard the footsteps approaching.

Taking a breath and holding it in, Steinmetz swung out from behind the door. The man's eyes widened when he saw it was not his partner. It was too late, though. Steinmetz leveled his Glock and fired. The bullet caught the man straight in the chest.

The agent fell backwards. Steinmetz charged out onto the stairs. He was over the man before he tumbled to the landing. His second shot struck right between the man's eyes.

Steinmetz let out his breath. He bent and found the second phone, accessing it the same way. He used it to phone Becker.

"Did you succeed," Becker said when he answered.

Steinmetz laughed. "I did. I have the girl. And when I'm done with her, I'm coming for you."

BALTIMORE, MARYLAND 2009

Lauren's eye flickered open. It was her right eye. Her left was swollen shut.

Her head pounded and the gash on her cheek pulled. Disoriented, she blinked but did not move her head. She sensed someone behind her and she vividly remembered seeing the man standing with Dr. Connor in his office.

All the betrayal, all the lies, built up inside her as she realized where she was. She was sitting in a wheelchair in the skywalk. How she had gotten there was beyond her. Regardless, she was not about to give up.

Breathing in slowly, silent, she leapt up from the chair. Spinning around, she lashed out with a fist. To her surprise, it caught Dr. Connor in the nose. He staggered back, equally hurt and startled.

"Bastard!" she screamed.

Connor bounced off the wall and then righted himself. He looked at Lauren for a second. His eyes told her everything. He was guilty and he was a coward. She was not surprised when he fled back toward the hospital.

For a second, she thought to follow. He would pay for what he did. She was sure of that. But the more immediate danger, however, was somewhere else. And she knew she had to get away.

She turned and ran toward the parking lot, checking her front pocket. Her car keys were still there. She would get to the top level and get out of there, then sort things out.

Before she reached the end of the skyway, however, he appeared. One second, she saw freedom and escape. The next, the man stood in front of her, blood staining his hands and the legs of his pants.

"Where are you going?" he asked, smiling.

Lauren froze. For a second she considered charging him, but then she noticed the gun extending from his blood-stained fingers. She started to back down the skyway toward the hospital.

"Not so fast," he said.

Lauren quickened her pace, still shuffling backwards and keeping an eye on Steinmetz. Then someone screamed behind her.

Lauren whirled around. A female resident stood a few feet away frozen and staring at the bloodied, armed man. There was a terrible clap like thunder and the woman flew backwards, blood spraying the wall.

Before Lauren could turn, an arm wrapped around her neck. She was dragged out of the skywalk and into the parking garage.

He had shot the resident. It had been so unbelievable when it happened that the fact finally dawned on her halfway up the stairwell. As she was dragged higher and higher, bent over and in a headlock, the true dread of the situation dawned on her. Something soft touched her cheek. Out of the corner of her eye, she saw her black silk stockings hanging half out of the man's pocket.

He was not going to just kill her. It would not be that easy. That fact gave her the resolve she needed. She would not go quietly. She would fight. If it meant she would be shot, so what. She now knew that it would be better than the fate the man had planned for her.

Up they went. His grip was like iron. It was not her chance yet. He would have to get her in a car, she assumed. When he did, she would strike, aim for his groin or his neck. Anywhere that might hurt.

As she was thinking about it, she stumbled. Looking down, a bloodied, mangled corpse was sprawled across the stairs. She cringed, nearly vomiting. But something caught her attention. A handgun rested beside one of the lifeless hands.

She had a chance. Obviously he was going through great lengths to take her alive for his own reasons. If she could get away from him, he might not shoot. Maybe she could get back to this place, grab the gun. A commanding voice silenced her plan.

"Let her go."

Lauren's heart missed a beat. The voice came from higher up the stairs. And she recognized it.

Struggling to look up, she saw Mark crouched behind a partially opened door. He had a gun in his hand and it was leveled at the man.

Just as suddenly, the man's gun was pressed against her temple. She was lurched up and thrust forward. The man pressed himself against her back, using her to shield him from Mark.

"Drop it or she dies," the man said in a calm voice.

Mark did not flinch. His gun pointed almost directly at her. The man seemed to sense the same thing. He moved his gun from her head and pointed it at Mark. There was a loud gunshot.

At first, she thought the man had fired at Mark. But what happened next was so fast that it blurred into one impossibly long second.

First, the man's arm, the one holding the gun, snapped back. Blood sprayed Lauren in the face. Mark had shot him. Then she was pushed forward, hard. Her forehead nearly struck the edge of one of the steps.

More gunfire erupted. She saw a bullet smash into the door. Mark appeared and fired again. No sooner than that, the man charged the door. Mark ducked back and the man slammed the door shut.

Lauren, still dazed from the blow to her head, let her body slide down two stairs. Her hand reached out, her eyes locked on the man. He turned to look at her but a bullet struck the door from the other side and he was forced to look away.

Her hand found the gun. Her fingers wrapped around it. Then the man was on her again. He yanked her up, one hand tearing at her chest as he pulled her toward the door. When he opened it, Mark was behind a car.

The man brought the gun up to Lauren's temple again. The burning hot metal touched her skin. It reeked of sulfur.

"I won't tell you again," the man said, cocking the gun.

Mark stood up. He lowered his gun. It dropped to the pavement.

The man did not pause. The second the gun slipped from Mark's fingers, his gun swung out. Mark seemed to know it was coming. He dove. The man fired.

The man never noticed the gun in Lauren's hand. He let go of her, charging after Mark, intent on killing him. She lifted the handgun and fired a single bullet into the back of his head. He dropped slowly. Red blood sprayed out through his matted hair. Lauren was surprised. Before that, she hadn't thought Steinmetz was human.

Bonn, Germany 2009

Kugler, sitting in the passenger side of the black sedan, glanced in the rearview mirror. He could just see the corner of Chandler's head. He took a deep breath and looked away.

How had it come to this? He held a senator of the United States captive while a rogue agent now held the man's daughter. On the brink of success, their well hidden plans were on the verge of being thrust out into the open.

"So what?" he thought. What if everyone learned the truth? Surely America would be outraged. Their self-righteous hypocrites would demand it. But what of the German people? They would stand behind him. He was sure of it. They would not care about the collateral damage. They would understand that he took the necessary steps to regain their pride, their strength, and ultimately, their rightful dominance.

Kugler reached up and tilted the mirror. He peered into Schmidt's lifeless eyes. Shaking his head, he looked at Becker.

"Kill him," Kugler said.

Becker did not look away from the road. "No."

"What?" Kugler asked, outraged.

"I said, 'no.'"

Kugler stared for a moment, unable to find the words to voice his anger. Becker spoke first.

"Steinmetz called."

"I know," Kugler said. "You said he had the girl, so it is over, now."

"'Fraid not," Becker said. "See, he has the girl, but he's not happy."

"What do you mean?"

Becker looked at Kugler for the first time. "He called from another agent's phone. One of the team I sent to kill him."

"So he knows?"

Becker nodded. "And he's coming here after us."

"Then you'll kill him," Kugler said.

"Yes, I will. But I can't guarantee what will happen with the girl. I have a plan. We are going to Frankfurt."

"Fine," Kugler said. "But what is the plan?"

"A little cat and mouse," Becker said with a grin.

Kugler looked suspicious. "Who's the mouse?"

Becker just laughed.

Baltimore, Maryland 2009

She sensed Mark coming toward her. Some part of her knew the drama, knew the anger she still felt, but that part of her laid buried under the weight of a single decision. She had pulled the trigger. She had taken a life.

Lauren had seen death before. She was not squeamish in the least. While others in her classes during medical school dreaded their first cadaver, she had found it interesting, nothing more.

But this was different. A single fire had burned inside of her, letting her risk everything to stop the madness she had discovered. She had taken an oath, and when she took it, she had meant it more than she had meant anything in her life. To some, she had learned, it may have been empty words. But to her it was a solemn oath to carry a mantle passed down from the dawn of civilization. That oath had been to revere and protect human life over everything else, even her own.

Mark touched her shoulder. She continued to stare at the dead man. A wisp of her black stocking still hung from the front pocket of his pants.

"You had to," Mark whispered.

She did not say anything.

"He was going to hurt you, Lauren. Bad."

She still did not respond. It was as if an endless hole opened up inside her and her soul teetered on the ledge. She knew that if she fell, she would never return. Mark seemed to know it, too.

"They have your father," he whispered.

The words echoed in her head. She remembered the day she had taken her oath. Why had it meant so much to her?

"If we don't do something, they are going to kill him," he said.

Her father, she tried to recall what she felt that day, that part of her life. It seemed so long ago. So much had happened, so much had changed. She had been alone, driven, and insecure. She used to have a burning need to make her father proud.

The oath had been the penultimate expression. To her, it had been the flag planted in the sand. It represented everything she had accomplished and it let her stand out from underneath his shadow.

Not any longer. She had found her strength. She had fought back and won, alone. Everything was different now. She clung to that, dragging herself away from the hole inside her. She looked at Mark.

"Where is he?"

"As far as I know, Germany," Mark said. "But I have to tell you something. I was here when Steinmetz, that's his name, killed those other men. I assume the head of Teleplunkt, Gerhardt Kugler, sent men to kill him. I heard Steinmetz tell them that he had you, and he was coming for them."

Lauren thought for a moment. "What do we do? If they are willing to kill their own men, why would they keep my father alive?"

Mark shook his head. "I don't know. I can hope that they haven't killed him yet because they didn't have you. But he told them he did."

Lauren frowned. "We need to make them think he doesn't. Then somehow, we need to get over there and find him before it's too late."

Before Mark could say anything, a phone rang. Lauren looked around. It was coming from the dead man, Steinmetz.

"Get it," she said to Mark. "Maybe they'll think it's him."

Mark found the phone and pulled it out of the corpse's pocket. When he answered on speaker, he did not say anything.

"Hello, Steinmetz," an icy voice said. "I have a deal for you."

Mark grunted.

"Our employer called the hit on you," the man said. "Against my advice. If you give me the girl, I'll give you Kugler."

"How?" Mark whispered.

There was a pause. "Are you okay? You sound injured."

Mark laughed.

"Oh," the man said. "Was I interrupting something with your prisoner?" He laughed. "I want her alive, though. Otherwise, I don't care. Listen, there is a Teleplunkt jet at BWI. Our American board member is flying over here. He's in a terrible rush." He laughed again. "Get her to the airport and on that jet. I'll meet you in the factory in Germany. You hand me the girl and I'll give you Kugler."

Mark looked at Lauren. "The father?"

"Senator Chandler? He's alive. Why do you care?"

"I'll be there."

Mark hung up.

"How do we get on the jet?" Lauren asked. "If we try, he'll know."

"Don't forget." Mark smiled. "I have friends."

Lauren frowned. "How could I forget?"

Mark had made the phone call from the parking garage. He led Lauren, who found it hard to make eye contact with him, to a large, dark colored sedan, the prototypical unmarked police car. He opened the passenger door and she got in without a word. As they raced toward the airport, she glanced at him. He looked sad.

"Thank you for helping me," she said.

"You're welcome. I was worried."

"You were tailing me again, weren't you?"

He nodded.

"Still on the job, huh?"

"Actually, no. I was on my way to Germany. Your father is good at giving people the slip, it seems. The agency was none too happy with the agent who let your dad get out of the country without him knowing. Seems they demoted him and promoted me. I was told to go find him and bring him back. They thought there was only one assassin."

Lauren's eyes flashed. "Why didn't you?" she snapped. "You could have protected him."

"I bowed out, Lauren. Someone else, a good agent, went."

"What do you mean you bowed out?"

"I didn't accept the promotion."

"What? Why?"

"Because," he said, looking away, "I should never have fallen for you. It was unprofessional."

She snorted. "Oh, you shouldn't have *fallen* for me? Lying was fine, though."

"That's not what I meant."

"It was you, all those years ago," she said.

"What?"

"When my car was broken into, and that lady was hassling me."

Mark blinked. "Yes."

"You lied about that, too."

"I know. It was just, when I saw you, I lost my head. I mean, what were the odds it would be you?"

"That whole thing at the beach, what was that? Some kind of entrapment? Or was it just a cheap thrill for you?"

"No, not at all. The higher ups suggested it. They thought that if you saw me there, you'd feel comfortable. So if you accidentally saw me at another time, it wouldn't tip you off."

"So it was an order, huh?"

"It was so much more than that. I know I was wrong, but when I saw you, and recognized you, I just . . ."

"Where they even your books in that house?"

He looked at her. She had never seen a man look so forlorn. He shook his head.

"You disgust me, Mark," she said. "I'm going to do what I need to do to save my father, but stay away from me when this is all done. I don't want to see you again."

"I understand," he said. "I just . . ."

He never finished. And she had no idea it was one of the last times she would hear his voice.

By the time they reached the Baltimore-Washington International Airport, there was an escort waiting for them in a black Lincoln. Mark followed the car out onto the tarmac toward a sleek white jet that sat alone on the runway reflecting the brilliant colors of the sunset.

As Lauren looked at the plane, she sighed. The entire drive to the airport, she had said nothing. She had not even looked at Mark. He had tried to talk to her once, but she had put a hand up, stopping him before he could start.

Their car came to a stop behind the Lincoln. A wheeled staircase led up to the plane's entrance. Two agents were escorting a man down the stairs. Lauren guessed that was the pilot.

Mark got out and Lauren followed him, still not making eye contact. The driver of the Lincoln waited for them. He was dressed in a black suit with a black tie. He wore dark sunglasses.

"We have a pilot on the way. We'll borrow our friend's clothes." He pointed at the man being escorted from the plane. "We have some people over there that . . ."

Mark interrupted the agent. "Look, we need to make sure they don't think something's wrong. The senator's life is at stake. Once we take off, keep everyone back."

The agent nodded. "That's the plan. But they'll be there when you need them."

"Excellent."

He handed Mark a packet. "Inside is the map to the factory and passports. We're getting a passenger off, then you two can board."

Lauren saw another agent appear at the hatch of the plane. He helped someone over the threshold. She smiled. It was Dr. J. Edgar Connor.

Lauren walked past Mark and the agent. She heard them protest but ignored it. Instead, she met Dr. Connor at the bottom of the stairs.

"Were you going somewhere?" she asked, a smug grin on her face.

Dr. Connor would not even look at her. He hung his head and was led past. Lauren turned around.

"I'll see you when I get back," she said.

The other agent approached her from behind.

"Seems he's been in on it from the start. According to what he said inside, his mother left Germany after the war. She told him story after story about his birthright. Did you know that the J in his name stood for Johan?"

She shook her head.

"Anyway," the agent said. "His chance came to make his mother proud. Gerhardt Kugler contacted him with his plan. Seems Connor was more than ready to betray his country."

"And his oath," Lauren added.

The agent looked confused. She turned back toward the plane. A surprising excitement took over her. She walked briskly up the stairs and into the jet. To her right the fuselage opened up into a comfortable seating area with white leather swivel chairs and two plush couches. A large flat screen television took up most of a three-quarter wall to the rear. She sat down.

A minute later Mark entered. He took a seat across the aisle from her. They sat in silence as the new pilot arrived. He told them they were cleared for take-off. Not long after that, they were flying high above the Atlantic heading for Frankfurt.

FRANKFURT, GERMANY 2009

The plane landed without incident. They made it through an abbreviated customs and hired a car to take them to a hotel near the Teleplunkt plant in Frankfurt. Mark put the room under a fake name, the one on his passport; and Lauren, uncomfortable for the first time, followed him up.

Inside the room, Mark sat down in the high-backed leather office chair beside the small desk by the window. He pulled out the cell phone he had taken from Steinmetz and placed it on the surface.

"Now, we wait," he said. "They'll know the plane landed by now, even though there was a routing "mistake" at the airport. They'll think their man was behind that. I figure they will set up a meeting at the factory. I'm going out once it gets dark to check it out, see if I can find a way inside."

"So, what do we do once they call?" she asked.

"We set the meeting."

"We can't just show up at it. They're expecting me, but not you," she said.

"That part I'm still working out."

"What if I showed up alone?" she asked.

"I think they'd kill you and your father."

"Would they?" She gave herself a minute to think. "Go with me here. What if I go in and tell them something like Steinmetz is prepared to go to the police if we don't call him within an hour. If anything happens to me or my father, it all goes public. I tell them that we are walking out."

Mark shook his head. "Too risky. Look, we haven't even been able to find out who this man is that's calling the shots. We know Kugler, and I do believe he's the one behind this plot. But he's not the muscle. This guy on the phone is. And whoever he is, he's professional enough not to be in the FBI or CIA databases."

"That's why this might just work. It's like playing cards. You can't bluff a clueless player. He'll never see the signs. But a pro, they can be bluffed. If we can just guess his most likely reaction, we can be ready for it."

Mark scratched at the stubble on his chin. "If I can find a way in, I can probably get a strike force inside the plant without anyone knowing. The German authorities have agreed to lend us agents. It's risky, but I'll be careful. If it doesn't look good, I'll abort.

"My guess is that this guy will never let you leave the plant, but he will be taken off guard. Something must have gone wrong with this Steinmetz for him to send a kill squad after him."

She blushed. "I think he got obsessed with me."

"What?"

"When he grabbed me, he had a pair of my stockings in his front pocket."

Mark laughed, but there was no humor to the sound. "So this guy must think Steinmetz is unbalanced at the very least. So the story would be believable. But he might know what you know. If that's the case, he'll call Steinmetz's bluff."

"How, though?" she asked.

"He'll grab you and your father. He'll assume Steinmetz doesn't have the proof."

"But he'll have to do it fast. What if I'm armed?"

"Lauren," Mark said in disbelief. "That's not legal. I know you're still dealing with what happened in the garage."

"Not a gun," she said with a smile. "Something else."

Mark had only been gone for a minute before someone knocked. Lauren's heart missed a beat. She inched toward the door trying to make no sound at all. When she peered through the keyhole, she saw the pilot from the plane. Someone stood beside him, an older, frowning gentleman with white balding hair.

Lauren did not know what to do. Before she could react, however, the door opened. The pilot walked in.

"Ms. Chandler, Mark sent me up," he said.

She looked at him with open suspicion.

"This is Hans Krauss. He is a colleague of your father. He came to us and we thought you should see what he has."

The older man walked in. He looked at Lauren with a shy smile.

"You look like your father," he said in practiced English. "He is a good man. I hope he is all right."

"Me, too," Lauren said, still off balanced.

"This may help you," Hans said.

He handed Lauren a manila packet.

"What is it?" she asked.

"Have a look."

Lauren opened the packet. At first she did not understand what she saw. There were a few pages typed in Asian. They looked to be a government report. After that, though, she recognized the statin formula she and Mark had found.

Her heart raced as her fingers picked through the papers. She saw the entire story unfold in undeniable proof. She had been right about everything, the cataracts, the lenses, the company, Dr. Connor, everything. The final piece of her plan had just fallen into her lap.

"Someone gave this to your father before he disappeared."

"What happened to my dad?"

Hans frowned. "He went to speak to a businessman, Gerhardt Kugler."

"Of Teleplunkt," Lauren said. "He must have figured it out, too." She turned to the pilot. "Can you get copies of this made and sent back to the States and to the German authorities in Berlin? And bring me back the original."

The agent nodded. She handed him the packet and he left. She smiled, but saw the look of concern on Hans' face.

"Don't worry," she said. "I'm going to get him back."

They called that night. Mark was at the plant. He had called her to let her know that the meeting was set for five o'clock that morning. He would have a team in the plant. She had to do what she could to move the meeting to the main factory floor. The rest was up to Lauren.

Lauren had what she needed. She placed it in the pocket of her jacket. Through everything that happened, she still had three pairs of the disposable shades with her. She left two at the hotel but put one on top of her head. She hoped everyone assumed they were normal sunglasses. She also tucked the manila envelope under her shirt.

She took a cab to the plant. When she reached security, she boldly announced who she was and that she was there on Steinmetz's behalf. They briskly ushered her toward a small security room. She balked.

"No," she said firmly. "To the factory floor."

The guard shook his head. Everything hinged on that moment. She knew that if they got her to a secure room, she was dead. All she could do was what she did best.

Lauren stumbled. The guard reached out to steady her. Prone like that, he was an easy target. She swung her arm down with everything she had. Her fist landed full force in the man's groin. She was off running before he doubled over in pain.

Lauren pulled out her phone as she ran through a dimly lit hallway. She dialed Mark. He didn't answer.

She had to find the factory floor. Slowing down, controlling her breathing, she tried to listen. A loud pressing sound filtered to her from ahead. She raced in that direction.

When she slammed open a set of double doors, the sound assaulted her like a slap to the head. She staggered back a little then rushed forward. When she reached the middle of the floor, she looked around.

Lauren had been to lens manufacturing plants before. They were generally well kept and clean. But this site took her breath away. The entire area was painted a pristine white. It looked so fresh that she assumed they must have meticulously cleaned it every day.

The machines lining the floor sparkled, their untarnished surfaces reflecting the bright lights above into tiny little prisms. She could tell everything was state of the art.

Near the far wall, just below a low hanging catwalk, she noticed a large white vat. Even to her limited knowledge, it looked out of place. She patted the front of her shirt where she had hidden her copy of the packet Hans had given her. She thought about the writing in an Asian language, and what Dr. Peterhagen had told her about the work the North Koreans had done on mind control. That vat, she was sure of it, held the chemical that made all of this possible. It was huge, towering over her like something out of a kid's nightmare. She shivered.

From behind her, she heard a commotion. Security officers, led by the one she had hit, rushed onto the floor. Lauren started to run further down the line. She caught movement on the catwalk above. She saw an older man in an expensive suit standing next to someone that looked more shadow than human. Then she saw her father standing behind them, straight and tall.

Lauren broke for a stairway leading up. She raced to the top well ahead of security. The older man took a step back and the ominous one moved forward.

"Call them off," Lauren said.

"Why should I?" the man said, smiling.

"Steinmetz sent me alone," she said, her voice quivering as she had practiced. "He told me to tell you that he'll go public with this whole thing. He's got the proof. If you don't listen to his demands, it goes to every major media in the U.S. and Germany."

The man did not react. The smile stayed on his face as he stared at Lauren. She felt that if she made even the slightest wrong move, he would know. She and her father would be dead.

She was about to speak when everything fell apart. Her mouth opened, but before any words came out, the sound of gunfire erupted. It came from somewhere further inside the factory. Someone screamed.

The man did not hesitate. He raced across the catwalk and seized Lauren before she could flinch. She struggled and he yanked her arm behind her back. A searing pan shot up her shoulder but that was not what stopped her. The manila packet came close to falling out of her pants. She could not let him see that, not yet.

Lauren let herself be dragged over toward her father, who pushed past the older man. He came up to Lauren and they hugged awkwardly. The man tore them apart.

"Take this," the man said to Kugler. The man gave him a handgun from a holster on his ankle. "Watch these two. I'll see what is going on."

More gunfire sounded as the man walked slowly away down the catwalk, his gun pointing downward. Lauren watched him go, knowing the time was not right. Not yet.

Kugler pointed the gun at the girl and her father. He watched Becker walk away. Something inside him knew things were not right.

When he started all of this, he knew violence could erupt. He was not so naïve to think he could ouster a world power without bloodshed. But he had not expected it in his factory, at least not so soon.

The gunfire flared again, this time closer. A door right below where he stood flung open. The security that had followed the girl in, three of his best, still stood on the floor. They pulled their guns and fired. Bullets struck metal right below his feet. Kugler threw himself against the wall, forgetting his prisoners for a second.

One of his officers went down, then another. A single man raced from the door below them. He rolled behind a set of crates. He fired again and the last security officer when down.

Kugler watched the man below. Where he hid behind the crates, Kugler had a clear shot. He took it.

When Mark burst onto the floor and shot the security guards, Lauren knew it was too soon. The strike team must have been seen. Now, she was stuck on the walk with Kugler and the other man, both armed, and Mark was alone below them.

Lauren saw Kugler level his gun. She lunged, striking him in the back just as he pulled the trigger. The bullet whirred into empty space.

Mark looked up at her. Their eyes met.

"Lau . . .

A gun fired. Mark's head whipped back. Blood shot from his throat as he fell behind the crates. Lauren screamed.

Benjamin Chandler recognized the man on the floor. It was his daughter's boyfriend. He was confused, but then remembered. If his earlier suspicions had been correct, the man was her FBI security detail as well. For the first time since seeing Lauren on the floor, a sliver of hope returned.

He heard the shot and saw the young man, he couldn't remember his name, take the bullet to his throat. His daughter screamed and he could feel her heart breaking.

Kugler struck her in the face. Lauren fell backwards. Anger boiled up inside Chandler. He lashed out.

He was on Kugler before the man had turned all the way around. The two fell to the catwalk. Chandler clawed at the gun in Kugler's hand.

The struggled went on. Kugler pushed against Chandler, bringing the gun nearly around to point at the senator's chest. Chandler growled and slammed the hand down. The gun popped free and rasped across the catwalk.

Chandler punched Kugler on the jaw. He lurched for the gun. His fingers touched the grip just as a foot came down on the barrel. Chandler looked up to see the other man, the one Kugler called Becker, glaring down at him. The muzzle of his Lugar aimed at the senator's head.

Chandler let go. Becker kicked him in the ribs. He groaned in pain, his only thought that he had utterly failed his daughter.

Lauren missed her chance. Kugler's gun was on the ground. The other man was close. It was time for her to act. But she couldn't.

Mark was dead, or at least dying. When the man kicked her father, she crumbled to her knees, grabbing her dad, making sure he was okay. Out of the corner of her eye, she saw the man pick up the other gun. The moment had passed. Worse, she knew there may not be another.

Absently, she reached up and touched her hair. The sunglasses were still there. She helped her father to his feet.

"Steinmetz, huh?" the man said, laughing. "You killed him, didn't you? I see it in your eyes. It's a shame I have to kill you now. I'd hire you in a second."

Lauren stared into the man's dead eyes. "Let us go."

"Can't do that," he said.

It was her turn to smile. "You can. There's no reason not to now. See, we know everything."

Slowly Lauren pulled the manila envelope out of her pants.

"It's all in here, the North Korean report, the secret board meetings. Your American member is already in custody. And this packet has been sent back to the States and to Berlin. The game's up. Let us go."

Kugler looked stricken. Lauren was shocked to see a look of recognition in the man's eyes. As if he had seen the envelope before. Kugler's face pleaded with the other man who paid him no attention at all.

"What will we do?" Kugler said. "This is too soon. We're not ready."

The man laughed. "I still can't let you live, sweetheart."

"Why?"

"Because, you know who I am. I can't let that happen. I have a business of my own, you know, one far more deadly than any of this."

Lauren knew she was about to die. It was now or never. Reaching, she scratched her head. The sunglasses fell down over her eyes. She acted like it was a nervous accident. With one hand, she moved to push them up. With the other, however, she took a small black disk out of her pocket. She activated it and dropped it to the floor in front of the other man.

FRANKFURT, GERMANY 2009

Kugler watched the black disk fall to the ground. He had no idea what it was. When it hit, though, the entire world turned a burning white. Pain lashed through his eyes into his brain. He screamed and covered his eyes.

The flash grenade, compliments of the FBI, detonated perfectly. She closed her eyes, not one hundred percent sure the glasses would be enough. At the same time, she grabbed her father and broke for the stairs.

A gun fired behind her. The bullet hit the railing ten feet away. Lauren threw the glasses off and pushed her father on. He moved awkwardly blinded by the flash.

Guiding him quickly down the stairs, she knew she had only a moment more. Looking over her shoulder, she saw the man with the gun rubbing at his eyes. His vision would clear. Hopefully it would be enough time.

When they reached the floor, she pushed her father forward. Another shot fired from above. This one sounded as if it was closer. Lauren looked at Mark.

His body was draped over the crates. Blood pooled on the floor. She looked at her father, then up at the cat walk. They had a minute at most.

"Go, dad," she screamed. "Run straight ahead. Don't stop until you run into something."

"Are you?"

"GO!"

She pushed him. He staggered across the floor, running in the general direction of the door. Lauren watched for a second and then turned around. She rushed to Mark.

Even before she reached him, she heard a gurgling noise. Mark's eyes were open. He was looking at her. A tear rolled down his cheeks.

He made a louder gurgling sound, as if trying to talk. She fell to her knees beside him, one hand gently caressing his bloodied cheek.

"Shhh," she said.

He got more agitated. He tried to push himself up. His face screwed up in concentration, he coughed out a word.

"Run!"

She shook her head. She went to work on the bullet wound to his neck, a serene smile on her face.

Lauren had no idea how close she came to dying. She applied pressure to Mark's wound and assessed that the bullet had missed his jugular but crushed his windpipe. He needed a tracheotomy. Going through his pockets, she found the utility knife she had given him so many months before.

Her heart missed a beat as she stared at the knife. It felt heavy and safe in her hand. And in that moment, more than anything, she needed to save Mark.

But she needed some kind of tube. Mark struggled to breath. Lauren bent over. She put her finger into the wound and found his trachea. She did mouth-to-windpipe resuscitation, warm blood dampening her cheeks.

The trachea cleared somewhat. She stood, looking around. She had to find something that would keep him from drowning in his own blood.

She used his collar to press the wound gently, hoping to stem the blood as best she could. She realized it was not coming from a main vessel. She propped herself on her knees, rapidly surveying the scene, trying to find something that would keep him from drowning on his own blood while establishing an airway.

She bent down. At the same instant, a gun fired. She felt something like fire burn through her shoulder. It was followed by an intense pain. It had been like someone hit her bone with a sledge hammer. She staggered but did not fall.

Lauren looked up. The man with the dead eyes stood on the catwalk. He was looking at her father, who was pulling open the door at the end of the floor. He fired but it was too late. Her dad was safe.

Suddenly the door below the catwalk opened again. Three agents from Mark's strike force rushed in. Lauren pointed up at the catwalk. Becker saw the agents first. He disappeared. So did Kugler. Two agents raced up the catwalk. They had to retreat under a hailstorm of gunfire.

Lauren looked at the machines still whirring and chugging in full motion. Her mind searched for something to help Mark. But she also realized she stood among the source. The place, she knew now, would be silent soon. She had won, but at what cost.

Then she saw the lens press. A sheet of plastic, clear as air, fed into the machine, set to be pressed into the tiny lenses needed for surgery. She looked at the raw film and she had it.

She motioned for one of the agents. The man came over.

"You've been shot," he said.

"Later," she snapped. "Get me one some of that plastic."

The man looked confused. "Pardon?" he said in a thick German accent.

Frustrated, she motioned toward the press. "The plastic, the clear film."

"Ah," the man said.

He rushed over to the press. Mark convulsed. She looked down and found he was having trouble breathing again. Taking the knife, she opened the ragged wound to the trachea. Clearing the pipe, she breathed into his throat again. He calmed.

While Lauren worked, the other two agents chased after Becker and Kugler. The third returned with a large piece of plastic. Lauren took it and cut it with Mark's knife into a usable piece. She rolled the still warm plastic into a cylinder. Piercing the trachea, she slid the plastic tube into place. Mark's eyes fluttered as clean, dry air reached his lungs.

Pressing lightly on the wound, she leaned forward and whispered into his ear.

"Everything is going to be okay."

Gerhardt Kugler sat in his conference room. The sun had set and the office was quiet. A single desk lamp glowed, illuminating one side of his worn face.

He looked up at the portrait of his father. It hung askew, as if the building had just survived an earthquake. His father's eyes seemed to stare back at him, mocking but not surprised. "How could you ever have thought to better me, boy?" it seemed to say.

Kugler rose, the chair shooting out behind him. He grabbed the heavy painting and swung it down atop one of the chairs. The oil covered canvas tore. Kugler slammed it down again and again until he fell exhausted into his chair.

The cleaning crew had arrived minutes before. He could hear them shuffling about, performing their menial tasks like lifeless golems. They sickened him. His stomach turned as he scratched at the day-old beard on his chin.

Everything had been lost. Becker had disappeared. The board had scattered. He was alone waiting, knowing the end had come.

As he stared into the gloom, a figured appeared at his door. At first, he thought they had come for him at last. When the person stepped into the light though, it was a cleaning lady.

Kugler stared at her. She wore the burqa of a Muslim. The black silk hid everything but her eyes. And she stared back at him. Although he knew it was impossible, he was sure it was the same woman from long ago.

"What do you want?" he hissed.

The hint of a smile appeared in her eyes. "Just to take away the trash."

Kugler's face burned red. He stood up. As he did, he saw the men crossing through the receptionist area. There were three of them, German police. He sighed and fell back down into his chair.

The woman hummed as she dumped his waste basket into a clear plastic bag. She turned her back on Kugler and walked away.

Becker stood across the street. He watched the police dragging Kugler out of his building like a common criminal. He smiled.

It had been a good job, he thought. Ultimately, though, the fun was over. The TeleLens was off the market. Teleplunkt would be disbanded. His paramilitary soldiers were slipping back into the obscurity of common criminals. Water purifiers were recommended for Bonn residents for the next three months and the water system was being filtered as well.

Even in America, it was over. Senator Brown was impeached and was being tried in civil court for taking bribes. And Kugler's buddy Dr. Connor had been disgraced. As for Becker, there would be other jobs. The only thing he truly regretted was killing his only friend, Walter. Maybe he would pay Alexandra a courtesy call. Picking up the scarred Anvil case, he walked away into the rising sun.

Washington, D.C. 2010

The Washington Monument rose into the sky, pointing up at the billowy white clouds rolling by. Lauren Chandler hit her stride as she ran along the reflecting pool outside the Lincoln Memorial. Glancing out across the sparkling water, it hit her.

Since returning from Germany, she had walked along the familiar path of her life in a kind of daze. It was as if she was trying to convince herself that everything was the same. But it wasn't.

Normally, her run would take her along the familiar route followed by tourists. Instead, she veered off the path. Her legs guided her down a side street, deeper into the more populated area of the city. The stunning architecture of the mall was replaced by shuttered windows and barred doors.

Lauren could feel the eyes on her as she passed the Civic Center. Her shoulder throbbed. She reached up and touched the scar through her clothes. The bullet had come out clean but the wound still bothered her on occasion.

Another turn and she raced down a street where people ran for far higher stakes than just exercise. When she saw a young man standing on the corner, her heart beat faster. Adrenaline coursed through her veins. She devoured the rush.

The young man took notice. He stepped out into the center of the sidewalk. His eyes glowed with a mixture of malice and entertainment.

"You musta taken a wrong turn," he said. White teeth flashed in a dangerous smile.

Lauren met the man's eyes. She ran straight at him. With everything she had been through, one guy wasn't a challenge any more. She pushed forward.

"Excuse me," she said.

The confidence behind her words opened a path. She jogged past him, so close that she brushed against his side.

Then she was past. She heard him say, "Damn." He laughed, but she could hear the respect in his tone. Lauren smiled.

The sun was setting behind the drab row homes that lined the street. She felt as light as air, as if she could run another twenty miles with no problem. Relishing the high, she let her mind totally relax. And for the first time since returning, she thought about Mark.

He had survived but may have lost the ability to speak forever. He was in line to get the first tracheal transplant. The only up side to the whole thing happened when he got back. His friends at the FBI hunted down the crooked Baltimore cop who shot him. The man was now facing some serious jail time.

She still felt awful for Mark but the intellectual side of her mind told her to forget him. How could she ever trust him again? Their entire relationship had been based on a lie. He had ample opportunity to come clean with her but he never did. On the other hand, how could she forget him after they spent what felt like a lifetime together dealing with an international crisis?

Yet there was another part of her that re-opened with the adrenaline. That part yearned to return to the excitement of the chase. She relived those final moments, when she thought Becker would kill her. To her surprise, there was no fear, no revulsion, only a strange yearning.

That side of her just might be able to forgive Mark.

As if in answer, her BlackBerry rang. Slowing down, she fished it out of the pouch in her running jacket. She recognized the number immediately.

"Hello."

"Hi," Mark said, but it was not his voice. It was the robotic buzz of a synthesizer pressed up against his trachea. It took a moment to get used to it.

She came to a stop. "Hi."

Lauren watched the sky ease toward night. The purple and rose streaks cut between the darkening silhouettes of the squat brick buildings across the street. She took a deep breath.

"Where are you?" he asked.

"Washington," she said.

"Oh," he said. "What are your plans? I heard you could be moving to Baltimore."

"I don't think so," she said. "I like Bethesda. But Hopkins offered me a clinical academic position."

"Really," he said. "That's great. You'll do great."

She closed her eyes. "I don't think I'm going to take it."

"No?"

"I'm not sure. I might travel instead. The NIH approached me about heading up a cataract team heading to Darfur. We're obviously using new lenses. I may join the part time faculty at Hopkins when I get back. But this is my home."

"Darfur? Wow." He paused. "You guys looking for a security detail?"

She smiled. "Darfur is a dangerous place."

"It is. Did you see the news?"

She knew what he was talking about. The Pentagon was already withdrawing troops from Germany and redeploying them in Afghanistan. If she didn't know better, she might have thought they lost. But the real battle had nothing to do with politics. It had to do with life, and an oath taken a long time ago.

Her father was retired. He left the Senate and was back in Danbury practicing law. Only a few people knew that he did it to be closer to her mother. After everything that happened, he had vowed to repair the damage he did.

"What about all the other people that drank the same water as those senators? Are they going to get cataracts, too?" Mark asked. "Will people still use those Teleplunkt lenses?"

"Well, I'm glad you reminded me," she said. "I made sure that the water in the metro area has been filtered to give maximum protection to the good citizens of the D.C. area. I learned from Pharmoletia that the statin drug deteriorates rapidly after five months. Anyone that is going to be affected already is. In my editorial in the Washington Post, I had already urged everyone to be wearing sunglasses during prime daytime exposure. And lastly, you can bet your bottom dollar that Teleplunkt lenses have been withdrawn from the market. What a nightmare.

"In hindsight how shrewd and malevolent people can be."

Thinking about the damage, she thought about Melanie. Hopkins let her go. She was somewhere in rural Maryland, supposedly opening her own practice. Lauren could only hope she'd never see her again.

As for Padma, she was in high demand. Dr. von Fricke had helped their recently revised paper on the cataract epidemic receive the outstanding award from the 2010 American Academy of Ophthalmology. Lauren had been in Darfur at the time, so Dr. Padma Patel received the award for both of them. Just like her hero, Semmelweis, true science was recognized in the end.

Lauren did not say anything for a moment. The two sides of her mind did battle. But the winner was already determined.

"Do you want to meet up for dinner?" she asked.

"I'd love to," he said in a tone of excitement.

"Too bad you're not still following me," she said tongue in cheek.

"Who said I'm not," he said.

THE END

COMING SOON—Follow the continuing adventures of Dr. Lauren Chandler.

LAST SIGHTING

She was jogging to release some of the tensions that had accumulated over the past two weeks working with NSA. He was the last person she was ready to confront in this remote area of Rock Creek Parkway. He was not here to talk as he aimed his menacing silencer adapted Lugar. When he shot twice, she attempted to roll down hill into the woods. Hit in the shoulder and arm, she rushed to her feet as he fired again at close range creating two red holes in the center of her back. Death was instantaneous. He collected the shells with a gloved hand and would have spit on her motionless body if it were not for the fact it might leave some evidence for the forensic boys.

The high profile murder was broadly featured two days later to all the major news outlets, but the trail was already cold. It would be three years until Dr. Lauren Chandler decided to apply her advanced research device to autopsy specimens of unsolved crimes. Her work with rabbits had been fruitful but she had controlled all aspects of the study. What she would soon learn in this case would bring back terrible memories and cause her to run for her life. The mind is a terrible thing to explore.

The other books by Robert Abel Jr MD

The Eye Care Revolution
The DHA Story
The One Earth Herbal Sourcebook
The Best Supplements For Your Health
Lumi's Book of Eyes